W. H. Carpe

MW01673796

The History of New York

Anatiposi

W. H. Carpenter, T. S. Arthur

The History of New York

Reprint of the original, first published in 1872.

1st Edition 2023 | ISBN: 978-3-38212-896-8

Anatiposi Verlag is an imprint of Outlook Verlagsgesellschaft mbH.

Verlag (Publisher): Outlook Verlag GmbH, Zeilweg 44, 60439 Frankfurt, Deutschland
Vertretungsberechtigt (Authorized to represent): E. Roepke, Zeilweg 44, 60439 Frankfurt, Deutschland
Druck (Print): Books on Demand GmbH, In de Tarpen 42, 22848 Norderstedt, Deutschland

THE

HISTORY OF NEW YORK

FROM ITS

Earliest Settlement to the Present Time.

BY

W. H. CARPENTER

AND

T. S. ARTHUR.

PHILADELPHIA:
CLAXTON, REMSEN & HAFFELFINGER.
1872.

STEREOTYPED BY L. JOHNSON AND CO.
PHILADELPHIA.

PUBLISHERS' PREFACE.

THERE are but few persons in this country who have not, at some time or other, felt the want of an accurate, well written, concise, yet clear and reliable history of their own or some other state.

The want here indicated is now about being supplied; and, as the task of doing so is no light or superficial one, the publishers have given into the hands of the two gentlemen whose names appear in the title-page, the work of preparing a series of CABINET HISTORIES, embracing a volume for each state in the Union. Of their ability to perform this well, we need not speak. They are no strangers in the literary world. What they undertake the public may rest assured will be performed thoroughly; and that no sectarian, sectional, or party feelings will bias their judgment, or lead them to violate the integrity of history.

The importance of a series of state histories like those now commenced, can scarcely be estimated. Being condensed as carefully as accuracy and interest of narrative will permit, the size and price of the volumes will bring them within the reach of every family in the country, thus making them home-reading books for old and young. Each individual will, in consequence, become familiar, not only with the history of his own state, but with that of other states: —thus mutual interest will be re-awakened, and old bonds cemented in a firmer union.

In this series of CABINET HISTORIES, the authors, while presenting a concise but accurate narrative of the domestic policy of each state, will give greater prominence to the personal history of the people. The dangers which continually hovered around the early colonists; the stirring romance of a life passed fearlessly amid peril; the incidents of border warfare; the adventures of hardy pioneers; the keen watchfulness, the subtle surprise, the ruthless attack, and prompt retaliation—all these having had an important influence upon the formation of the American character, are to be freely recorded. While the progressive development of the citizens of each individual state from the rough forest-life of the earlier day to the polished condition of the present, will exhibit a picture of national expansion as instructing as it is interesting.

The size and style of the series will be uniform with the present volume. The authors, who have been for some time collecting and arranging materials, will furnish the succeeding volumes as rapidly as their careful preparation will warrant.

PREFACE.

THE history of New York, the wealthiest and, from its happy geographical position, the most important of all the confederated States, has hitherto been but imperfectly known even to its own citizens. This defective knowledge cannot be said to have originated from any want of interest on the subject, but rather from the difficulty of obtaining the requisite information within a moderate compass, and in a connected form; the narrative of events being scattered through numerous volumes, all of which are in their nature fragmentary.

To supply this want—to place before the general reader a clear, succinct, and impartial history of the State, from its earliest settlement to the present day, is the object of this volume, which will not be found a mere compilation, but a work originally treated, and elaborated with care and impartiality. Brief as it is, it yet contains every event of marked historical importance; nothing being omitted but those obtrusive speculations, and dry legislative details, which, in a work intended for popular use, are neither valuable nor interesting.

CONTENTS.

CHAPTER I.

CHAPTER II.

CHAPTER III.

CHAPTER VI.

CHAPTER VII.

CHAPTER VIII.

CHAPTER IX.

CHAPTER X.

CHAPTER XI.

CHAPTER XIV.

CHAPTER XV.

CHAPTER XVI.

CHAPTER XVII.

CHAPTER XVIII.

CHAPTER XIX.

CHAPTER XX.

CHAPTER XXI.

CHAPTER XXII.

CHAPTER XXIII.

CHAPTER XXIV.

HISTORY OF NEW YORK.

CHAPTER I.

Columbus—Voyages of the Cabots—John and Sebastian Cabot discover the Continent of North America—Voyage of Sebastian Cabot—His exploration of the coast—Newfoundland fisheries—Patent from James I. to the Virginia Companies—Settlement of Jamestown—Voyage of Verrazzani, under the auspices of James I.—Sails from Madeira—Reaches America—Lands in North Carolina—Friendliness of the savages—Their humanity—A child kidnapped—Arrival of Verrazzani at Sandy Hook—His description—Conference with the natives—Bay of New York—Harbour of Newport—Description of the natives—Exploration inland—Departure for Europe—Claims of France—Cartier and Roberval—First permanent French settlement—Quebec founded by Champlain—The Five Nations—Policy of Champlain—Joins a war-party of Hurons and Algonquins—Discovery of Lake Champlain—Defeat of the Iroquois—The consequence.

FIVE years after the discovery of the Bahamas by Christopher Columbus, John Cabot, a native of Venice, and an expert navigator, then residing at Bristol, in England, was authorized, by letters patent from Henry the Seventh, to take five English ships, in any haven or havens of the realm, to explore the seas east, west, or north, in search of any countries hitherto unknown to Christians, and to plant the English banner on any part of the land thus newly found.

Under this license, John Cabot, accompanied by his son Sebastian, subsequently celebrated as a daring mariner, left Bristol in the early part of May, 1497, and on the 24th of June, first came in sight of the continent of North America.

On reaching the coast, which is supposed to have been that of Labrador, they found it rocky and sterile, abounding with the white polar bear, and with deer far larger than any they had ever seen before. After satisfying themselves that this cheerless region was inhabited only by savages clothed in the skins of beasts, and armed with the primitive weapons of bows and clubs, the Cabots returned to England with the tidings of their success.

The following year a second expedition was fitted out, the command of which was given to Sebastian Cabot. Being furnished with several small vessels, freighted with such articles of merchandise as were thought best suited for purposes of traffic with an uncivilized people, he again embarked for the newly-discovered land, and after a voyage of several weeks, approached the continent in the latitude of fifty-eight degrees.

Proceeding north, he penetrated that portion of the arctic region since known as Hudson's Bay; when, finding his further progress seriously obstructed by masses of floating ice, he yielded to the loudly-expressed fears of his men, and shaping his course southward, sailed along the shore until he reached the southern limit of Maryland. After having thus ranged the coast through thirty degrees of latitude, his provisions growing short, he sailed for England. It was from these two voyages of John and Sebastian Cabot, that Great Britain acquired the title to nearly the whole continent of North America.

For upward of a century, however, no advantage was derived from the discoveries thus made, beyond the establishment of fisheries off the coast of Newfoundland. The first successful attempt at colonization was made in 1606, when James the First, disregarding all previous patents, granted to two rival associations of adventurers, embodied under the respective titles of the London and Plymouth Companies, permission to settle plantations on any part of the North American continent lying between the thirty-fourth and forty-fifth degree of north latitude.

The settlement of the London, or South Virginia colony, was to be made at any point between Cape Fear and Long Island, while that of the Plymouth, or North Virginia colony, was restricted to the region embraced between Delaware Bay and Halifax.

The following year, three small vessels, bearing one hundred and five colonists, sent out to Virginia by the London Company, entered the Chesapeake Bay, and after exploring the James River, selected a small peninsula, thirty-two miles from its mouth, where, on the 13th of May, 1607, they laid the foundation of Jamestown. No settlement was made by the Plymouth Company until thirteen years afterward.

Profiting by the discoveries of Cabot, French mariners, from the ports of Brittany and Normandy, sailed early to the coast of Newfoundland, where they shared with the English in the lucrative fisheries of that region.

Desirous of opening a wider field of commerce for his subjects, and, perhaps, emulous of the renown acquired through their discoveries by England and Spain, Francis the First ordered John Verrazzani, a Florentine mariner, to take command of four vessels, and explore the region concerning which so many marvellous stories were circulating throughout Europe.

Three of his vessels, having become separated in a storm, Verrazzani sailed from the island of Madeira on the 17th of June, 1524, with one small caravel, containing fifty men and provisions for eight months. After weathering with great difficulty a fierce tempest, he succeeded, at the end of fifty days, in approaching a low sandy shore, which, from the numerous fires scattered along the coast, he concluded to be thickly inhabited. Running southward fifty leagues without finding a harbour, he turned again toward the north, and anchored in latitude 34°, off the coast of North Carolina. A large concourse of the natives immediately collected on the beach, and, encouraged by their evident friendliness, Verrazzani ventured to land for a short time and take a closer survey of the country. Re-embarking, he continued his course to the north, everywhere greeted with signals of welcome by groups of savages gathered admiringly on the shore. Nor were they less humane than hospitable. One of the sailors, in an attempt to swim to them with a few presents, being thrown by a heavy sea half dead upon the beach, was caught up in the arms of the savages, and borne to a place of safety. Soothing his fears by gentle caresses, they kindled a fire to facilitate his recovery, and after drying his clothes, led him with many an affectionate embrace back to the beach. They then retired to an eminence, from whence they kept an anxious watch until they saw him return in safety to the ship.

Proceeding north fifty leagues, Verrazzani anchored off the seaboard of Maryland, and sent twenty men on shore to explore the country. They penetrated inland some six miles, but the natives had fled affrighted deeper into the forest. Hidden in the long grass they found two women and six children. They seized one of the latter to take with them to France, and attempted also to bear off the younger of the women, who was tall of stature and very beautiful; but fearing her outcries would endanger their safety, they released her, and kidnapped the child only. After this outrage, so strikingly in contrast with the guileless tenderness exhibited by those who were called barbarians, Verrazzani kept coasting northward until he arrived at Sandy Hook, "a very pleasant place, situate among certain little steep hills, from amidst which there ran down into the sea an exceeding great stream of water, which within the mouth was very deep, and from the sea to the mouth of the same, with the tide—which they found to rise eight feet—any great ship laden might pass up." When they had held a brief conference with the natives by signs, and had sufficiently admired the beautiful bay of New York, which Verrazzani describes as "a most pleasant lake, about three leagues in compass," the anchor was again weighed, and dropped within the fine semi-circular harbour of Newport, where they met "the goodliest people, and of the fairest conditions," of any they had found in their voyage. They were of noble proportions, some "of the colour of brass, and some inclining to whiteness: black and quick eyed, of sweet and pleasant countenance, imitating much the old fashion."

During the fifteen days they remained at this place, exploring parties, guided by the hospitable savages, often ventured five or six leagues inland, where they found extensive plains, the soil of which was very fertile, and forests "so great and thick that any army, were it never so great, might have hid itself therein;" the trees being of oak and cypress, and of other kinds unknown in Europe.

Taking leave of the courteous and charitable inhabitants of Rhode Island, Verrazzani, still coasting northward, sailed along the shores of New England, and at length terminated his explorations at the island of Newfoundland, after having ranged the North American continent for a distance of seven hundred leagues. In July, 1524, he reached the port of Dieppe, from whence he wrote to the king an account of his remarkable voyage; and upon the discoveries alleged to have been made by him at this time, the claims of France to a wide extent of territory on the Western continent were subsequently founded.

The voyages of Cartier and Roberval followed. The river St. Lawrence was discovered by the former in 1534, and various efforts at colonization were subsequently made, all of which proved unsuccessful, until the spring of 1605, when the first permanent French settlement was established at Port Royal, on the island of Nova Scotia. In 1608, the energetic Champlain founded Quebec. The following year, being desirous of securing the friendship of the Algonquins and Hurons, he joined them in an expedition against the Iroquois, or Five Nations, a powerful confederacy, which had been for many years a terror to the surrounding tribes.

When Champlain first entered Canada, this

renowned confederacy, consisting of the Mohawk, Oneida, Onondaga, Cayuga, and Seneca nations of Indians, occupied, by conquest from the Mohican tribes, the middle, northern, and western portions of the territory which was subsequently included within the limits of the province of New York.

Knowing how formidable the proximity of this haughty and warlike Indian republic would be to a feeble French colony, settled on their immediate borders, he conceived the design of humbling the power of the Iroquois, by rendering assistance to their hostile but weaker neighbours, and of inducing them by this means to unite in a general league of amity with the French.

Influenced by what appeared to be the wisdom of this policy, he joined a war-party of his savage allies, and leaving Quebec, then an insignificant village, consisting of a few scattered cottages in the midst of newly-cleared fields and gardens, ascended the river Sorel to the rapids near Chambly. Notwithstanding he had been kept in utter ignorance of this obstruction to the course of his vessel, he determined to proceed. Sending most of his party back to Quebec, he crossed the portage with his allies, and re-embarked in one of their frail canoes, attended only by two Europeans After travelling in this manner for several days, he entered, for the first time, the lake which now bears his name, and traversing its whole extent, suddenly discovered near Ticonderoga a number of canoes filled with Iroquois. Both parties with wild shouts of exultation pulled rapidly for the shore, where they commenced selecting their ground for the battle. As it was then late in the night, the Iroquois, in answer to a challenge from the allies, declined fighting until the next day, when they could see themselves.

In the gray of the following morning, Champlain placed his two countrymen, supported by a small detachment of savages, in ambush, on the flank of the enemy. Both parties were about two hundred strong; but the Iroquois, being unconscious of the powerful aid which the Hurons and Algonquins had received in the firearms of the Europeans, were confident of an easy victory. Previous to the onset, Champlain had been requested by his allies to single out the three leaders of the enemy, who could readily be distinguished from their followers by the superior size of their feathered ornaments. This having been arranged, the Huron and Algonquin warriors sounded the war-whoop, and, darting out in a body from their cover of fallen timber, advanced some two hundred feet in front of the enemy, and then, deflecting to the right and left, displayed to the astonished gaze of the Iroquois the first white man they had ever beheld, clad in strange apparel, and armed with weapons of singular shape and unknown power. But their amazement was changed into extreme terror, when they saw fire issue from the levelled tube, first from the arquebuss of Champlain in the centre, and then from those of his two companions on the flank, and beheld two of their chiefs fall dead, and the third reel back dangerously wounded. The allies charged immediately, and the Iroquois, after receiving a few more vollies from the Frenchmen, fled panic-stricken from the field. In the pursuit many were killed, and some few prisoners were taken. At length the victors desisted from following the fugitive enemy any longer, and returning to the field of battle, passed two hours in celebrating their triumph, by songs and dances. Not a single one of the allies had been killed, and but very few wounded. Satisfied with their success, they now returned homeward; but amused themselves with torturing one of their prisoners by the way. Shocked at the horrible barbarities to which he was a witness, Champlain suddenly put an end to the agony of the sufferer, by despatching him with his own hand.

Such was the commencement of the feud between the Iroquois and the French. The policy of Champlain, carried out in several similar expeditions during the succeeding year, instead of humbling the Five Nations to sue for peace, instigated them to revenge, and engendered that intense hatred of the Canadian colonists, which made them fast allies of the Dutch and English, during the whole period that the French retained possession of the northern territory.

CHAPTER II.

Voyage of Henry Hudson—Attempts to reach Nova Zembla—Is impeded by ice—Ranges the North American coast southward—Reaches Penobscot—Trades with the natives—Attacks and plunders them—Rounds Cape Cod—Is blown off the Capes of Virginia—Returns north—Discovers Delaware Bay—Enters Sandy Hook—Death of Colman—Discovers the Great North or Hudson River—Explores it—The Palisades—West Point—The Catskills—Traffic with the natives—Their hospitality—The exploration continued—Hudson arrives in the vicinity of Albany—Is visited by numbers of Indians—Singular expedient to test their friendliness—Scene of intoxication—The Iroquois tradition concerning it—Return of Hudson—An Indian killed—Ambush near Harlem River—Skirmish with the Manhattans—Departure.

About the same time that Champlain was on his first expedition against the Iroquois, Henry Hudson, an English mariner in the employ of the Dutch East India Company, was penetrating the arctic regions in the vain search for a northern passage to India. With a small yacht, or fly-boat, called the Crescent, manned by a mixed crew of Englishmen and Hollanders, he attempted to reach Nova Zembla; but being impeded by masses of ice, he changed the course of his vessel to the south-west, ran down the coast of Acadia, and on the 17th of July, 1609, anchored off the

Bay of Penobscot. Finding a good harbour near by, he entered it the following day, and remained there a week, preparing a new foremast and mending the tattered sails. While he was thus engaged, a large concourse of natives arrived in two French shallops and in canoes, and proposed to traffic furs for such European commodities as he might have on board. Something or other soon occurring to elicit suspicion of their intentions, Hudson ordered a strict watch to be kept. The day before he left the harbour, having refitted his yacht, he sent out a boat with six men to capture one of the shallops, while twelve men, armed with muskets and light field-pieces, went ashore in a second boat, and driving the savages from their huts, plundered them of all the valuables they contained.

Leaving at once the immediate scene of this outrage, Hudson glided out to the mouth of the harbour, from whence he set sail on the following day. Running down the coast, he rounded the promontory of Cape Cod, and steering a southerly direction reached the Capes of Virginia on the 18th of August. Being driven out to sea for eight days by a succession of severe gales, he did not land and visit the colony of his countrymen, which he knew to have been settled on the James River two years before; but turning northward, discovered the Delaware Bay, examined its currents, soundings, and the aspect of the land; and then, without going on shore, continued his course northwardly until the 2d of September, when he came in sight of the highlands of Neversink, and entering the next day the southern waters of New York, anchored during the same afternoon within the harbour of Sandy Hook.

He was immediately visited by the natives, some of whom were clad loosely in pliant deer-skins, while others were dressed in furs, and wore mantles of feathers. They brought on board small supplies of maize and green tobacco, which they exchanged for trifles.

While remaining at anchor in this harbour, he sent a boat with five men to sound through the Narrows, and examine the nature of the country beyond. They found a fertile soil, covered with luxuriant grass and goodly trees, and adorned with such a profusion of wild flowers that the air was filled with their fragrance. As the boat, however, was returning, its small crew was suddenly assaulted by a number of Indians in two large canoes, and John Colman, one of Hudson's veteran seamen, shot with an arrow in the neck. Two others were also wounded, but not mortally. This sad accident is supposed to have arisen from the Indians having been suddenly surprised at the appearance of strange men within their waters, and not from any preconcert on their part; for as soon as they had discharged their arrows, they fled with great speed. Two days afterward the traffic with the natives was resumed. But Hudson, a strict, stern, cautious man, was no longer willing to hazard the safety of his vessel and crew among a people of whose pacific intentions he began to entertain serious doubts Weighing anchor, and passing through the Narrows on the 11th of September, he entered New York Bay, "an excellent harbour for all winds," where he remained until the next afternoon. Having determined to avoid all intercourse, as far as it was possible, with the savages who resided on the island of Manhattan, he sailed up the great North River two leagues, and, on the 13th, proceeded with a light wind and flood tide as far as Phillipsburg. Here he anchored for the night. The following day he continued his voyage, having on his left the Palisade rocks, presenting through a distance of thirty miles, unbroken save by the valley of the Nyack, a lofty perpendicular front, varying in altitude from three to seven hundred feet; while on his right he beheld the river bounded by a low undulating border, fringed with noble trees, whose foliage was just beginning to be tinted with the rich colours of autumn. Sailing onward, he saw the river gradually expand into a bay, contract again, and again expand, until in the distance before him it appeared to be abruptly shut in by a barrier of mountains. The bold heart of the mariner sank within him as he saw what seemed to him the termination of his voyage. At length he discovered a deep, narrow, winding river, up which he sailed until he came to West Point, where he dropped anchor, and waited until daylight for the farther prosecution of his discovery. As soon as the mist of the morning had cleared away, he continued his voyage fifty miles farther up the river, where, in full view of the Catskill Mountains, he remained until the following evening, trafficking with the natives, "very loving people," who spoke the language of the Mohawks. Going with them on shore in one of their canoes, he was conducted to a house made of the bark of trees, exceedingly smooth, and well finished both within and without. Near the house, he saw a quantity of corn and beans drying in the sun, sufficient to have freighted three ships. The Indians received their visitors with great hospitality, spread mats for them to seat themselves upon, and brought them some food in wooden bowls painted red, while two men were despatched in search of game, who speedily returned with a brace of wild pigeons. A fat dog was also killed, and skinned with shells taken from the water. These preparations were made in expectation of Hudson and his companions remaining during the night; but they determined to return on board their ship. Apprehensive that they had been influenced to this course through fear of their bows and arrows, the noble-hearted savages immediately broke them into pieces, and threw them into the fire. But the prudence of Hudson was proof against even this act of friendliness, and he persisted in taking his leave. Soon after, he proceeded up the river two leagues, when meeting with shoal water, he anchored off the flats, opposite to which the city of Hudson now stands. Continuing on his course by short stretches, during the three following days, he reached, on the 19th of September, the vicinity of Albany, where he remained with his yacht, trafficking with the natives for provisions and furs, while the mate with four men ascended the river in a boat, and sounded the depth of the channel as far up as the junction of the Mohawk with the Hudson, or opposite the present town of Lansingburgh.

Hudson arrived at Schenectadea, now called Albany, about noon. The natives immediately came flocking on board, bringing with them grapes and pumpkins, together with otter and beaver skins, which they exchanged for hatchets, beads, knives, and other trifles.

Desirous of testing if any of the chiefs were disposed to be treacherous, Hudson resorted to the singular expedient of plying them freely with wine and strong liquors. Under the influence of these strange potations, they all grew exceedingly merry, and one of them became intoxicated. On beholding him stagger and fall, the natives became dumb from utter astonishment. They all hurried ashore in their canoes, and did not again return to the ship until noon of the next day, when, finding their chief perfectly restored, they were highly gratified. Renewing their visit in the afternoon, they brought with them presents of tobacco and beads, and sending for a platter of venison, caused Hudson to eat with them. When he had done so, they all departed except the old chief, who still remained on board, in the hope of obtaining another draught of that attractive but poisonous fire-water, the knowledge of which was thus first introduced to the Indians of New York.

The tradition of this scene of intoxication, on the arrival of the first ship, exists among the Iroquois Indians until this day. One relation transfers the locality from Albany to New York, and is as follows: "A long time ago, before men with white skins had ever been seen, some Indians fishing at a place where the sea widens, espied something at a distance moving upon the water. They hurried ashore, collected their neighbours, who together returned and viewed intensely this astonishing phenomenon. What it could be baffled all conjecture. Some supposed it a large fish, or animal; others, that it was a very big house floating on the sea. Perceiving it moving toward land, the spectators concluded it would be proper to send runners in different directions to carry the news to their scattered chiefs, that they might send off for the immediate attendance of their warriors. These arriving in numbers to behold the sight, and perceiving that it was actually moving toward them, they conjectured that it must be a remarkably large house, in which the Manitto, or Great Spirit, was coming to visit them. They were much afraid, and yet under no apprehension that the Great Spirit would injure them. They worshipped him. The chiefs now assembled at York Island, and consulted in what manner they should receive their Manitto. Meat was prepared for a sacrifice. The women were directed to prepare the best of victuals Idols or images were examined and put in order A grand dance they thought would be pleasing, and, in addition to the sacrifice, might appease him if angry.

"The conjurors were also set to work to determine what this phenomenon portended, and what the result would be. To these, men, women, and children looked up for advice and protection. Utterly at a loss what to do, and distracted alternately by hope and fear, in their confusion a grand dance commenced. Meantime fresh runners arrived, declaring it to be a great house of various colours, and full of living creatures. It now appeared certain that it was their Manitto, probably bringing some new kind of game. Others, arriving, declared it positively to be full of people of different colour and dress from theirs, and that one in particular appeared clothed altogether in red. This then must be the Manitto. They were lost in admiration, and could not imagine what the vessel was, whence it came, or what all this portended.

"They are now hailed from the vessel in a language they could not understand. They answer by a shout, or yell, in their way. The large canoe stops. A smaller canoe comes on shore with the red man in it, some stay by his canoe to guard it. The chiefs and wise men form a circle, into which the red man and two attendants approach. He salutes them with a friendly countenance, and they return the salute after their manner. They are amazed at their colour and dress, particularly with him, who, glittering in red, wore something—perhaps lace and buttons—they could not comprehend. He *must* be the Great Manitto, they thought; but why should he have a white skin?

"A large, elegant bottle is brought by one of the supposed Manitto's servants, from which a liquid is poured into a small cup or glass, and handed to the Manitto. He drinks, has the glass refilled, and handed to the chief near him. He takes it, smells it, and passes it to the next, who does the same. The glass in this manner is passed round the circle, and is about to be returned to the red clothed man, when one of them, a great warrior, harangues them on the impropriety of returning the cup unemptied. 'It was handed to them,' he said 'to drink out of as he had. To follow his example would please him; to reject it, might provoke his wrath; and, if no one else would, he would drink it himself, let what would follow; for it was better for one even to die, than that a whole nation should be destroyed.'

"He then took the glass, smelled at it, again addressed them, bidding them adieu, and drank its contents. All eyes were now fixed upon him. He soon began to stagger. The women cried, supposing him in fits. He rolled on the ground. They bemoaned his fate; they thought him dying. He fell asleep. They at first thought he had expired, but soon perceived he still breathed. He awoke, jumped up, and declared he never felt more happy. He asked for more; and the whole assembly imitating him, became intoxicated.

"While this intoxication lasted, the whites confined themselves to their vessel; but when it ceased, the man with red clothes returned, and distributed beads, axes, hoes, and stockings. They soon became familiar, and conversed by signs. The whites made them understand that they would now return home, but the next year they would visit them again with presents, and stay with them a while; but that as they could not live without eating, they should then want a little land to sow seeds, in order to raise herbs to put in their broth.

"Accordingly, a vessel returned the season following, when they were much rejoiced to see each other; but the whites laughed when they saw the axes and the hoes hanging as ornaments to their breasts, and the stockings used as tobacco pouches. The whites now put handles in the axes, and cut down trees before their eyes, and dug the ground, and showed them the use of the stockings. Here, they say, a general laugh ensued, to think they had remained ignorant of the use of these things, and had borne so long such heavy metal suspended round their necks. Familiarity daily increasing between them and the whites, the latter now proposed to stay with them, asking them only for so much land as the hide of a bullock, spread before them, could cover or encompass. They granted the request.

"The whites then took a knife, and beginning at one place on this hide, cut it into a rope not thicker than the finger of a little child. They then took the rope, drew it gently along in a circular form, and took in a large piece of ground. The Indians were surprised at their superior wit, but did not contend with them for a little ground, as they had enough. They lived contentedly together for a long time, but the new-comers from time to time asked for more land, which was readily obtained. And thus they gradually proceeded up the Mahicannittuck, or Hudson River, until they began to believe they would want all their country, which proved eventually the case."

Such is the interesting tradition, of the Iroquois, of their earliest interviews with the whites, and the incidents which rendered those meetings memorable.

After having passed several days in friendly intercourse and profitable trade with the natives, Hudson, finding he could proceed no higher up the river in his vessel, set out on his return. His ship again grounding opposite the spot where the city of Hudson now stands, and also suffering detention for some days by reason of adverse winds, he went ashore and explored the western bank of the river, where he found a rich soil, covered with goodly oak, walnut, chestnut, and cedar trees, with abundance of slate for houses, "and other good stones."

On the 26th, he was visited by two canoes, in one of which came the old chief who had been intoxicated at Albany. He had descended the river thirty miles to testify his love, bringing with him another old man bearing strings of beads as a present. Hudson caused them, and the four women by whom they were accompanied, to dine with him. Two of the latter were young girls, some sixteen or seventeen years of age, who behaved themselves "very modestly." Dropping down the river on the 27th, he anchored on the 29th in the vicinity of Newburgh, of which he took particular notice, as a "pleasant place to build a town in." Here he remained bartering with the natives, until the afternoon of October 1st, when he sailed with a fair wind through the Highlands, and after descending the river seven leagues, the wind failing, he anchored at the mouth of Haverstraw Bay.

The Indians of the Highlands, whose chief village was in the vicinity of Anthony's Nose—a name which has been given to an elevated peak on the east side of the North or Hudson River—soon came crowding on board in great numbers. One of them, dissatisfied with the trifles he had received in payment for his furs, and desirous of displaying to his friends something of a different character, lurked in his canoe about the stern of the ship, for the purpose of carrying off some article or other from this wonderful floating structure.

Watching his opportunity, he clambered up the rudder, and entering the cabin window, stole a pillow and a few articles of wearing apparel. For this act, so venial in a poor ignorant savage, he was immediately shot down by the brutal mate. His companions, panic-stricken, took to flight. In an effort to recover the articles, another Indian had one of his hands cut off, and was drowned.

Leaving the scene of this disaster, Hudson continued on his way, stopped for the night off the mouth of Croton River, sailed again at daybreak, and descending the river twenty-one miles, came to an anchor near the upper end of the island of Manhattan.

Previous to exploring the great river which now bears his name, Hudson, perhaps in retaliation for the death of Colman, had made prisoners of two Manhattan Indians, designing to hold them either as hostages for the future pacific behaviour of their tribe, or with a view of carrying them to Europe. Opposite West Point, as he went up the river, these prisoners had escaped, and making their way back with all speed to their friends, collected a large party of armed warriors, who lay in wait for the return of the vessel in the neighbourhood of the inlet of Harlem River.

Near to this inlet the ship was now hove to. One of the savages who had escaped, accompanied by many others, came out in two canoes; but not being suffered to approach the vessel, they fell back near the stern, and discharged a volley of arrows at the crew. A fire was immediately returned from the vessel, by which two or three of the savages were killed. Finding the numbers on shore increasing, the ship was at once got under way. As it moved along, the main body of Indians ran to the point upon which Fort Washington was subsequently erected, and continued the assault by another volley of arrows. The discharge from a cannon killing two of them, the rest fled into the woods; but a dozen of the boldest speedily returned, and entering a canoe, advanced resolutely against the ship. The cannon was fired a second time, and the ball, passing entirely through the canoe, killed one of the warriors. A fire from the deck about the same time killing several others, the fight terminated, with the loss of nine Indians. Hudson, soon after, descended to the mouth of the river, and on the 4th of October put to sea, shaping his course south-east by east.

CHAPTER III.

Hudson returns to Europe—Reaches Dartmouth—Communicates with his employers—Sails on a new voyage of discovery—Enters Hudson's Bay—Reaches its southern limit—Searches for an outlet—Is frozen in—Scarcity of his provisions—Mutinous condition of his crew—He sails for the mouth of the bay—Mutiny—Abandonment of Hudson and his companions—Signal retribution—The Dutch traffic with the Indians—Captain Argall—New explorations—Blok coasts Long Island—Discovers the Housatonic and Connecticut Rivers—Returns with Christiaanse to Manhattan—Fortified posts erected at Manhattan and Albany—May examines the Delaware Bay—Alliance with the Iroquois.

After leaving Sandy Hook, Hudson held a consultation with his crew, as to whether they should continue their search for a new route to the Pacific, or return to Europe. Finding their opinions discordant, he concluded to sail for Amsterdam, and report to his employers. The voyage across the Atlantic was prosperous; but, as he approached the coast of England, his men became mutinous, and compelled him to put into Dartmouth, where he arrived on the 7th of November, 1609.

He immediately wrote to the directors of the Dutch East India Company, transmitting them his journal, together with an account of his discoveries. He also proposed to them the plan of another voyage, which he volunteered to undertake upon certain conditions; but before they had decided whether to accept or decline his offer, the English government forbade him from again entering into the service of the Dutch.

Early the following year, a London company, in whose employ Hudson had made two previous voyages in search of a new route to India, engaged him to explore the inlets to the west of Davis's Straits, through one of which it was conjectured that a passage might be found to the South Sea.

Embarking on board a ship called the Discovery, with a crew of twenty-three men, Hudson left Blackwall on the 17th of April, 1610, and passing Greenland, Iceland, and Frobisher's Straits, entered, on the 2d of August, the straits which now bear his name. After having encountered many perils from storms, and driving ice, and a great whirling sea, he penetrated into Hudson's Bay, exulting in the belief that he had found the long-sought passage to the Pacific. Doomed to disappointment by reaching at length the southern limit of the bay, he shaped his course northward. Difficulties occurring soon after between himself and his crew, made it necessary for him to cashier both the mate and the boatswain, and advance others to their offices. Disheartened and perplexed at finding himself embayed, he wasted the remainder of the summer in unavailing efforts to discover an outlet to this great inland sea. Sailing to and fro, and with not more than six months' provisions on board, the season became so far advanced, that on the 1st of November, he was compelled to moor his ship in a small cove, where, in ten days, it was completely frozen in. Here they remained, arctic prisoners, until June, 1611.

In the mean time, the difficulties between Hudson and his crew had increased. For the first few months they subsisted principally on wild fowl; but when these were gone, many of the men fell sick, and the others, emaciated by want of food, searched the surrounding country, and ate with avidity even the most loathsome things to appease their hunger. At the breaking up of the ice, they received, for the first time, a visit from one of the natives, who, after obtaining some presents, promised to return in a few days; but although anxiously expected, he never came back. Seeing the woods on fire to the south and south-west, Hudson embarked in the shallop with eight men, in the hope of obtaining such supplies from the Indians as would enable him to prosecute his voyage. Disappointed in his endeavours to come up with them, for they fled before him, he returned disconsolately to his vessel, and prepared to leave the dreary and inhospitable region which he had wasted seven months in examining.

Dividing among his crew the last remaining bread, amounting only to a pound for each man, he wept while he gave it to them. Quitting his winter harbour about the middle of June, he steered north-west from the mouth of the bay; but meeting with ice, and baffled by contrary winds, was soon after compelled to come to an anchor.

During the week he was thus detained, the discontent which had for a long time existed among his crew, broke out into open mutiny. Headed by his deposed mate, Henry Green, the mutineers, at daybreak on the 21st of June, seized Hudson, his youthful son, and six seamen, and thrust them into the shallop. A fine moral incident now occurred. Philip Staffe, the carpenter, —a man of a brave, hopeful spirit, and generally beloved—after attempting in vain to turn the conspirators from their purpose, determined, in opposition to their wishes, to share the fate of his commander, whatever that fate might be. The wind proving favourable about this time, the anchor was weighed, and as soon as the ship, having at her stern the shallop, had become partially free from the surrounding ice, the rope was cut, and Hudson and his eight companions were mercilessly abandoned, to be swallowed up by the waters of that wild arctic bay which they were the first to discover, to meet a lingering death by starvation, or to fall victims to the fury of the savages, whose fires had been discovered to the south-west. Not one of them was ever heard of after.

This cold-blooded act on the part of the mutineers was destined to meet with a signal retribution. After beating about for a month, and barely escaping shipwreck on three several occasions, they at length reached, on the 19th of July, the vicinity of Cape Diggs, where they fell in with a number of savages in seven canoes. Being welcomed with a great show of hospitality, and apprehending no treachery, Green, Wilson, and Thomas, the chief conspirators, went ashore the next day, unarmed, to meet the savages, some of whom had gathered on the beach, while others were dancing and gesticulating on the hills beyond. Two others of the mutineers, Perce and Moter, landed at the same time, and ascended the rocks to gather sorrel. The boat was left in charge of one Prickett, a lame man, who had only been passively implicated in the desertion of Hudson and his unfortunate companions. While this guard was seated at the stern, some savages came out from an ambush near by, the leader of whom sprang upon Prickett and wounded him in several places; but the latter, having succeeded in drawing a Scotch dagger, stabbed the savage with so direct an aim that he fell dead on the boat. At this juncture, Green and Wilson, beset on all sides, came staggering across the beach, and tumbled into the boat, mortally wounded. Moter sprang from the rocks into the sea. Perce, badly hurt, fought with a hatchet his way to the boat, pushed it from the shore, and helped Moter in. A cloud of arrows was now poured in upon the fugitives, by one of which Green was shot dead. Wilson and the other wounded, with the exception of Prickett, died the same day, leaving only one of the ringleaders alive, and he perished miserably by famine before the ship reached England.

Such was the tragic end of Henry Hudson, the renowned arctic discoverer, and the first explorer of the great river of New York, and such the fate of the principal mutineers.

It was not until after the lapse of several years, that the United Provinces laid formal claim to the country watered by the Hudson and its tributaries; but in the mean time, a profitable traffic in furs had been carried on with the natives, the ships of the Dutch often wintering at Albany, or

Beaverwyck, as it soon came to be called, where they exchanged with the Iroquois, or Five Nations, guns, ammunition, blankets, and trinkets, for the beaver and other valuable skins which were then obtained abundantly in that region.

The first voyage, undertaken in 1610, proving extremely lucrative, led to an extension of the traffic. The Iroquois, bitterly hostile to the French settlement in Canada, cemented a close friendship with the Dutch; while the Manhattans, though the hereditary foes to the Mohawks, the most important of the Five Nations, so far relaxed their enmity toward the Netherlanders as to permit them to erect trading-houses on their island.

In 1614, Captain Argall, the kidnapper of Pocahontas, while returning from an expedition against the French settlement at Port Royal, discovered a few rude warehouses and huts on the island of Manhattan, and compelled the traders by whom they were occupied to acknowledge the authority of England. The few Dutch residing on the island, being too weak to resist, sought safety by submission; but soon as Argall had taken his departure, they again hoisted their own flag.

A few months previous to this, the States General of the Netherlands, having granted to such as should discover new lands an exclusive trade to them for four successive voyages, a company of merchants fitted out five ships for exploration and traffic. The chief command of this little fleet was intrusted to Hendrik Christiaanse, who sailed with three of the vessels on an exploring expedition to the north of Cape Cod, while the remaining two, under Captains Blok and May, steered for the harbour of New York. Shortly after his arrival, the ship commanded by Blok, being accidentally destroyed by fire, he built on the coast a yacht of sixteen tons burden, and passing through the East River, to which he gave the name of Helle-Gadt, coasted Long Island, and determined its insular situation. Meeting with one of the ships belonging to the squadron of Christiaanse, he embarked on board of it, leaving his yacht to be used by a fishing party. Having discovered the Housatonic, and explored the Connecticut, which he called Fresh River, he next examined Narraganset Bay, and finally returned with Christiaanse to the harbour of New York. Here, on the southern point of Manhattan Island, a small fort was erected during the autumn of this year, and in the course of the year following, a similar redoubt, surrounded by a ditch, and mounted by thirteen small pieces of artillery, was erected upon a small island a little below the present city of Albany.

While Christiaanse and Blok were exploring to the north and east, May steered south and examining the Delaware Bay, gave to the northern cape his own name. His exploration was continued soon after in the new yacht built by Blok, by Hendricksen, who ascended the river as far as the mouth of the Schuylkill.

The chief command of these fortified trading posts thus established was given to Christiaanse, Jacob Elkins, formerly a merchant's clerk in Amsterdam, receiving the appointment of lieutenant, or commissary.

The redoubt at the island near Albany, being found subject to overflow during high floods, it was abandoned in 1617, and another fortification constructed soon after on the mainland four miles south. At this place a treaty was concluded between the Dutch and Iroquois, to which the Delawares and Mohicans were also parties. This important alliance with the Five Nations was productive of the most beneficial results, both to the Dutch themselves and to the English, who succeeded them. It was maintained in good faith for many years; and by opposing a barrier of friendly Indians to the encroachments of the French, effectually precluded them from inflicting more than a temporary injury upon the frontier settlements, while it secured a prompt and sanguinary retaliation.

CHAPTER IV.

The English Puritans in Holland—First project of a settlement —Agents sent to England to treat with the Virginia Company—Embarkation at Delfthaven—The Mayflower—Accidents to the Speedwell—Arrival off Cape Cod—Plymouth settled—Dutch West India Company incorporated—Forts built on the Hudson and the Delaware—Arrival of Governor Minuits—The first colonists of New Netherland—Increase of the fur trade—Commercial relations with New Plymouth—Embassy of De Razier—Dutch scheme of colonization—Provision concerning Patroons—Swanandael purchased—Pavonia—Renselaerwyk—Colony of De Vries near Henlopen—Its massacre by the savages—Return of De Vries—The colony re-established—Removal of Minuits—Administration of Wouter Van Twiller—Trading-post established on the Connecticut—Emigration to New England—Settlements on the Connecticut—Difficulties with the Patroons—The manors of Pavonia and Swanandael revert to the company—Removal of Van Twiller—William Keift appointed governor.

WHILE the Dutch were thus busily engaged in profiting by the explorations of Hudson and subsequent navigators, a number of English Puritans, who had taken refuge in Amsterdam and Leyden from religious persecution at home, unable to accommodate the rigid austerity of their own religious tenets to the looser though more liberal opinions of the Hollanders, determined at length to emigrate to some new country, where they could maintain in its integrity the form of worship to which they were attached, and preserve, at the same time, the morals of their children from corruption. At first they thought of settling in Guiana, but preferring a country where their own language was spoken, they sent Robert Cushman and John Carver to England to treat with the Virginia Company for a place of settlement. Failing to obtain from the king a guarantee of protection in their religious principles, the negotiation languished. It was, however, subsequently renewed, and in 1619 a patent was obtained in the name of John Wincob for the northern parts of Virginia; but owing to the detention of the latter in England, this patent was never used.

The establishment of a colony in America having been decided upon, a part of the Leyden congregation, under the guidance of Elder Brewster, left Delfthaven, in a small vessel called the Speedwell, toward the close of June, 1620, and crossing over to Southampton, were there joined by the Mayflower, an English ship freighted with their provisions and outfit. When the passengers had been distributed between the two ships, they set sail on the 5th of August, but had not proceeded far on their voyage before the Speedwell was found to leak so badly that they were obliged to return to port and refit.

On the 21st of August, the anchors were again weighed; but the Speedwell proving leaky a second time, they put back into Plymouth, and abandoned the vessel as unseaworthy. The remaining vessel not being sufficiently large to accommodate the whole of the company, a portion of them were now left behind. The others embarked on board the Mayflower, and on the 6th of September the voyage was resumed.

After a rough and tedious passage, which lasted nine weeks, the Mayflower entered, on the 9th of November, the harbour of Cape Cod. Finding they had arrived at a part of the continent which was not embraced within the limits of their patent, they concluded before landing to form themselves into a government distinct from that of Virginia. When they had drawn up and signed a written contract, by which they mutually agreed to yield obedience to all just laws and ordinances as should be thought most proper and convenient for the general good of the colony, they chose John Carver for their first governor, and immediately afterward sent out exploring parties to examine the face of the country, and to select a fit place to establish a settlement.

After coasting about for nearly five weeks, they at length fell in with the harbour of Plymouth; and on the 11th of December, 1621, Governor Carver went ashore, attended by several of the principal immigrants. Finding the situation better suited to their purposes than any they had yet seen, the whole of the company, one hundred and one in number, were disembarked, and commenced erecting soon after, of timbers hewn from the living trees of the adjacent forest, the first houses built in the town of New Plymouth.

While this little colony was struggling with privations under which one-half of their number prematurely perished, a great change was taking place in the commercial relations of the Dutch with the North American continent. The Amsterdam licensed trading company, which had hitherto enjoyed a monopoly of this lucrative traffic, was superseded by a great national association, which, under the title of the Dutch West India Company, was incorporated with exclusive privileges of trade and settlement.

To that portion of the continent embraced between the Delaware Bay and Cape Cod, was now given the name of New Netherland. In 1623, the first ship sent out by the new company arrived in the North River, and during the same year two new forts were built; one called Fort Nassau, on the Delaware River, and the other Fort Orange, on the west bank of the Hudson, where the town of Albany now stands.

In 1624, Peter Minuits arrived at Manhattan Island, as Director or Commercial Governor of New Netherland. He brought with him in two vessels a number of Walloons, or French Protestants, so called from their ancestors having fled from religious intolerance in their own country, and settled upon the banks of the river Waal, in Guelderland. These Walloons, the first permanent colonists of New Netherland, established themselves on Long Island, at Walle-Bocht, or Foreigners' Bay, now called Wallabout.

During the six years that Minuits was governor of New Netherland, he was actively engaged in extending the commercial operations of the company; but although the territory over which he claimed jurisdiction was recognised as a "delightful land, full of fine trees and vines," its colonization proceeded slowly, until some of the directors, among the most prominent of whom were John De Laet and Kilian Van Renselaer, formed an association for that especial purpose.

In the mean time, the quantity of furs exported by the vessels of the company had been doubled within the first four years. The trade with the natives extended northward to Quebec, Fort Orange constituting the chief mart for the interior of the province. A coasting trade was also carried on by small vessels, which gradually extended itself from Cape May to Cape Malabar.

Six years after the settlement of New Plymouth, Governor Minuits attempted, for the first time, to open commercial relations with that colony. Letters were accordingly written to the people of New Plymouth, congratulating them upon the success which had attended their efforts to establish a plantation in the wilderness, and offering to supply them with any wares they should be pleased to deal for. The answer being friendly,

Isaac de Razier, secretary of New Netherland, "a person of a plain and genteel behaviour," embarked with great formality on board a small vessel called the Nassau, attended by a body-guard of soldiers and trumpeters, to support the dignity of his mission. Landing on the north side of Cape Cod, he crossed over to the southern shore, where he met with a boat despatched to receive him and his retinue, and crossing the bay, entered Fort Plymouth, "honourably attended by a noise of trumpeters."

Meeting with a welcome reception, he remained several days, but failed in his efforts to arrange a treaty of peace and commerce, as Governor Bradford and his council doubted the claim of the Dutch to the country they occupied, and recommended that so important a treaty should be agreed upon between their respective nations. This expression of opinion did not, however, mar in the least degree the good feeling existing between De Razier and his Puritan friends. With considerate kindness he offered them the assistance of the New Netherland troops against the French, if it should at any time be required, and urged them to abandon the barren soil of Plymouth for the more fertile banks of the Connecticut.

When he took his departure, he was accompanied to his vessel by a number of the colonists, who purchased from him some articles of merchandise for their own use, and a quantity of seawan, or Indian shell money, to exchange with the natives for peltry and provisions.

In 1629, a scheme of colonization was drawn up by the directors of the Dutch West India Company, and ratified soon after by the States General. Under this charter of liberties and exemptions, any person who within the space of four years established in New Netherland, at his own expense, a colony of fifty persons, acquired the right to purchase from the Indians an extent of territory stretching sixteen miles along one side of a navigable river, or eight miles on each bank, running as far inland as he thought proper. The land thus bought and settled, he was entitled to hold as absolute proprietor, with the honourable appellation of Patroon, or Lord of the Manor. All other persons willing to emigrate on their own account, were at liberty to take up as much land as they had the ability properly to improve. The company reserved to itself the trade in furs, and the possession of the island of Manhattan, promising to complete the fort without delay, and to supply the colonists with negro slaves; but binding themselves to do so no longer than the traffic might be found convenient or lucrative.

This charter of privileges was no sooner promulgated, than several of the directors of the company bestirred themselves to take advantage of its provisions. Two of them, Godyn and

Bloemart, in anticipation of its passage, had already commissioned their agents in America to purchase from the natives the tract of land extending from Cape Henlopen to the mouth of the Delaware, a distance of thirty-two miles. In May, 1630, they made a second purchase of the country around and including Cape May, sixteen miles in length, and the same in breadth, from the Indian owners of that territory. These two tracts received the name of Swanandael, or the Valley of Swans.

In April, the agent of Kilian Van Renselaer, in consideration of certain cargoes or parcels of goods, purchased the lands on both sides of the Hudson River, above and below Fort Orange, subsequently known as Renselaerwyk. This territory, with additions made a few years afterward, was twenty-four miles in length and forty-eight in breadth, and included the present counties of Albany and Renselaer, with a part of Columbia. During the months of June and July of this year, Pauw, another of the directors, obtained in a similar manner a grant of Hoboken and Staten Island, to which he gave the name of Pavonia.

Companies were soon after formed for the speedy settlement of these manors. De Vries, one of the owners under Godyn's patent, established a colony of thirty persons at Swanandael, or Valley of Swans, a short distance from Cape Henlopen, at a place called Hoarkill, now known as Lewistown. A number of emigrants, sufficient to make good the titles of the patroons, were also settled at Pavonia and Renselaerwyk.

After remaining a year in the country, De Vries returned to Holland for supplies, leaving his colonists to the care of Gillis Osset, a rash and ignorant man, who, instead of endeavouring to conciliate the affection of the surrounding Indians, quarrelled with them because one of their chiefs had innocently appropriated to his own use a tin-plate stamped with the arms of Holland, which had been affixed to a post in Swanandael, as a sign of sovereignty. Finding the offence regarded as serious, the Indians cut off the head of the chief who had committed it, and brought a token of the deed to Osset.

Grieved that his intemperate speech should have led to so sanguinary a result, the Dutch commander told the messenger they had done wrong, and that a simple reprimand would have been all-sufficient. The friends of the murdered chief, attributing his death to the clamour raised by Osset, now concerted together to avenge themselves upon all the colonists. While the latter, thirty-two in number, were engaged in the fields attending to the cultivation of their tobacco and grain, the commander Osset and a single sentinel remained in charge of the palisaded fort, where the settlers all lived together. Accordingly, the Indians, having assembled to carry out their purpose, sent three of their warriors to the fort, as if for purposes of trade. Bearing in their arms parcels of beaver skins, they passed the sentinel, and cautiously avoiding a large bull-dog which was chained outside of the house, they approached the commander, who stood near the door, and with smiling countenances offered to barter their furs for merchandise. A bargain having been struck, Osset proceeded to the garret where the public stores were deposited, for the purpose of obtaining the commodities agreed upon. While he was absent, the Indians stationed themselves near the staircase, and awaited impatiently his reappearance. The moment he descended, one of them cleft his head with a tomahawk, and he fell dead on the floor. The sentinel and the dog were next despatched; the latter, of whom they stood in great terror, being shot at from a distance, until he was pierced through and through with more than a score of arrows. Possession of the fort having been thus obtained, they now arranged their plans for the murder of the colonists at work in the fields. Collecting together into one body, they advanced leisurely toward their victims, whom they approached with an air of idle curiosity, as if desirous of witnessing them at their labours. Watching their opportunity, they fell upon the workmen suddenly, and, by a simultaneous movement, massacred the whole of them. The fort was immediately destroyed, the palisades torn up, and the southern shore of the Delaware Bay was once more in complete possession of the natives.

On returning from Holland with additional immigrants in December, De Vries, entering the bay where he had left in peaceful security his industrious settlers, found nothing but silence and desolation. Ascending the creek in his boat, he found the valley beyond strewed with the remains of his murdered countrymen. A few Indians making their appearance at a distance, he greeted them with words of peace, but it was not without hesitancy that they advanced to meet him. Desirous of recovering their friendship, De Vries distributed some presents among them, and formed a treaty of peace and reconciliation. Disembarking the few settlers he had brought with him, he sailed up the river to trade with the natives for supplies. Fort Nassau, built upon Timber Creek, near Camden, which had been some time before deserted by its garrison, he found filled with Indians, of whose sanguinary intentions he was providentially forewarned. A large number of them entered his boat, some playing on reeds, and others bearing beaver skins for sale. After startling them by avowing his knowledge of their intentions, he compelled them to return to shore, under threats of being fired on if they resisted. When they had reluctantly obeyed his orders, sixteen of their chiefs formed a circle on the bank, and declared themselves disposed to be friendly. From motives of policy he concluded a treaty of peace with them, and accepting at their hands the presents customary on such occasions, offered them others in return. These, however, they refused to take, stating coldly that they did not bestow gifts for the purpose of receiving others.

Failing to obtain on the banks of the Delaware the provisions he required, he sailed to Virginia, where he was not only furnished with supplies, but received from the governor six goats, which he took with him to New Amsterdam. They constituted the first live stock owned by the colonists of Manhattan.

The administration of Governor Minuits not proving satisfactory to the Dutch West India Company, he was removed from his office in the spring of 1633, and Wouter Van Twiller appointed director-general in his place. This new officer had just arrived, and by him De Vries was welcomed to the fort, and hospitably entertained during the remainder of his stay.

Under the government of Van Twiller, new trading-posts were established, to meet the increasing traffic with the Indians. A profitable trade in furs springing up with the Pequods and their neighbours upon the Connecticut River, led to the purchase of land from the former, and the erection of a fortified post called the House of Good Hope, not far from the present city of Hartford.

In the mean time, the colony of Plymouth having received large accessions of immigrants from abroad, a commercial rivalry between the latter and the Dutch was gradually undermining the good feeling which had hitherto existed between them. Winthrop, the governor of the new colony settled in Massachusetts Bay, protested against the occupation of the Connecticut by the Dutch, on the ground that the King of England had already granted it to certain of his subjects. Van Twiller, in reply, deprecated any contention about "a little part or portion of these heathenish countries," and proposed to refer the dispute for settlement to their respective governments.

The colony of New Plymouth now took up the matter, and proceeded to assert a right to the territory in question by building a trading-house at Windsor, a short distance above the post erected a few months previous by Van Twiller.

Indignant at this contemptuous defiance of his authority, the latter immediately despatched a force of seventy soldiers to break up the English establishment; but as the Puritans evinced a sturdy determination to defend their new possession, the Dutch commander very prudently recalled his troops, and contented himself with issuing a vigorous protest.

Finding his English neighbours obstinately bent on appropriating to themselves the rich meadows of the Connecticut, Van Twiller busied himself in strengthening and improving New Amsterdam. During the year 1634, he rebuilt the fort, erected barracks for the accommodation of the garrison, constructed a church and parsonage-house, together with various windmills and dwellings for the use of the colonists, and opened several farms, or boweries, in the interior of the island. But this sudden display of energy soon subsided, and, while seeking to aggrandize himself, he gradually suffered the affairs of the company to fall into neglect.

In the mean time, a quarrel had been progressing between the Dutch West India Company and the patroons, or large proprietaries; the former contending for a monopoly of the fur trade, while the latter claimed the exclusive right of traffic within the limits of their own territories. The company finally put an end to the dispute by repurchasing the Swanandael lands belonging to De Vries and others, and by resuming their authority over Hoboken and Staten Island. The manors of Pavonia and Swanandael being thus abolished, that of Renselaerwyk alone remained.

But while the Dutch were thus busily employed with their commercial adventures, large numbers of immigrants were flocking into the New England colonies, and encroaching upon the territory of New Netherland. The trading-post established by Van Twiller on the Connecticut still remained in the charge of his officers; but the country around it was fast settling by the English. In 1634, the latter built a fort at the mouth of the river; and the following year the congregation of Mr. Hooper, one hundred in number, settled upon its western bank, and in the vicinity of Van Twiller's house of Good Hope, founded the town of Hartford.

The administration of Van Twiller not proving satisfactory to the company, he was superseded in 1638 by William Keift, who immediately went to work with great energy to remedy the disorder into which the affairs of the province had fallen.

CHAPTER V.

Difficulties of Governor Kieft—Delaware settled by the Swedes—Arrival of Minuits—Fort built on Christiana Creek—Action of Dutch West India Company—Occupation of Long Island by the Puritans—Fort Nassau reoccupied—Indian disturbances—A retaliatory murder—Kieft demands the fugitive—Preparations for war—Failure of the first expedition against the Raritans—Trouble with the Hackensacks—Two Hollanders murdered—Indemnity offered and refused—Massacre of the Raritans and Hackensacks—Confederation of the river tribes—Indian war—Deplorable condition of the Dutch—Long Island and Manhattan devastated—Unpopularity of Kieft—Attempt upon his life—Negotiations for peace—Speech of an Indian chief—Renewal of the war—Expeditions of Underhill—Destruction of Indians at Tappan and on Long Island—Interposition of the Mohawks—Treaty of peace.

KIEFT had scarcely assumed the government of New Netherland before he found himself involved in a perfect network of difficulties. While the encroachments of the English at the north were rapidly contracting the limits of the Dutch claims in that direction, the Swedes had made their appearance on the Delaware, and were exercising an independent authority over that region.

This new colony owed its existence to Minuits. Indignant at having been superseded by Van Twiller, Minuits sailed to Sweden, and proposed to Oxensteirn, the celebrated minister of Queen Christina, the settlement of a colony on the shores of the Delaware. His services were promptly accepted. Two vessels, the Key of Calmar and the Griffin, were placed under his orders. Leaving Sweden toward the close of the year 1637, he touched at Virginia for wood and water, and then proceeding to the Delaware, sailed up the river, purchased from the Indians the lands on the western shore of the bay, from the southern cape to the falls near Trenton, and, building a fort near the mouth of Christiana Creek, there planted his little colony early in the spring of 1638. Keift immediately issued a series of sharp protests against the occupation of the territory by the Swedes; but as Minuits paid no heed to his remonstrances, he hesitated to resort to forcible measures, until he had first advised with his employers.

But the Dutch West India Company had the sagacity to foresee that a state of hostilities with the English and the Swedes was by no means calculated to benefit their American trade, and that the only way whereby they could hope to compete with their new rivals was to encourage the growth of New Netherland by offering additional advantages to actual settlers. This was done; and under the more liberal provisions of the new charter of privileges, a large number of immigrants arrived at New Amsterdam. The colony was further increased by persons from Virginia and New England.

In the mean time, the English had settled New Haven, and farms were springing up all about the Dutch trading-post on the Connecticut, until the lands around it were restricted to thirty acres. Long Island was also occupied under a grant from Lord Stirling; the arms of the Dutch torn down from the tree to which they had been affixed, and, in bravado, a roughly-carved fool's-head was set up in their place.

But this insult was too flagrant to be suffered to pass without punishment. The intruders were taken prisoners by a party of Dutch troops, and were not released until they had humbly apologized for their offence, and promised to quit the territory. They did not, however, leave the island, but, retiring to its eastern end, founded the town of Southampton. Another company of Puritans landed on the island in 1641, and settled the village of Southold. Against these encroachments, Kieft, a passionate, headstrong man, complained bitterly, but failed of obtaining any redress. In despite of all his protests, settlers from Connecticut spread themselves more and more over the territory of New Netherland during the year 1642; while, at the same time, numerous families of Swedes and Fins established themselves along the shores of the Delaware. But though the Dutch asserted their right to the country by reoccupying Fort Nassau, Printz, the new Swedish governor, garrisoned a similar work on Tinicum Island, a few miles below, as a place of residence for himself, and a protection to the settlers in its vicinity.

At any other period, it is possible that the possession of either shore of the Delaware might have been disputed by the Dutch governor of New Netherland; but when those settlements took place, Kieft was too busily engaged in another quarter, to show his resentment in any manner more forcible than words. Indian disturbances had broken out. An Indian of the Raritan tribe, having witnessed during his boyhood the robbery and murder of his uncle by one of the servants of Minuits, had nursed a desire to revenge his kinsman's death as soon as he was grown up. In 1641, he fulfilled his vow of retaliation by killing an old Dutchman. Kieft immediately demanded that the assassin should be given up; but his people refused to surrender him, and justified the act.

In this emergency, Kieft summoned a meeting of the principal citizens and farmers, to take the subject into consideration. They chose twelve of their number to advise with the governor; but as the board, thus popularly appointed, commenced an active inquiry into existing abuses, Kieft speedily dissolved it, as infringing upon his authority. A detachment of eighty men was sent against the Raritans; but the guide lost his way, and the expedition came to nothing. De Vries and other moderate men counselled a more pacific policy; and the Indians themselves, finding they were threatened with hostilities, evinced a disposition to conciliate matters, by offering to surrender the murderer. Unfortunately, while the adjustment of this affair was pending, a Hackensack Indian, the son of a chief of that tribe, who had been made drunk and then robbed by the Dutch, revenged himself by shooting down the first two white men he chanced to meet.

Desirous of making immediate atonement, a deputation of chiefs waited on Kieft, and offered two hundred fathom of wampum as an indemnity for the crime. The wampum was refused, and a peremptory demand made for the murderer. The chieftains declined to surrender him. "You yourselves," said they, "are the cause of this evil. You ought not to craze the young Indians with brandy. Your own people, when drunk, fight with knives and do foolish things; and you cannot prevent mischief till you cease to sell strong drink to the Indian."

Notwithstanding the obvious truth of this remonstrance, Kieft would listen to no terms of accommodation that did not include the surrender of the fugitive. The chiefs were equally inflexible in shielding him. While the anger of the Dutch governor was at its height, his allies, the

Mohawks, descended upon the Raritans, and forced them to throw themselves upon the mercy of the Dutch. Their forlorn condition awakening a feeling of pity, some of the more compassionate of the colonists supplied them with food. Fearing to return to their former homes in the vicinity of Tappan, the fugitives took shelter among the Hackensacks. The two tribes most obnoxious to the Dutch being thus brought near to each other, the war party among the colonists determined upon their massacre; and, in defiance of the remonstrances of De Vries and many of the most influential inhabitants of New Amsterdam, preparations were at once made to carry their sanguinary purpose into effect.

Acting under the authority of the passionate and overbearing governor, two armed parties, composed respectively of troops and volunteers, crossed the Hudson on the night of the 25th of February, 1643, and fell suddenly upon the Indian encampments. Taken entirely by surprise, scarcely any resistance was offered; and in the stillness of the night, the noise of the musketry and the shrieks of the victims could be distinctly heard by the inhabitants of the island of Manhattan. No mercy was shown. Men, women, children, all were indiscriminately slaughtered. Infants bound in their bark cradles were flung into the icy river; and the poor frantic mothers, who had plunged into the water to their rescue, were mercilessly forced back from the shore until they were drowned. This fearful massacre continued throughout the following day. The wounded, who during the darkness of the night had crawled into secret hiding-places, were hunted out and killed in cold blood. Nearly a hundred Indians, of all ages, perished in this barbarous onslaught, and some thirty others were taken prisoners to New Amsterdam.

But the triumph of the Dutch was only temporary. All the tribes around Manhattan made common cause with the Raritans and Hackensacks, and commenced a war of retaliation. In every direction plantations were destroyed, villages burned, the men and women murdered, and the helpless children hurried away into captivity. The settlements on Long Island were laid desolate. Those on the opposite shore of the Sound shared the same fate. Ruin and despair stared the harassed colonists in the face. Many sought safety in flying from the country. "Mine eyes," says Roger Williams, "saw the flames of their towns, the frights and hurries of men, women, and children, and the present removal of all that could to Holland."

The fury of Kieft was succeeded by terror and remorse. He was charged with having been the cause of the massacre. He threw the blame on Adriansen, an old freebooter, who had headed the ferocious attack on the Raritans. Rendered furious by this accusation, Adriansen, armed with cutlass and pistol, attempted the life of the governor. His assault being frustrated, he was seized and sent a prisoner to Holland. In this fearful state of things, all the colonists were enrolled into service, and a day was set apart for a solemn fast.

Happily, the vengeance of the combined tribes was satiated. Offers of peace were made and accepted. A deputation, led by De Vries, met the principal chiefs of Long Island at Rockaway, on the 5th of March, 1643. In the council which was held soon after their arrival, one of the chiefs arose, bearing in his hand a bundle of small sticks. Addressing himself to De Vries and his companions, he said:—

"When you first arrived on our shores, you were destitute of food; we gave you our beans and our corn; we fed you with oysters and fish; and now, for our recompense, you murder our people." Here the chief put down one little stick. Having thus indicated that this was his first accusation, he continued:—

"The traders whom your first ships left upon our shore to traffic till their return, were cherished by us as the apple of our eye; we gave them our daughters for their wives; among those whom you have murdered were children of your own blood." This closed the orator's second charge, and he laid down another stick. Many other complaints of a similar nature remained behind, as was shown by the number of sticks which he still held in his hand.

A truce was at length agreed upon, to which the river tribes assented soon after; but it was only of brief duration. Their wrongs had been too great for the Indians to settle down quietly, and the presents they received as an equivalent for the damage they had sustained bore no proportion to the losses they had incurred. "The price of blood has not been paid," said an old chief sadly, and the war broke out anew.

In September, the confederated tribes recommenced their devastations upon the frontier settlements, and Kieft was again compelled to call upon the colonists for assistance and advice. A board of eight men were appointed by the popular voice to consult with and aid the governor in the conduct of the war. John Underhill, an English soldier, who had already distinguished himself by his bravery in the Pequod war of New England, was chosen to command the Dutch troops.

Never were energetic measures more imperatively needed. Nearly all the settlements upon Long Island were deserted and destroyed; and of the plantations upon Manhattan Island, only three remained. The distressed colonists, flying before the fury of the savages, were now huddled around the fort at New Amsterdam, where, half famished for want of provisions, and in daily fear of an attack, which they felt themselves incompetent to successfully resist, they dragged out for nearly two years a miserable and precarious existence. Fearful of being utterly exterminated, they applied for assistance to the colonists of Connecticut, and to the Dutch West India Company. But the former were unwilling to embroil themselves with their savage neighbours; and the latter, having suffered serious military disasters in the Brazils, was unable to afford any relief.

Underhill and his subordinates were, however actively engaged to the best of their ability. The Indian villages on Long Island were attacked with partial success. The natives of Tappan were harassed, their corn destroyed, and their forts burned to the ground. Two other expeditions to Long Island, in 1644, were still more effective. In the first, one hundred Indians were killed, and several taken prisoners to New Amsterdam. In the second, Underhill, with one hundred and twenty men, made a sudden descent upon a large Indian town, and falling upon the inhabitants while they were celebrating one of their annual festivals, slew five hundred of them, and set fire to their wigwams.

By these fierce but energetic measures, the spirit of the confederacy was subdued. Several of the tribes solicited peace, but others still resolutely held out. A reinforcement of Dutch troops from Curacoa, arriving in June, 1645, placed the colonists of New Netherland in a better condition to carry on the war. The Mohawks at length interposed. They sent an envoy to Manhattan, to use his influence in favour of a peace. The overtures were successful. On the 30th of August, 1645, delegates from the hostile tribes met in council in the vicinity of Fort Amsterdam, and by a solemn treaty put an end to a war which had been conducted with equal ferocity by both parties.

CHAPTER VI.

Close of the Indian war—Unpopularity of Keift—His recall and shipwreck—Governor Stuyvesant—Condition of New Netherland—Beaverswyk—New Amsterdam—Negotiations with New England—Provisional treaty—War between England and Holland—Prudent policy of Massachusetts—The Dutch solicit assistance from the Narragansetts—Reply of one of their chiefs—Swedish settlements on the Delaware—Fort Cassimer erected—Contentions with the Swedes—Capture of Fort Cassimer—Reduction of the Swedish province by Stuyvesant—Flourishing condition of New Netherland—Internal dissensions—Arbitrary rule of Stuyvesant—Claims of Maryland—Sale of Delaware to the city of Amsterdam—Political privileges granted by Stuyvesant—Patent of Charles II. to the Duke of York—English force sent to take possession of New Netherland—Surrender of the province.

THE close of the Indian war was celebrated with great rejoicings by the harassed colonists of New Netherland; but Kieft, who laboured under the imputation of having provoked the disasters they had undergone, grew daily more unpopular. His arbitrary temper and reckless policy produced numerous complaints among the colonists, and fostered a general desire for his removal. Fully conscious that the condition of antagonism which existed between the people of the province and their governor was greatly prejudicial to their commercial interests, the directors of the West India Company sought to restore harmony by the recall of Kieft, and the appointment of Peter

Stuyvesant in his place. At the same time, the few remaining commercial restrictions were abolished, and the trade thrown open to all competitors.

Stuyvesant arrived in the province during the early part of May, 1647, and in the fall of the same year, Kieft sailed for Europe. The ship in which he embarked, laden with a valuable cargo of furs, was cast ashore on the coast of Wales, and the sanguinary governor, together with some eighty others, perished in the waves.

The new director-general, or governor of New Netherland, Peter Stuyvesant, was possessed of many estimable qualities. He was a brave, frank, honest, and tolerably well-educated soldier. The commencement of his rule was marked by a more tolerant policy toward the neighbouring Indians, though he soon showed himself disposed to regard the poorer settlers with a feeling pretty closely allied to contempt. In comparison with the neighbouring English colonies, that of Manhattan could not be said, up to this period, to have flourished. Its settlement, lucrative as the fur trade had proved itself at first, had not only absorbed the profits of the traffic, but had cost the Dutch West India Company a considerable sum besides. New England already contained twenty thousand inhabitants; while the whole of the settlers within the jurisdiction of New Netherland did not exceed three thousand. A few houses were clustered about Fort Orange, or Beaverswyk, as the present town of Albany was then called. The island of Manhattan was still mostly forest land, many of the cleared plantations having been abandoned during the prevalence of the Indian war, and only some five or six of them, on the arrival of Stuyvesant, continued to be successfully worked. New Amsterdam, the seat of government, was nothing but a mere village of huts, roughly constructed, protected by palisades, and by the fort of the same name, itself hardly in a defensible condition.

One of the first duties which devolved upon Governor Stuyvesant was the arrangement of the long-pending territorial dispute with New England. This, however, was found to be a difficulty by no means easy to be settled harmoniously. The Puritan colonies were already powerful, both in numbers and unity of action; and they were but little disposed to regard the protests of a weaker neighbour, whose title to any territory at all they had always questioned. To war, the Dutch West India Company were decidedly averse, both from the expense attendant upon its prosecution, and from the consciousness that a successful prosecution of it was altogether hopeless.

Finding that negotiation from a distance made but slow progress, Stuyvesant bent his pride to the occasion, and visited Hartford in person. At this place, on the 11th of November, 1650, he succeeded in concluding a provisional treaty, by which the New England commissioners consented to the partition of Long Island between themselves and the Dutch, the boundary between the two colonies being settled to begin in the vicinity of Greenwich on the main, and to extend to Oyster Bay. The treaty received the consent of the Dutch West India Company, and was accepted by the States General; but it failed of being ratified in England.

When the war broke out between England and Holland in 1651, it was at first supposed that it would involve the English and Dutch colonies in a similar struggle; but Massachusetts restrained the ardour of the western settlements, who were anxious for the reduction of New Amsterdam, and urged it upon the colonies, as the safest and most prudent policy, "to forbear the use of the sword, but to be in a posture of defence."

Deeply apprehensive of such an attack, the Dutch West India Company had authorized Governor Stuyvesant to purchase the aid of the Narragansetts; but the latter firmly refused to render any assistance. When pressed by the offers of the Dutch, Mixam, one of the chiefs, nobly replied: "I am poor, but no presents of goods, or of guns, or of powder and shot, shall draw me into a conspiracy against my friends the English."

Fortunately, the peace of 1653 put an end to all apprehension of an invasion from New England, and also effectually prevented the sailing of an expedition against New Amsterdam, which had been authorized by Cromwell.

In addition to his difficulties with the New England colonies in relation to boundaries, and the subsequent danger of hostilities, Stuyvesant became uneasy at the growth of the Swedish settlements on the Delaware. At first, harassed by the prospect of a more imposing peril, and acting in obedience to the pacific policy of his superiors, he restricted himself merely to protecting the Dutch commerce in that quarter, by building Fort Cassimer, near the mouth of the Brandywine.

As Fort Christiana was not more than five miles distant, the proximity of the rival garrisons speedily led to annoyances and contentions. These petty quarrels were kept up until 1654, when Risingh, the Swedish governor, drove out the Dutch troops, and took possession of their fort. The news of this high-handed measure was no sooner made known to the West India Company, than Stuyvesant was ordered to drive the Swedes from the river, or compel their submission. Such great preparations were accordingly made for this undertaking, that it was not until September, 1655, that the expedition was completely organized. Sailing from New Amsterdam with a force of six hundred men, Stuyvesant entered the Delaware, and reduced fort after fort, without meeting with any resistance. Risingh capitulated on honourable terms, and the whole Swedish colony, amounting to seven hundred persons, acknowledged the jurisdiction of the States General, and were confirmed in the possession of their lands and personal property.

From this period the province of New Netherland steadily advanced in numbers and prosperity. The Dutch themselves began to appreciate its value; and immigration to the banks of the Hudson was encouraged by wise and liberal regulations.

The religious tolerance extended to all comers influenced persons from all parts of Europe to take up their residence in the favoured land. Bohemia, Germany, England, France, Switzerland, and Italy aided to increase the population of New Netherland; and the little village of thatched huts on the island of Manhattan speedily exchanged its rude and primitive dwellings for structures of a more imposing character. Fugitives from persecution in other lands found welcome and a home at New Amsterdam. Mechanics, "farmers and labourers, foreigners and exiles, men inured to toil and penury," were invited to assist in building up the colony, by the offer of a free passage from the old world to the new; and the directors of the company had soon the satisfaction of perceiving that their liberal policy was productive of the most beneficial results.

The province of New Netherland, previously retarded in its growth by restrictions and monopolies, now began to assume an importance which justified the most sanguine predictions of its future greatness. Agriculture flourished, timber was exported, mechanical labourers were in steady demand, and peace and plenty rewarded the toils of all.

Among other commercial enterprises in which the West India Company were engaged at this period, was a traffic in slaves. A portion of these soon found a market at New Amsterdam. Others continued the property of the company, and these latter, after a certain period of service, were settled upon small farms, upon the condition of paying annually a stipulated amount of produce.

But in the midst of all this tolerance of opinion, the people of New Netherland were far from enjoying the same political privileges which were exercised by the neighbouring English colonies. In this respect, the directors of the company still continued arbitrary and unwise. The delegates elected to advise with the governor during the dangerous period of the Indian war had been tolerated no longer than their services were actually necessary; and although several attempts were subsequently made by the people to obtain some concessions of authority, all such efforts were stigmatized as factious, and speedily repressed.

After numerous complaints had been made, commercial privileges were extended, but political enfranchisement was steadily denied. A convention, called by the people to assert their right to share in the enactment of laws for the proper government of the province, was dissolved by Stuyvesant, who regarded the demand as an innovation from New England, and fraught with the most dangerous consequences. In answer to a petition which was presented to him, requiring that no new laws should be enacted but with the consent of the people, he haughtily told the deputation that the directors would never make themselves responsible to subjects, and that his authority was derived "from God and the West India Company," and not from the pleasure of the wavering multitude.

In this bold and arbitrary avowal, Stuyvesant was fully and amply sustained by the directors in Holland. They instructed him to pay no regard to the clamours of the people; but to let them fully understand that they must "indulge no longer the visionary dream that taxes could be imposed only with their consent." But the discontent had already taken root, and although the acts of the sturdy old governor were sullenly tolerated, the sentiment of loyalty was weakened, and a change of rulers began to be regarded not only without aversion, but as an object of desire.

The western shore of the Delaware being claimed by Lord Baltimore, the proprietary of Maryland, the West India Company, fearful of encroachments from that quarter, and desirous of building up a barrier against any aggressions on their southern frontier, transferred their claim to all that portion of Delaware lying between Cape Henlopen and the falls of Trenton to the city of Amsterdam, which immediately proceeded to colonize it, principally with indented servants. This scheme, however, soon proved partially unsuccessful. A condition of freedom, under the more liberal government of Maryland, induced many of the Dutch settlers to break through the restraints imposed upon them by their task-masters, and seek refuge in the territory of the English. During the year 1659, Fendall, the governor of Maryland, laid formal claim to the possession of Delaware; but he was answered by the Dutch envoy, that his people had purchased and colonized the territory in dispute, before the patent of Lord Baltimore was in existence. The reply of Fendall being of a threatening character, and the claim of Lord Baltimore being pertinaciously reasserted by his agents, the directors of the West India Company adopted the spirited resolution to defend their rights, "even to the spilling of blood."

Similar troubles were already in agitation at the north. Massachusetts claimed the right to extend the territory of that colony to the upper waters of the Hudson, and thence westwardly as far as they thought proper; while Connecticut had no sooner obtained a royal charter than claims were asserted under it to a considerable portion of territory over which the Dutch had previously exercised undisputed jurisdiction.

Conscious of his inability to resist by force of arms the encroachments of his English neighbours, Stuyvesant went in person to Boston, in order to try what he could effect by negotiation. He met a convention of the New England colonies at that place, in September, 1663; but was compelled to return as he went, without being able to obtain, either then, or during the subsequent month at Hartford, the recognition of any territory at all, as belonging of right to the province of New Netherland. To the cautious Puritan diplomatists, the Dutch province was a fiction, inasmuch as the English laid claim to the whole of the continent discovered by Cabot.

In the midst of these proprietary disputes, Stuyvesant, foreseeing the danger that was impending over the colony, sought to restore harmony among the people of New Netherland themselves, by granting them certain privileges which he had heretofore indignantly refused. In 1663, a popular assembly was conceded, which met in November of the same year, and in fuller numbers during the spring of 1664. But that confidence which the government had superciliously alienated was not to be so easily regained. The privilege which had been extended to the "wavering multitude" had been extorted from the fears of the governor, and not from his sense of justice. An alarming invasion was threatened, and it was necessary to conciliate the people, in order to prevail upon them to take up arms in defence of the province. But the concessions came too late.

In 1664, Charles II. granted to his brother James, Duke of York, a patent for all the mainland of New England, beginning at St. Croix, extending thence to the Pemaquid, and stretching across and embracing the whole territory, from Connecticut River to Delaware Bay.

Without any previous declaration of war against the Dutch, three ships, with six hundred men, were despatched from England to take possession of New Netherland in the name of the Duke of York. These ships, having three commissioners on board, reached Boston in July; and toward the close of the following month, the troops pitched their camp on Long Island, on the site of the present city of Brooklyn.

Governor Stuyvesant had received early intelligence of the sailing of this expedition and its destination; but all his efforts to arouse the spirit of the colonists were unavailing. Indeed, many of the latter, elated at the prospect of obtaining the same political privileges which were enjoyed by the neighbouring provinces, boldly denied that the Dutch had ever any right to the country.

No sooner had one of the frigates entered Gravesend Bay, than Stuyvesant despatched a letter to the English commander, desiring to know the reason of his approach and anchorage in the harbour, without giving the customary notification. Sir Richard Nichols responded by a summons of surrender, on the condition of security to the inhabitants of their estates, lives, and liberties.

The governor, a brave old soldier, who had lost a limb in the service of the States, was desirous of making a sturdy defence; but the council and burgomasters, whom he had convened for consultation, being well aware that any resistance they could offer would be of no avail, advised submission, provided the terms offered in the summons were such as the inhabitants could accept.

The fiery governor struggled hard to induce them to change their determination. He refused to let them know the liberal conditions which had been offered, and upon their demanding a sight of the summons, his wrath knew no bounds; suddenly producing the latter, he passionately tore it into shreds before their eyes. Finally, however, after much contention, and aided by the good offices of Winthrop, the aged governor of Connecticut, Stuyvesant was driven to consent to a capitulation. The other settlements on the Hudson and Delaware swore allegiance to the English soon after, and the conquest of New Netherland was completed.

CHAPTER VII.

New Netherland becomes New York—Colonel Nichols governor—Meeting on Long Island—Incorporation of the city of New York—Arbitrary system of government established—Lovelace appointed governor—War with the Dutch—New York reconquered—Administration of Colve—Retrocession of New York—Government of Andros—Difficulties with Connecticut—Spirited conduct of the Puritans—Disaffection of the people—A representative government demanded—Reply of the Duke of York—Description of the province—Its prosperity—City of New York, its population and public buildings—Character of the people—Andros recalled—Dongan appointed governor—Concession of political privileges—Indian affairs—Convention at Albany—Designs of the French—Instructions of the Duke of York—Conduct of Dongan—Invasion of the Five Nations by the French—Peace solicited—Speech of De la Barre—Reply of Garrangula.

New Netherland having thus, without bloodshed, become subjected to the English crown. Colonel Sir Richard Nichols took upon himself the government of the conquered province as deputy-governor, and in honour of the proprietary, that portion of the territory retained by him, together with the little capital of New Amsterdam, acquired the name of New York.

All the tract of land previously belonging to New Netherland, which was bounded by the Delaware Bay on the west, by the ocean and the Hudson River on the east, and by the present state of New York on the north, having been granted by the duke to Lord Berkeley and Sir George Carteret, became henceforth a separate and distinct jurisdiction, under the name of the province of New Jersey.

During the short period that Nichols remained governor of New York, commissioners, appointed for that purpose, determined the boundary between the latter province and Connecticut, and under their decision the whole of Long Island was included within the territory of the new proprietary.

On the 1st of March, 1665, a convention of delegates was held at Hempstead, on Long Island, for the purpose of adjusting the limits of their respective townships, and the appointment of proper local officers. Three months later, the city of New York was incorporated, the exercise of municipal authority being intrusted to a mayor, five aldermen, and a sheriff; but the people themselves derived no political privileges from a change of rulers. The governor, and a council devoted to his interests, retained the sole right to impose taxes, and to enact or modify such laws throughout the province as they thought proper. This arbitrary mode of government was productive of the usual discontent; but Nichols, busied for the most of the time in confirming the ancient Dutch grants, paid no heed to the murmurs of "factious republicans."

Returning to England in 1667, he was succeeded by Francis Lovelace, who, following out the system adopted by his predecessor, took upon himself both the executive and judicial functions, and instructed his deputy on the western shore of the Delaware to repress all disaffection in that quarter, by laying such taxes upon the people as might give them "liberty for no thought but how to discharge them."

Adopting this principle as his rule of action, Lovelace imposed a duty of ten per cent. upon all imports and exports. But this high-handed measure was met by a vigorous protest from eight of the Long Island towns, who boldly expressed their aversion to all taxes levied under the sole authority of the governor and council, and demanded a participation in the government of the province by means of an annual assembly. Lovelace and his subservient subordinates responded to the protest by ordering it to be publicly burned by the common hangman.

The affairs of the province continued to be administered in this despotic manner until 1673, when Charles II., having been drawn by the intrigues of Louis XIV. into a war with the Dutch, a small squadron belonging to the latter, and commanded by Cornelius Evertsen, anchored, on the 30th of July, in the vicinity of Staten Island.

Lovelace appears to have been absent at this time, and Manning, the commandant of the fort, no sooner received a summons to surrender, than he sent a messenger to arrange the terms of capitulation. Not a blow was struck. The people of New Jersey quietly returned to their old allegiance, and the Swedes and Fins followed their example. The whole territory of New Netherland having thus quietly submitted to the arms of the States General, Anthony Colve was appointed governor-general, and Lovelace obtained permission to return to England in the Dutch fleet. Manning was subsequently tried by court-martial for treachery and cowardice, and found guilty. Having, however, in the mean time, made interest in England with the king and the Duke of York, he escaped being sentenced to death, but was adjudged to have his sword publicly broken over his head, and to be incapable of serving the crown for the future in any civil or military capacity.

Governor Colve retained his office but a short period, for at the close of the war, which took place in February, 1674, it was agreed by treaty mutually to restore all conquests. To remove any disputes which might subsequently arise in respect to his title in consequence of the previous surrender of the province, the Duke of York obtained from the king a new patent, covering the same lands which had been granted him in 1664. On the 1st of August, two days after this patent was executed, the duke appointed Major Edmund Andros to receive possession of the province at the hands of the Dutch authorities, and to renew the absolute authority of the proprietary. On the 31st of October, this was quietly accomplished. Hoping to obtain some concessions from the new governor, the inhabitants petitioned to be allowed an assembly, and Andros favoured the prayer; but it was disapproved of by the proprietary. The settlers of the eastern portion of Long Island, preferring the jurisdiction of Connecticut to that of New York, also petitioned Andros to be allowed to unite themselves with that colony; but, instead of their wishes being acceded to, the governor soon afterward organized an expedition for the purpose of asserting the claim of the Duke of York to all that territory embraced within his patent as far as the Connecticut River. As soon as these intentions were made known to Laet, the deputy-governor of Connecticut, he called the assembly together, who promptly ordered Captain Bull, in command of the colonial troops at Saybrook, to resist the advance of Andros. The order reached Saybrook almost simultaneously with the appearance of Andros before the town.

He summoned the fort to surrender, and the sturdy Puritan commandant responded by hoisting his flag. Conscious that his force was too weak to carry the place by assault, Andros resorted to persuasion; but when he directed his commission and the duke's patent to be read in the hearing of the colonial troops, he was ordered to desist. Finding neither threats nor expostulations of any avail, he suffered himself to be escorted to his boat by the armed provincials, and set sail for New York.

The exercise of his authority being continually clogged with difficulties, especially by the people of Long Island, many of whom were of Puritan descent, Andros strongly urged upon the Duke of York the policy of conceding to the people a representative form of government. To this wise and judicious counsel, the duke replied by letter, dated the 1st of January, 1679:—

"I cannot but suspect that assemblies would be of dangerous consequence; nothing being more known than the aptness of such bodies to assume to themselves many privileges which prove destructive to, or very often disturb the peace of government when they are allowed."

Such being the decision of the short-sighted proprietary, Andros was too obsequious a servant to persist in urging the popular demand. The province continued to prosper notwithstanding. It consisted at this time of twenty-four towns and villages, in six precincts, ridings, or courts of sessions. The number of its militia amounted to two thousand men. Its annual exports consisted of sixty thousand bushels of wheat, besides peas, beef, pork, tobacco, and furs.

The city of New York contained some three thousand five hundred inhabitants, and about three hundred and fifty houses, almost all of which presented their gables to the streets, the most important public buildings being erected in the foreground, so as to be the more readily seen from the river. The chief part of the town, at this period, lay along the East River, and on the slope of the ridge forming the line of Broadway. In front of the town were constructed three half-moon forts, called Rondeels, which were erected at equal distances from each other, between Coenties Slip and Wall Street, the latter deriving its name from the line of palisades which stretched from that point to the junction of Grace and Lumber Streets, where the North River limits terminated in a redoubt.

Apart from the unhappy dissensions arising from the denial of the right to govern themselves, the inhabitants of the province of New York were both peaceful and prosperous. Having but few wants, and simple in their tastes, "a wagon gave as good content as in Europe a coach, and their home-made cloth as the finest lawns. The doors of the low-roofed houses, which luxury never entered, stood wide open to charity and the stranger." A merchant worth five thousand dollars was accounted an opulent man; and a farmer worth half that sum in personal property was regarded as rich; but the merchants were not many, the slaves were few, and servants greatly in demand.

But the consciousness of being deprived of those political rights which were enjoyed by all the other English colonies was a constant source of unhappiness and disaffection, especially among the people of Long Island, who had struggled for many years to obtain the same liberty of self-government which was exercised by their kindred of Connecticut. It was therefore with feelings of the utmost gratification that they hailed the recall of Andros in 1682, and the appointment of Colonel Dongan as governor of the province.

Repeated importunities and petitions having at length convinced even the obtuse mind of the Duke of York, that his narrow provincial policy was fast bringing his authority into contempt, and alienating the affections of the people, he condescended to take counsel of William Penn, and instructed Dongan to convene a general assembly. After many delays, the new governor reached New York on the 27th of August, 1683, and almost immediately afterward issued a proclamation to the freeholders, empowering them to elect delegates to the legislature.

On the 17th of October, 1683, the first assembly met. It consisted of the governor, his council of ten, and seventeen members chosen by the people, to form the house of representatives. The most important act of the session was the adoption of a declaration of rights. This charter proclaimed that, "Supreme legislative power shall for ever be, and reside, in the governor, council, and people, met in general assembly. Every freeholder and freeman shall vote for representation without restraint. No freeman shall suffer but by judgment of his peers; and all trials shall be by a jury of twelve men. No tax shall be assessed on any pretence whatever, but by the consent of the assembly. No seaman or soldier shall be quartered on the inhabitants against their will. No martial law shall exist. No person professing faith in God by Jesus Christ shall at any time be any ways disquieted, or questioned, for any difference of opinion." Such was the language of the earliest popular charter of New York. The despotism under which the people had so long groaned had taught them a just consideration for the liberty of others.

The spirit of discontent being appeased by the concession of political privileges, Governor Dongan next turned his attention to Indian affairs. For a long series of years the French in Canada had vainly endeavoured to break down the power of the Iroquois, and detach them from their alliance, at first with the Dutch, and subsequently with the English. But neither hostile invasions nor the preaching of Jesuit missionaries could win those proud and independent warriors to acknowledge the supremacy of France. But even while disposed to maintain a friendship with the English, they were not insensible of the neglect which they had met with at the hands of Lovelace, and in their war-parties along the frontiers of New York, Maryland, and Virginia, had resented the aggressions of the whites. Soon after the commencement of Dongan's administration, the principal chiefs of the Five Nations were invited to meet in grand convention at Albany, for the purpose of renewing the old treaty of peace, and putting an end to this desultory warfare. In the mean time, the French, under De la Barre, were organizing a large army, with the avowed purpose of utterly exterminating the Five Nations, and Governor Dongan received instructions from the Duke of York to throw no obstacles in their way. Too conscientious to regard any such ruthless orders, Dongan warned the Indians of the impending danger, and promised them assistance.

In accordance with their previous agreement, deputies from the Mohawks, Oneidas, Cayugas, Onondagas, and Senecas, met the governors of New York and Virginia at Albany, on the 13th of July, 1684, where a treaty of peace was made with the offending tribes, the Mohawks and Senecas, "never having broken the ancient chain," being witnesses to the same.

The warriors had scarcely dissolved the council and returned to their villages, before De la Barre invaded the Iroquois territory with an army of seventeen hundred men. Bad provisions, however, and the miasma arising from the marshes of Ontario, had so weakened his troops by sickness, that, after a delay of six weeks at Fort Frontenac, he crossed the lake, and invited the chiefs of the Five Nations to meet him and conclude a treaty of peace.

The Mohawks and Senecas, acting under the advice of Dongan, refused to attend; but the Oneidas, Onondagas, and Cayugas, influenced by the Jesuit missionaries, concluded to visit the French governor in his camp, and hear what he had to say.

Two days after their arrival a council was held. Addressing himself to Garrangula, an Onondaga chief, De la Barre said: "The king, my master, being informed that the Five Nations have often infringed the peace, has ordered me to come hither with a guard, and to send Ohguesse to the Onondagas to bring the chief sachems to my camp. The intention of the great king is, that you and I may smoke the calumet of peace together; but upon this condition: that you promise me in the name of the Senecas, Cayugas, Onondagas, Oneidas, and Mohawks, to give entire satisfaction and reparation to his subjects, and for the future never to molest them.

"This is what I have to say to Garrangula, that he may carry to the other chiefs the declaration which I make. The king, my master, does not wish them to force him to send a great army to Cadaracqui Fort, to begin a war, which must be fatal to them. He would be sorry that this fort, which was the work of peace, should become the prison of your warriors. We must endeavour, on both sides, to prevent such misfortunes. The French, who are the brethren and friends of the Five Nations, will never trouble their repose, provided that the satisfaction which I demand be given, and that the treaties of peace be hereafter observed. I shall be extremely grieved if my words do not produce the effect which I expect from them; for then I shall be obliged to join with the Governor of New York, who is commanded by his master to assist me, and burn the castles of the Five Nations, and destroy you. This belt confirms my words."

Unmoved by the threat with which De la Barre had closed his address, the proud Onondaga chieftain, perfectly aware of the weak condition of the army which had marched so exultingly from Canada to exterminate his people, walked five or six times round the circle, and then, halting before the French governor, who was seated in an elbow chair, he answered with the most sarcastic irony:—

"Yonnondio, I honour you, and the warriors that are with me likewise honour you. Your interpreter has finished his speech; I now begin mine. My words make haste to reach your ears: hearken to them. Yonnondio, you must have believed, when you left Quebec, that the sun had burnt up all the forests which render our castles inaccessible to the French; or that the lakes had so far overflowed their banks that they had surrounded our castles, and that it was impossible for us to get out of them. Yes, Yonnondio, surely you must have dreamed so, and the curiosity of seeing so great a wonder has brought you so far. Now you are undeceived, since I and the warriors here present are come to assure you that the Senecas, Cayugas, Onondagas, Oneidas, and Mohawks are yet alive. Hear, Yonnondio. I do not sleep. I have my eyes open; and the sun, which enlightens me, discovers to me a great captain at the head of a company of soldiers, who speaks as if he were dreaming. He says that he only came to the lake to smoke the great calumet with the Onondagas. But Garrangula says, that he sees the contrary; that it was to knock them on the head, if sickness had not weakened the arms of the French."

Continuing his speech in the same strain of

ierce sarcasm, he told De la Barre that the Great Spirit had saved the lives of the French by afflicting them with sickness; for if they had not been thus stricken down by a higher Power, the very women, and children, and old men of the Iroquois wouid have stormed the heart of the French camp. In answer to the accusation of being subject to the English, he said proudly: "We are born free; we neither depend upon Yonnondio nor Corlear. We may go where we please, and carry with us whom we please; and buy and sell what we please; if your allies are slaves, use them as such. This belt preserves my words." When he had justified the wars of the Five Nations with the Indian tribes friendly to the French, he thus concluded:

"Hear, Yonnondio. What I say is the voice of the Five Nations. Hear what they answer; open your ears to what they speak. The Senecas, Cayugas, Onondagas, Oneidas, and Mohawks say, that when they buried the hatchet at Cadaracqui, in the presence of your predecessor, and in the middle of the fort, they planted the tree of peace in the same place, to be there carefully preserved; that instead of a retreat for soldiers, the fort might become a rendezvous for merchants; that in place of arms and munitions of war, beavers and merchandise should only enter there.

"Hear, Yonnondio. Take care for the future, that so great a number of soldiers as appear there do not choke the tree of peace planted in so small a fort. It will be a great loss, if, after it had so easily taken root, you should stop its growth and prevent its covering your country and ours with its branches. I assure you, in the name of the Five Nations, that our warriors shall dance to the calumet of peace under its leaves, and shall remain quiet on their mats, and shall never dig up the hatchet till their brother Yonnondio or Corlear, shall, either jointly or separately, endeavour to attack the country which the Great Spirit gave to our ancestors. This belt preserves my words; and this other, the authority which the Five Nations have given me."

Then turning to Le Main, the interpreter, he said: "Take courage, Ohguesse; you have spirit, speak; explain my words; forget nothing; tell all that your brethren and friends say to Yonnondio, your governor, by the mouth of Garrangula, who loves you, and desires you to accept of this present of beaver, and take part with me in my feast, to which I invite you. This present of beaver is sent to Yonnondio on the part of the Five Nations."

And so ended this remarkable speech, one of the finest examples of barbarous eloquence to be found in any language. Utterly confounded by the bold reply of the Onondaga chieftain, De la Barre hastily accepted a treaty, the terms of which he was not in a condition to dispute, and retired with his shattered forces to Montreal.

CHAPTER VIII.

Canadian affairs—Denonville supersedes De la Barre—Prepares for war—Marches against the Iroquois—Is attacked—Retires into Canada—Fate of the French garrison at Niagara—Retaliation of the Iroquois—Negociations for peace—Reply of Governor Dongan—Speech of Garrangula—Council at Montreal—Stratagem of the Dinondadie Indians—Renewal of hostilities—Dreadful massacre of the French—Affairs of New York—Disaffection in England—Landing of William, Prince of Orange—Flight of James—Revolution in the provinces—Dongan recalled—Agitation in New York—The fort seized by Leisler—William and Mary proclaimed—Leisler governor—Count Frontenac appointed governor of Canada—Negotiates with the Five Nations—War between England and France—Burning of Schenectady—Difficulties in New York.

THE unsuccessful expedition of De la Barre and its disgraceful termination were no sooner made known in France, than a reinforcement of troops was ordered into Canada, and the Marquis Denonville appointed to supersede De la Barre in the government of that province. An energetic soldier, extolled for his courage, uprightness, and piety, Denonville speedily sought to retrieve the honour of the French arms. In order to control the Iroquois, and, at the same time, command the fur trade of the lakes, he suggested to the French government the propriety of establishing a fort at Niagara. In the mean time he prepared for active operations against the Five Nations, by pushing forward extraordinary supplies to Fort Frontenac.

Penetrating at once the design of the new French governor, Dongan wrote to warn him, that any attack upon the Indian confederacy would be resented by the English, whose allies they were. Affairs remained in this disturbed condition until 1687, when the Miamis being threatened with war by the Iroquois, Denonville determined, by invading the latter, to force them to forego their purpose. Collecting at Montreal two thousand troops and six hundred friendly Indians, he sent orders to the commanders of outposts to meet him with reinforcements at Niagara, for an expedition against the Senecas. The Five Nations immediately prepared for war. Embarking his whole army in canoes, Denonville set out from Fort Cadaracqui on the 23d of June, and sailing down the lake in two divisions, landed at Tyrondequait, and marched against the principal town of the Senecas, seven leagues distant. In the mean time, Monsieur Companie, with an advance party of some three hundred Canadians, had surprised two villages of the Onondagas, who, reposing upon the good faith of the missionary Lamberville, had settled themselves peacefully about eight leagues from the lake. To guard against their giving the alarm to their countrymen, these Indians were ruthlessly seized and carried to the fort. Reserving thirteen of the principal warriors to be sent as galley slaves to France, the remainder were tortured at the stake, where, singing their death-song to the last, they died heroically.

Throwing forward a detachment of traders and friendly Indians as scouts, Denonville followed with the main body, which was composed of the regulars and militia. On the second day of the march, the vanguard reached the vicinity of the town. Seeing no one, and supposing the place to have been deserted, they quickened their pace to overtake the fugitives. Suddenly, five hundred Senecas sprang from their ambush, and, raising the war-cry, charged upon the advance, and upon the main body which hastened up to its support. In a moment all was confusion. Rolled back upon each other by the unexpectedness of the attack, the French retreated in disorder, and took refuge in the neighbouring woods. The firmness of the Indian allies alone retrieved the fortunes of the day. Gathering courage from the example of the latter, the regulars under Denonville were rallied, and again led to the attack, which finally ended in the repulse of the Senecas.

But the victory was dearly bought. Disheartened by his losses, and the sturdy resistance he had met with, Denonville contented himself with burning the Seneca village, and torturing two old men found in it. Afraid to pursue the fugitives, he retired with his army to the south-east side of the straits, at Niagara, where he built a fort; and leaving within it a garrison of one hundred men, under the command of the Chevalier de la Troye, returned into Canada with the remainder of his army.

He had no sooner evacuated the country of the Iroquois, than the Senecas reoccupied it, and investing the garrison of Niagara, succeeded in cutting off the communication, until all but eight men perished miserably by famine.

Lamberville, the missionary, who had been the unconscious cause of the massacre of the Onondagas at Fort Cadaracqui, was soon after summoned by some aged chiefs into their presence. "We have much reason," said one of them, "to treat thee as an enemy; but we know thee too well. Thou hast betrayed us, but treason was not in thy breast. Fly, therefore; for when our young braves shall have sung their war-song, they will listen to no voice but the swelling voice of their anger." Humanely considerate for his safety, even in the midst of their own sorrow, they ordered trusty guides to conduct him secretly to a place of security.

On the 5th of August, Governor Dongan met the chiefs of the Five Nations in council at Albany, and warmly commended the courage they had exhibited in defending their country against the advance of the French. He advised, that the Christian Indians who had removed into Canada should be invited to return and settle themselves within the limits of their own territory, and strongly cautioned his allies to make no peace with the French, except through his agency.

Throughout the whole of 1688, the Senecas, Onondagas, and Mohawks continued a fierce retaliatory war upon the Canadians. Fort Chambly was beset, the houses in the vicinity burned to the ground, and the warriors returned in triumph with numerous captives to Albany. Several French soldiers were captured near Fort Frontenac, by the Onondagas, and held by them as hostages until their sachems should be returned to their own country, unharmed, from the galleys of Marseilles.

Denonville applied, through Pere le Vaillant, to Governor Dongan, to negotiate a peace and use his influence for a restoration of the captives. Dongan answered, that no peace could be made with the Five Nations until the Onondaga sachems were released from the French galleys and sent home, the Christian Indians returned to their own country, the forts at Niagara and Frontenac razed, and compensation made to the Senecas for the damage they had sustained.

Denonville indignantly refused to purchase a peace on any such humiliating terms, and Garrangula immediately advanced at the head of five hundred warriors. "I have always loved the French," said the scornful chieftain. "Our war riors proposed to come and burn your forts, your houses, your granges, and your corn; to weaken you by famine, and then to overwhelm you. I am come to tell Yonnondio he can escape this misery, if, within four days, he will yield to the terms which Corlear has proposed." Thus haughtily threatened, Denonville yielded. A truce being proclaimed, twelve hundred warriors met the French governor in council at Montreal, and dictated a treaty of peace on the conditions previously offered by Governor Dongan. As the Mohawks and Senecas were not represented at the council, Denonville required that deputies from them should also come forward and ratify the treaty on the part of their respective nations. To this requisition the other chiefs agreed, and the terms of the treaty having been arranged, the convention was dissolved.

But while the prospects of peace were thus brightening, a singular artifice, adopted by a tribe of Indians friendly to the French, suddenly inspired the Iroquois with sentiments of the bitterest hostility.

The Dinondadies, an Indian tribe at war with the Five Nations, desirous of preventing a good understanding between the French and the Iroquois, executed the following stratagem to effect their purpose. One hundred warriors, led by Adario, their chief, suddenly intercepted the deputies of the confederated cantons, at the falls of the Cadaracqui, or Ontario River, while they were on their way to Montreal to ratify the treaty of peace previously agreed upon. Some were killed, and the remainder taken prisoners. Adario then boasted to the latter that he owed his success to the French governor, who had given him timely information of the approach of fifty Iroquois warriors. Surprised at this apparently treacherous conduct, the ambassadors communicated to the chief the peaceful object of their journey. Feigning the utmost indignation and remorse at having been made an instrument of the basest treachery, Adario instantly ordered the captives to be set free. "Go, my brethren," said he; "I untie your bonds and send you home again, though our nations be at war. The French governor has made me commit so black an action, that I shall never rest easy until your people shall have taken a full revenge."

Giving implicit credence to the story told by Adario, the Five Nations no sooner heard of the outrage which had been committed upon the persons of their ambassadors, than, animated by the keenest thirst for revenge, they collected twelve hundred warriors, and on the 26th of July, 1688, landed on the south side of the island of Montreal, burned, sacked, ravaged, and plundered all the surrounding settlements, up even to the very gates of the city; slew one thousand of the inhabitants, and carrying off twenty-six captives, tortured them to death at the stake. Not content with this terrible retaliation, they returned again to the island in October, and committed further devastations of the most sanguinary and barbarous character. Perfectly paralyzed with terror, the French made no resistance; and the confederates, gaining increased confidence with success, swept over the whole of Canada, carrying destruction wherever they went. Only a few fortified places remained, and these owed their safety more to the ignorance of the savages in the art of attacking them, than to the courage of their respective garrisons. Of the neighbouring Indian tribes, only two remained faithful to the French in their adversity. All the others repudiated their alliance, and made peace with the Iroquois and the English. Had the latter rendered the least assistance to the Five Nations, the whole French dominion in Canada would have been at an end. As it was, the cities of Quebec, Montreal, and Trois Riviéres alone remained; the whole country south of the lakes being permanently conquered by the confederated warriors.

During the progress of these events, great political changes were taking place in the provinces. The attempt of James II. to bring about a restoration of the Catholic religion, had rendered him odious to the English people; and the birth of a son in 1688, having destroyed all hope of a Protestant succession, William, Prince of Orange, the champion of Protestantism in Europe, who had married Mary, the eldest daughter of James, was invited to take upon himself the government of the kingdom. Complying with the popular wish, William landed in England in the fall of 1688, and James, deserted even by his own children, was compelled to take refuge in France.

The news of this great Protestant revolution reached Boston on the 4th of April, 1689. Andros, who had been appointed governor of that province, was immediately deposed; the charter, of which he had deprived the people, was resumed; and the aged Bradstreet, whom Andros had superseded in office, reinstated as chief magistrate. During the month of May, Connecticut followed the example of Massachusetts, deposed the royal governor, and re-elected Robert Treat. Rhode Island adopted similar measures. Virginia hesitated for a short time, but at length proclaimed William and Mary "Lord and Lady" of the province.

In New York, the tidings occasioned great agitation. The wise and politic Dongan having been recalled by James, a short time previously, the government of the province had been transferred into the hands of his deputy Francis Nicholson. A rumour was spread, that the friends of the deposed king intended to confirm his authority by a massacre of the disaffected; a fierce popular excitement was created; a mob paraded the streets; five militia companies, the only military force in the city, surrounded the house of Jacob Leisler, a merchant, and their senior captain, and demanded that he should place himself at their head and seize the fort. It was captured on the 1st of June, with the stores and public money; and the companies took upon themselves garrison duty alternately. Nicholson, deprived of his authority, sailed for England. A committee of safety was immediately formed, and Leisler appointed captain of the fort, with gubernatorial powers, until such time as an officer, duly commissioned, should be sent from England.

After proclaiming William and Mary at the sound of the trumpet, Leisler wrote to the king, explaining his proceedings, and accounting for the use he had made of the money found in the fort. At this period, Milbourne, the son-in-law of Leisler, a man of great energy and ambition, arrived from England, and was made secretary of the province. The old council, finding it impossible to resist, with any hope of success, the self-constituted authorities of New York, retired to Albany, where a convention was held, which proclaimed allegiance to William and Mary, but rejected the authority of Leisler, and refused to surrender the fort to Milbourne, who, with an insufficient force, had been sent up to demand it.

Soon after this, a letter reached New York,

addressed to Nicholson, or in the event of his absence, to "such as for the time being take care for preserving the peace, and administering the law in New York." In this letter a commission as governor was enclosed for Nicholson; but as the latter had already sailed for England, Leisler, under the supposed sanction of the superscription, continued in authority.

In the mean time, the disasters of Denonville in Canada had led to his recall, and the appointment of Count Frontenac as governor-general. Although then in his sixty-eighth year, Frontenac, within a few days after his landing at Quebec, started in a canoe for Montreal, to animate the desponding inhabitants, and renew the French alliances with the neighbouring Indian tribes. This was the more necessary as the French monarch had espoused the cause of the exiled James, and had declared war against England. Messengers were also sent into the Iroquois territory to conciliate the friendship of the Five Nations. A council was accordingly held on the 22d of January, 1690, at Onondaga, at which eighty chiefs of the confederated cantons were present. During the conference the Indian delegates professed themselves disposed to listen to terms of peace, but evaded the desire of Frontenac to negotiate a treaty.

Desirous, by a display of energy and courage, to force the proud warriors to regard an alliance with France in a more favourable light, Frontenac determined to carry the war into the English provinces.

Three separate expeditions were accordingly organized, the first of which, led by De Mantet and Sainte Helene, was to make a sudden and unexpected descent upon New York. The second, led by Hertel, was to surprise the settlement at Salmon Falls, on the Piscataqua; while the third, commanded by Portneuf, was ordered to attack the fort and settlement at Casco Bay. They were all successful. The war party under De Mantet and Sainte Helene, and consisting of one hundred and ten French and Indians, left Montreal about the middle of January, 1690. After a march of twenty-two days over the frozen surface of the wilderness, during which they subsisted upon parched corn, and such game as could be procured by their hunters, they entered, just before midnight, the village of Schenectady, on the Mohawk River. Passing within the palisades, the gates of which were open and unguarded, they divided themselves into parties of six or seven each, and while the inhabitants were buried in profound slumber, the war-whoop was suddenly raised, and the doors of the houses burst forcibly opened. An indiscriminate massacre was immediately commenced. Men, women, and children were put to death in a manner too barbarous to relate. The whole village was set on fire, and by the flames, the rifle, and the tomahawk, sixty persons perished, and twenty-seven were carried off into captivity. Those who escaped the fury of the assailants, fled, half-clad, through a driving snow, toward Albany, twenty-five of whom subsequently lost their limbs, through their exposure to the severities of the weather during that dreadful night. The enemy remained in possession of the village until noon the following day, when, fearful of being intercepted on their return by the Iroquois, they retreated hastily into Canada.

The citizens of Albany, alarmed at this daring invasion, and weakened by internal discord, no longer held out against Milbourne, who was approaching a second time; but passively submitted the fort into his hands. Unhappily, the province still continued to be torn by dissensions; and while the popular faction clamorously sustained the measures of Leisler, the tory or aristocratic party placed themselves in direct and vehement opposition.

CHAPTER IX.

Invasion of Canada resolved upon—Failure of the expedition—Arrival of Ingoldsby at New York—The fort blockaded—Arrival of Governor Sloughter—Arrest of Leisler and his council—Leisler and Milbourne tried and sentenced to death—Their execution—Appeal to the king by the son of Leisler—Report of the commissioners—Appeal to parliament—Reversal of the sentence against Leisler and Milbourne—Death of Sloughter—Fletcher appointed governor—His character—Frontenac invades the country of the Five Nations—His march from Montreal—Falls upon the Mohawk villages—Returns to Canada—Activity of Schuyler—Of Fletcher—His popularity with the Indians—Convention at Albany—Conduct of Fletcher toward the provincial assembly—Resistance of the latter—Activity of Frontenac—Invades the Onondagas—Torture of an aged chief—Meagre results of the expedition.

THE terrible loss effected by the French detachment upon the frontier settlements, proving to the English provinces the necessity of united action, a convention of delegates from Massachusetts and Connecticut was held at New York, on the 1st of May, 1690, when it was resolved that a force of nine hundred men, from Connecticut and New York, should march overland against Montreal; while Massachusetts despatched a fleet and army against Quebec. Both expeditions proved signally unsuccessful. A disagreement between the leaders occasioned insubordination among the troops, and the land forces separating, returned home, exasperated by mutual misunderstandings. The command of the naval expedition was intrusted to Sir William Phipps. He sailed up the St. Lawrence with a fleet of thirty-two vessels, and anchoring before Quebec on the 18th of October, sent a messenger to Frontenac, demanding a surrender of the town. "I'll answer your master by the mouths of my cannon," was the reply of the brave old governor. Two attempts were immediately made to land below the town, but they were both repulsed with loss. The forts opening their fire soon after, the provincials were compelled to abandon the assault and retire with precipitation.

In January, 1691, Ingoldsby reached New York, from England, bearing a commission as captain. On his arrival he demanded possession of the fort; but Leisler refused to give it up, contending that Ingoldsby had exhibited no order from the crown, or from Sloughter, who was known to have received the commission of governor, though he had not yet made his appearance in the province. Irritated at finding his authority disputed, Ingoldsby, supported by the royalists, blockaded the fort with his troops, and issued a proclamation denouncing the governor and his garrison. The passions of the militia being aroused, shots were exchanged during the investment, by which, greatly to the grief of Leisler, several lives were lost.

On the 19th of March, Sloughter reached New York. In the disordered state of the province, an able and energetic governor would have speedily remedied many of the evils which had been fostered by the violence of contending factions. Sloughter was neither able nor energetic; but licentious, avaricious, and poor. Prepossessed against Leisler before his arrival, he declined to receive his messengers, or to recognise him in any other light than as an usurper, and Ingoldsby was at once ordered to arrest the obnoxious governor and his council. Soon after their arrest, a special court was organized for their trials. Six of the prisoners were found guilty of treason, but reprieved. Leisler and Milbourne denied the jurisdiction of the court, and appealed to the king. Leisler insisted that the letter addressed to "such as for the time being take care for preserving the peace and administering the laws in their majesties' province of New York," justified his retaining the office of lieutenant-governor; and the obsequious judges referred the argument to the opinion of the governor and council. They decided that no such interpretation could be put upon the superscription; and the unfortunate governor and his son-in-law were condemned to death for high treason. One hope of escape from an ignominious death yet remained. Sloughter had pronounced them great villains, but hesitated to order their execution until the pleasure of the king should be made known.

The friends of Leisler boldly defended his conduct, and denounced the malignity of his enemies; but the latter, now grown numerous, supported as they were by the influence of the new governor, demanded that the law should be put in force. In the midst of these disturbances the assembly met. It was soon found to be composed of persons attached to the aristocratic faction, and, of course, bitterly hostile to Leisler and his son-in-law. A motion was made for their reprieve; but resolutions were passed on the 17th of April, 1691, declaring the conduct of the prisoners illegal and arbitrary, and imputing to their usurpations the burning of Schenectady, and the ruin of various merchants. The council then demanded of Sloughter their immediate execution, as essential to the welfare of the province. As the governor still hesitated, the enemies of Leisler adopted a stratagem to effect their purpose. A dinner party was given, to which the governor was particularly invited. While he was under the influence of wine, he was cajoled into signing the death-warrants, and before he recovered his senses the sentence was carried into effect.

On the 16th of May, in the midst of a cold drizzling rain, the prisoners were led to the gallows, which stood outside the city wall. Guarded by the troops, the sad procession moved on, thronged about by weeping friends, and exulting enemies. "Weep not for us," said Leisler to the sorrowing populace, "we are going to our God; but weep for yourselves, that remain behind in misery and vexation." The handkerchief was bound about his face. "I hope," said he, "these eyes shall see our Lord Jesus in heaven." They were his last words. Milbourne's were not less pathetic. "I die," he exclaimed, "for the king and queen, and the Protestant religion in which I was born and bred. Father, into thy hands I commit my spirit." In the midst of torrents of rain, the people rushed forward to obtain some memento of their leaders.

The appeal to the king, which Leisler had not been permitted to take, was prosecuted by his son. It was referred to the Lords Commissioners of Trade, who, after a patient hearing, decided, on the 11th of March, that the "deceased were condemned and had suffered according to law;" but declared their families to be fit objects of royal compassion. The report was approved, but the estates of the victims of party animosity were ordered to be restored to their families. Not satisfied with this decision, the friends of Leisler appealed to parliament for redress, and in 1695, the petition being strongly supported by Sir William Ashurst and Constantine Phipps, an act was passed by which the attainder was reversed. Three years subsequent to this, the bodies of Leisler and Milbourne were disinterred, and after lying in state with great pomp for several days, were reburied in the old Dutch church.

The judicial murder of these popular leaders led to a result widely different from that which had been anticipated by their enemies. The principles they had espoused and supported were only implanted deeper in the minds of the people. Out of this signal act of tyranny grew a hatred of oppression, and an abhorrence of the royalist, or aristocratic party, which gradually gained ground in the midst of fierce animosities, and finally ended in the triumphant assertion of popular rights.

The war with Canada still continued, sustained principally by the efforts of the Mohawks under Schuyler. But the vigorous energy, foresight, and activity of Count Frontenac, were more than a match for the feeble and ill-conducted attempts made against him by the English provinces. After an inefficient and distracted administration of four months, Sloughter died, and in the absence of Dudley, the president of the council, the control of affairs was committed to Captain Ingoldsby.

In September, 1692, Colonel Benjamin Fletcher, a man of strong passions, feeble talents, active, and avaricious, arrived, as governor, bringing with him presents for the Indians, military supplies, and an addition of two companies of soldiers. Fortunately for his subsequent conduct of Indian affairs, Fletcher early made the acquaintance of Major Schuyler, who had succeeded to the influence which old Corlear once exercised over the Iroquois, and from whom the English governors were subsequently entitled "Corlear" by the Indians. Major Schuyler, or "Quidder," as the Mohawks called him—for they could not pronounce his Christian name of Peter—was a brave, active, intelligent, and humane man; and his unbounded authority over the wild tribes on the frontier, rendered him eminently serviceable to the governor, who judiciously admitted him of his council.

During the period that Fletcher was reorganizing his government, and creating various issues with the assembly, Count Frontenac was busily preparing for an expedition against the Five Nations. On the 15th of January, 1693, he set out from Montreal, with a force of seven hundred French and Indians, and passing Schenectady on the 6th of February, entered the first fortified village of the Mohawks the same night, and captured five men, and a few women and children. Most of the warriors of that nation being at this time on a visit to Schenectady, a second village was captured equally bloodlessly; but at the third, about forty Indians were surprised during a war dance, and a battle ensued, in which the French were victorious, though not until after they had sustained a loss of forty men. Satisfied with his success in this sudden foray, Frontenac now set off on his return to Canada, bearing with him about three hundred captives.

The tidings of this invasion was no sooner known to the Mohawks at Schenectady, than they called upon the inhabitants to assist them in pursuing the retiring enemy. The people were timid, and hesitated, much to the anger of their savage allies; but their cowardice was atoned for by the activity of Schuyler, who hastened to the relief of his friends, at the head of two hundred men. Being joined on the 15th of February by three hundred Indians, he followed in pursuit of the foe, sending back to Albany for reinforcements and provisions. On the 17th he came up with the rear guard of the French, and a series of trifling skirmishes ensued. Two days afterward, his force being increased by the arrival of eighty regulars, with the much needed supply of provisions, Schuyler resumed the pursuit; but the enemy had taken advantage of the delay, and succeeded in reaching the north branch of the Hudson, through a driving snow storm. Provisions again falling so short that the Indians were compelled to subsist upon the dead bodies of the enemy, all further advance was rendered impossible, and Schuyler returned to Albany, after having retaken about fifty of the captives.

The activity of Fletcher on this occasion gained

him great credit with the Five Nations. He no sooner heard of the approach of the French, than embarking with three hundred volunteers, he landed at Albany, a distance of one hundred and sixty miles from New York, within five days. He was too late to be of any service, but his zeal gratified the Indians, who bestowed upon him the name of "Cayenguirago," or the Great Swift Arrow.

Reinforcements of troops and munitions of war reaching Canada from France soon after this inroad, the Oneidas sued for peace, and even the faithful Mohawks wavered. To prevent the other nations of the Iroquois from submitting to the energetic Frontenac, and to confirm them in their old alliance with the English, Fletcher met the chiefs of the Five Nations at Albany, in July, 1693, where he distributed the presents with which he had been intrusted, and renewed the ancient covenant. This attention was well-timed, and the Indians expressed their gratitude. "Brother Cayenguirago," said they, "we roll and wallow in joy, because of the great favour your king and queen have done us, in sending us arms and ammunition, at a time when we are in the greatest need of them."

But if Governor Fletcher succeeded in acquiring the affections of the Indians, he failed in inspiring any attachment, either to his person or government, on the part of the provincial assembly. With the latter he was coarse, passionate, and overbearing; and the liberal principles which were rapidly spreading throughout the colony, were met by him with the most pointed and vigorous rebukes. "There are none of you," said he, "but what are big with the privileges of Englishmen and Magna Charta." Having desired them to provide for a ministry in each precinct throughout the province, a scheme was at length agreed upon, which was transmitted to him for his approval. He returned it with an amendment, vesting in himself the power of inducting every incumbent. The house refusing to accept the additional clause, Fletcher summoned the members before him, and in a fit of passion prorogued the assembly. "You take upon you as if you were dictators," said he.

The dissensions between the governor and succeeding assemblies increased in violence, until at length, in 1695, it broke out into an open rupture.

While Fletcher was thus contending with the people in the assertion of their rights, Frontenac was rebuilding the fort at Cadaracqui, which was called after his name.

The continual alarms to which the province of New York had been subjected by the unceasing activity of a bold and enterprising enemy, led to the project of calling upon the several colonies for assistance. The demand made upon each was proportioned according to wealth and population, but it was only partially responded to.

Unsuccessful in his efforts to form a treaty of peace with the Five Nations, Frontenac had no sooner strengthened the fort at Cadaracqui, than he determined upon an invasion of the Iroquois territory with all the regulars and militia under his command. Accompanied by a large force of friendly Indians, he left Montreal in July, 1696. The vanguard of this imposing army was composed of two battalions of regulars, under De Callieres, and a scouting force of Indians. The main body consisted of a large party of volunteers, and four battalions of militia, commanded by De Ramezai, the governor of Trois Riviéres. Two battalions of regulars and a small number of Indians brought up the rear. So formidable a military force had never before been seen upon Lake Ontario. Crossing to Oswego, the army reembarked upon Oneida Lake, and separating into two divisions, coasted both shores, to deceive the Indians in regard to the point where the landing was to be effected. Entering the country of the Onondagas, the latter at first prepared to defend themselves; but on being apprized of the strength of the French, they set fire to their village, and retired deeper into the forest.

Learning that the savages were flying before him, Frontenac, borne in an elbow chair in the rear of the artillery, pressed forward and entered the deserted village. One aged chief alone remained within the rude fortification to receive them. He was at once delivered over to the French Indians to be put to death. Although upward of one hundred years old, he bore the tortures they inflicted upon him with the most unflinching firmness. Exasperated by his stoical indifference, one of the savages at length stabbed him with a knife. "You had better," said he, "let me die by fire, that these French dogs may learn to die like men. You Indians, you dogs of dogs, think of me when you are in a like condition."

The death of this one aged and heroic Onondaga was the only result of an invasion which threatened the entire extermination of the Iroquois.

As soon as Frontenac commenced his return to Canada, the Onondagas harassed his rear, and succeeded in cutting off several of his batteaux. A desultory warfare followed, which was terminated in 1699 by the peace of Ryswick.

CHAPTER X.

Arrival of Bellamont—Ordered to suppress piracy on the coast—Fletcher discountenanced—Exultation of the popular party—Captain Kidd commissioned to apprehend the pirates—Turns pirate himself—Appears in Boston—Is arrested and sent to England for trial—Commotion in England—Address of Bellamont to the assembly—His popularity—Engages in a controversy with Frontenac—French treaty with the Indians—Law passed by the assembly against Roman Catholic priests—Death of Bellamont—Nanfan lieutenant-governor—Appointment of Cornbury—His character—Attaches himself to the Royalists—Is granted a donation—Second intercolonial war—Money appropriated for fortifying the Narrows—Embezzled by Cornbury—Difficulties with the assembly—Distrust of Cornbury—His profligate career—Petitions for his recall—Arrival of Lord Lovelace—Cornbury arrested for debt—His return to England.

On the 18th of June, 1697, Richard, Earl of Bellamont, received a commission as Governor of New York; but meeting on his voyage with contrary winds, did not arrive in the province until the 2d of April, 1698. Having been one of the committee to which was intrusted an examination into the conduct of the party by which Leisler and Milbourne had been sacrificed, he was already tolerably well informed in relation to the affairs of the province. As his commission embraced also the provinces of Massachusetts Bay and New Hampshire, in order that he might be enabled the more effectually to suppress the piracy which had for a long time been notoriously encouraged on the coasts of North America, he brought over with him his kinsman, John Nanfan, as lieutenant-governor of New York.

The administration of Fletcher had given as little satisfaction in England as it had in the province over which he had exercised the authority of governor. The impunity with which the buccaneers had visited the harbour of New York was imputed to his encouragement and connivance. Bellamont, an able and upright man, soon exhibited his abhorrence of such proceedings, by regarding Fletcher and his adherents with disfavour. Elated at finding themselves once more under an executive who was disposed to consult the good of the province, rather than the elevation of an aristocratic faction, the popular party hailed his administration with delight; and the friends of the murdered Leisler, favoured by Bellamont, soon found themselves in a majority, both in the council and in the assembly.

In view of his orders to suppress piracy in America, Bellamont, previous to his leaving England, had made the acquaintance of Robert Livingston, who recommended that the apprehension of the pirates should be intrusted to Captain Kidd, a shipmaster of New York, who was well acquainted with their haunts, and whom he vouched for as a man of courage and integrity. The proposal was submitted to the king; but as all the vessels in the royal navy were required to operate against the French, for the war had not then closed, the project could not be entertained by the Admiralty. Livingston then proposed the formation of a company, to be indemnified out of the recaptures, and offered to defray the fifth part of the cost and charges of a vessel, and to enter into bonds for the faithful performance of his commission by Kidd. To evince his approval of the design, the king took a tenth share himself, and Somers, the Lord Chancellor, the Duke of Shrewsbury, the Earls of Romney, Oxford, and others joined in the adventure, and raised the sum of six thousand pounds to carry it into effect. In April, 1696, Kidd, duly commissioned, sailed for Plymouth; but turning pirate himself, carried the vessel into the eastern seas, where he committed great depredations. After securing the wealth thus villanously acquired, he burned his ship, and returning to America, took up his residence at Boston. At this place, in 1698, he was arrested by Bellamont, who having advised the English government of the capture, a man-of-war was sent over to convey the prisoner to England. Being driven back to port in a storm, a rumour was spread that the ministry then in power were in collusion with the buccaneers, and were afraid to have Kidd brought back to England, lest he should implicate the whig lords as having confederated with him for piratical purposes. These suspicions becoming general, a motion was made in the House of Commons, that all who had been concerned in the original adventure with Kidd, should be deprived of their offices under the government. This motion being lost by a large majority, several of the adventurers were next impeached in the House of Lords. They were soon after put upon their trial, and from the facts then elicited, were honourably acquitted by their peers.

The first assembly convened by Bellamont, met on the 18th of May. In his opening address, the new governor pointed out the disorderly condition into which the province had fallen through the culpable negligence, favouritism, and covetous spirit of his predecessor. Reminding the members that the revenue required to be provided for, he added: "It would be hard if I, that come among you with an honest mind, and a resolution to be just to your interest, should meet with greater difficulties in the discharge of his majesty's service than those who have gone before me. I will take care that there shall be no misapplication of the public money. I will pocket none of it myself, nor shall there be any embezzlement by others; but exact accounts shall be given you, when, and as often as you require."

The custom adopted by Fletcher of influencing elections by his personal presence, was firmly discountenanced by Bellamont, who recommended the assembly to provide by law for the reformation of such abuses. Confident that they had at length obtained a governor sincerely desirous of promoting the general welfare of the province, the members of the assembly passed a warm address of thanks for his speech; but were soon after engaged in controversies among themselves, which led to the secession of six of the delegates, and obliged Bellamont to dissolve the house on the 14th of June.

During the year 1699, the governor was engaged in a spirited correspondence with Count Frontenac, relative to the exchange of prisoners consequent upon the peace of Ryswick. Bellamont included in his demand the Indians detained in captivity in Canada, claiming their liberty as British subjects. Frontenac insisted upon considering the Five Nations as independent, and therefore not subject to the provisions of the late treaty. Bellamont persevered in demanding their release, and threatened to recommence the war if his claim was not admitted. "If it is necessary," he wrote, "I will arm every man in the provinces under my government to oppose you, and redress the injury that you may perpetrate against our Indians."

While the dispute was pending Frontenac died; and De Callieres, his successor, terminated the difficulty by treating with the Iroquois in person, without admitting the right of the British governor to intermediate. When the French commissioners reached Onondaga to perfect the treaty, they were met outside of the palisades by Decanesora, an Iroquois chief, who presented them with three belts of wampum. "By the first," said he, "we wipe away your tears for the French who have been slain in the war; by the second, we open your mouths that you may speak freely; and by the third, we clear the mat on which you are to sit, from the blood which has been spilled on both sides." The commissioners in attendance from Albany were then invited to witness the conference that ensued; and when Bruyes, a Jesuit, expressed a desire to remain in the nation, the chiefs, true to their old allegiance, replied coldly: "We have already accepted Corlear's belt, by which he offers pastors to instruct us."

The virulent hatred inspired by the influence which the French missionaries exerted over the minds of the Indians, strongly exhibited itself in New York, during the summer of 1700, when the assembly passed an act for the hanging of every Roman Catholic priest that came voluntarily into the province.

Respected by the people, and in harmony with his council and the assembly, the latter exhibited their confidence in the integrity of the governor by voting a revenue for six years, and placing it in his hands for disbursement. Notwithstanding this honourable proof of popular confidence, the activity of Bellamont in preventing any violation of the navigation acts, made him many enemies among the merchants of the province, who, regarding those laws as oppressive and unjust, had heretofore been accustomed to violate them with impunity. The display of ill-feeling occasioned by these differences ceased only with the death of the governor, which took place suddenly on the 5th of March, 1701.

He was succeeded by Lieutenant-governor Nanfan, during whose brief administration a court of chancery was organized, and a Protestant minister, paid by the province, directed to devote his services to the instruction of the Indians. Unhappily, party animosities also revived at this time, which led to acts of violence and disorder. Livingston and Bayard, the leaders of the anti-Leislerian faction, were treated with great harshness by the popular party then in power, and the result would in all probability have ended seriously to the latter, but for the arrival, in 1702, of the needy and unprincipled Cornbury, as governor of the two provinces of New York and New Jersey.

Claiming kindred with royalty, weak-minded, arrogant, and vicious, Cornbury immediately united himself to the aristocratic faction, which, strengthened by his powerful support, soon acquired a majority in the assembly. To his opening address the members heartily responded by providing an annual revenue for seven years, by voting him a donation of two thousand pounds to defray the expenses of his voyage, and by increasing his annual salary to twelve hundred pounds.

War having been proclaimed by England against France and Spain, on the 4th of May, 1702, the assembly, which met in April, 1703, granted an appropriation of fifteen hundred pounds for the erection of two batteries at the Narrows. But though it was distinctly specified that the money should be appropriated "for no other use whatever," his lordship neglected to build the fortifications. Dishonest and extravagant, he drew the amount from the treasury by his warrants, and applied it to his private purposes.

To guard against any misapplication of the public funds in future, the assembly of 1704 refused to make any further appropriations until the previous grant was accounted for. Angry discussions followed. The members asserted their rights, and Cornbury responded haughtily, by saying: "I know of no rights that you have as an assembly but such as the queen is pleased to allow you."

A treaty of neutrality existing between the French in Canada and the Five Nations, there was in reality no pressing necessity for voting the sums of money which Cornbury was repeatedly soliciting; but when, in 1705, a French privateer entered the harbour of New York, the alarm into which the province was thrown, induced the assembly to pass bills for raising an amount sufficient to defray the expenses of fortifications, and a corps of scouts and rangers, to be stationed on the frontiers.

Warned by the previous embezzlements, not to trust the public funds in the hands of the governor, they agreed to sanction the grant only upon the condition that it should be disbursed by a treasurer appointed by themselves. To this Cornbury reluctantly assented, and the arrangement was subsequently permitted by the English government, but only so far as it applied to specific appropriations. The firm and decided stand taken by the assembly on this occasion, led to its sudden prorogation.

In 1706 the house was again called together; but the members being found equally intractable, a dissolution speedily took place. No further session was convened until 1708, and in the mean time, the profligate career of Cornbury had rendered him odious to all parties. He had been rebuked for his tyrannical interference in matters of religion, for his peculations in office, and for his exaction of illegal fees, and no longer was any confidence placed either in his honour or his honesty. For some time he endeavoured to maintain his authority by a greater display of imperiousness and arrogance; but falling deeply into debt, he suffered himself to be humbled by the assembly whose rights he had so haughtily disputed, and became contemptible in the eyes of the people, by parading the fort dressed in the clothes of a woman, and by similar acts of recklessness and folly.

Disgusted alike with his antics and his knavery, the public indignation at length vented itself in clamorous petitions for his recall. Their efforts were successful; and in 1709, Lord Lovelace arrived at New York commissioned to supersede Cornbury in the government of the province. Losing with his office his immunity from arrest, Cornbury had no sooner recognised the commission of his successor, than his creditors threw him into the custody of the sheriff of New York, where he remained until he succeeded, by the death of his father, to the earldom of Clarendon. He then returned to England, bearing with him the unenviable distinction of having been one of the worst provincial governors that had ever received an appointment from the English crown.

CHAPTER XI.

Lovelace demands of the assembly a permanent revenue—An annual grant substituted—Death of Lovelace—Administration of Ingoldsby—Abortive attempt to invade Canada—Discontent of New York—Address to Queen Anne—Colonel Schuyler repairs to England, accompanied by five Mohawk chiefs—Reception of the latter in London—Their interview with the Queen—Governor Hunter arrives at New York—The assembly refractory—Expedition against Canada—Its shameful failure—Activity of De Vandreuil—The provincial troops disbanded—Indignation of England and the colonies—Charges brought against St. John and Harcourt—Controversy between Hunter and the assembly in relation to a permanent revenue—The point carried by the governor—Gloomy condition of the province—Negro insurrection—Peace of Utrecht—Permanent revenue granted—Hunter's popularity—His return to England.

THE first assembly convened by Lord Lovelace met in April, 1709. In his opening address to the members, he demanded, on behalf of the crown, the grant of a permanent revenue, the discharge of the debts of the provincial government, and, for his own satisfaction, a full examination of the public accounts, in order that he might be exonerated from debts which were not of his contracting.

The assembly responded by congratulating Lovelace on his arrival among them, and by assuring him of their desire to consult the good of the country and his satisfaction; but as the loose and unprincipled conduct of Cornbury had taught them the policy of retaining in their own hands an entire control over the appropriations, they declined voting any more moneys than were necessary for the annual support of the government.

As this placed the governor and the other servants of the crown entirely at the mercy of the assembly, there is no doubt that Lovelace would have resisted an innovation by which his prerogative was restricted within such narrow limits; but having contracted a disorder in crossing the ferry at New York, on his first arrival in the province, he died the 5th of May, 1709, while the assembly was in session, and was succeeded by Richard Ingoldsby, the lieutenant-governor.

The brief administration of Ingoldsby was only remarkable for another abortive attempt to invade Canada, for which large preparations had been made by New York and the New England provinces.

The design being to co-operate with a strong British fleet, in a simultaneous attack upon Quebec and Montreal, troops from Massachusetts, Rhode Island, and New Hampshire, assembled at Boston, and awaited the arrival of the promised squadron, while the quotas of New York, New Jersey, and Connecticut, numbering some fifteen hundred men, marched to Wood Creek, near the head of Lake Champlain, where they erected fortifications, and stored their provisions.

As usual, unforeseen obstacles occurred. Just as the expedition was about to set sail from England, an alarming defeat, suffered by the Portuguese, rendered it necessary for the British ministry to despatch the fleet and troops intended for America, to the support of their ancient ally. Deeply mortified at having been thus foiled in the prosecution of a favourite project, the colonial levies were recalled and disbanded.

New York was particularly disconcerted at this unexpected result. The province had been lavish of its means to make the invasion as effective as possible. The expenses it had incurred amounted to twenty thousand pounds. Besides maintaining its quota of volunteer and independent companies, it had enlisted six hundred Iroquois warriors, and supported at Albany, during the period of their absence, one thousand of their wives and children.

Disappointed at the failure of an enterprise upon the success of which the security of the frontiers so much depended, the assembly declined to assist in an attack upon Acadia, which was agreed upon soon after, during a congress of colonial governors held at Newport, in Rhode Island. Believing that in the spread of the French from the region of Canada westward, the greatest danger was to be apprehended by the British colonies, the assembly, in the month of

October, 1709, drew up an address to the queen, setting forth their views upon the subject.

"It is well known," they wrote, "that the French can go by water from Quebec to Montreal. From thence they can do the like, through rivers and lakes, at the back of all your majesty's plantations on this continent as far as Carolina. And in this large tract of country live several nations of Indians who are vastly numerous. Among those they constantly send emissaries and priests, with toys and trifles, to insinuate themselves into their favour. Afterward they send traders, then soldiers, and at last build forts among them; and the garrisons are encouraged to intermarry, cohabit, and incorporate among them; and it may easily be concluded, that upon a peace, many of the disbanded soldiers will be sent thither for that purpose."

About this time, Colonel Schuyler having expressed his determination to proceed to England, at his own expense, for the purpose of urging personally upon the government the necessity of the conquest of Canada, the assembly entered warmly into his views by passing an unanimous resolution testifying to his long and faithful public services, and by intrusting to his charge their address to the crown.

Accompanied by five Mohawk chiefs, Schuyler reached England early in the spring of 1710. The presence of the stately savages created a great sensation throughout the kingdom. Multitudes flocked to see them. Followed everywhere by a dense throng of people, they paraded the streets of London, dressed in black clothes, over which were flung gay scarlet mantles edged with gold. On the 19th of April, they were introduced by the Lord Chamberlain to Queen Anne, when one of them, after referring to the failure of the expedition against Canada, continued as follows:—

"We were mightily rejoiced when we heard our great queen had resolved to send an army to reduce Canada, and immediately, in token of friendship, we hung up the kettle, and took up the hatchet, and with one consent assisted Colonel Nicholson in making preparations on this side the lake; but at length we were told our great queen, by some important affairs, was prevented in her design at present, which made us sorrowful, lest the French, who had hitherto dreaded us, should now think us unable to make war against them. The reduction of Canada is of great weight to our free hunting; so that if our great queen should not be mindful of us, we must, with our families, forsake our country and seek other habitations, or stand neuter, either of which will be against our inclinations."

When he had closed, the orator presented the queen with belts of wampum, in proof of the sincerity of the Five Nations. He received a gracious reply, and the audience was ended.

On the 14th of June, Brigadier Robert Hunter arrived at New York, bearing the commission of governor. A native of Scotland, Hunter first entered upon the business of life as apprentice to an apothecary; but running away from his master, he enlisted in the army as a common soldier. His fine talents, handsome person, and graceful address, won him the friendship of Swift and Addison, and the hand of Lady Hay. Married to a peeress, military promotion soon followed. His first colonial appointment was in 1707, as lieutenant-governor of Virginia; but being captured by the French while on his voyage to that province, he was commissioned, on his return to England, to succeed Lovelace in the government of New York and New Jersey.

Hunter brought over with him, at the expense of the crown, three thousand Germans, who had taken refuge in England the year previous, from the wars which had laid desolate their homesteads on the Rhine. Many of these immigrants settled in the city of New York. Of the remainder, some ascended the Hudson River, where they commenced cultivating a tract of several thousand acres on the manor of Livingston; while others, migrating into Pennsylvania, wrote from thence such favourable accounts of the country to their friends abroad, that the latter came flocking over in numbers so great as to form extensive agricultural communities in the western parts of that province.

Hunter met his first assembly in September, 1710; but following out instructions similar to those which had been given to his predecessor, he soon found himself threatened with a controversy in relation to a permanent revenue, which he only avoided by a prorogation of the house until the following spring.

While this discussion was at its height, the New England states were vigorously prosecuting the conquest of Acadia. Thirty transports, bearing four provincial regiments, supported by six English vessels, having on board five hundred marines, sailed from Boston in September, and toward the close of the month cast anchor in the harbour of Port Royal. The command of this expedition had been given to Colonel Nicholson, formerly lieutenant-governor of New York under Sloughter. It proved signally successful. The French garrison, feeble in numbers, and already mutinous from a scarcity of food, being more disposed to desert to the besiegers than to offer an ineffectual resistance, Subercase, their commander, capitulated on the 12th of October, and on the 16th, evacuated, with his ragged and half-famished troops, one of the strongest fortresses in all North America. The inhabitants of the surrounding districts immediately submitted to the conquerors, who, in retaliation for the sufferings which their own countrymen had experienced at the hands of the French, treated them with but little mercy. Vetch, the second in command to Nicholson, being left with four hundred men to occupy the fortress, the remainder of the forces returned in triumph to Boston.

The bloodless acquisition of Acadia, still further stimulating the desire of the English colonies to obtain possession of Canada also, Nicholson, at the instance of the provincial governors, repaired to England, and urged upon the ministry an immediate prosecution of the long contemplated enterprise.

His appeal being strongly supported by the secretary of state, St. John, subsequently known as Lord Bolingbroke, seven regiments of regulars and a battalion of marines were ordered to be embarked on board a fleet of fifteen ships-of-war and forty transports, the command of the land forces being given to Brigadier-general Hill, while that of the squadron was intrusted to Admiral Sir Hovenden Walker. The fleet reached Boston on the 25th of June, 1711, where a month was wasted in embarking the colonial forces, and in providing supplies.

In the mean time, fifteen hundred provincials and eight hundred Indians, commanded by Nicholson, assembled at Albany, preparatory to an attack on Montreal. But with the usual fatality which had attended every attempt to conquer Canada, the fleet which was destined to operate against Quebec, did not commence ascending the St. Lawrence until the middle of August. The wind blowing fresh, Walker put into the Bay of Gaspe, until the 20th, when he again set sail. On the evening of the 22d, a thick fog setting in, the pilots advised that the vessels should lie-to, with their heads pointing to the southward. The admiral, inefficient and self-willed, countermanded the order and directed that the fleet should head north. The consequence was that, during the mist and darkness, eight of the transports were wrecked among the Egg Islands of the St. Lawrence, with a loss of eight hundred and eighty-four men. Alarmed at a disaster brought about in a great measure by his own incompetence, Walker now put back into Spanish River Bay, where he called a council of war. Acting upon their advice, which was evidently in accordance with his own wishes, he concluded to abandon the expedition and return home, congratulating himself that by the loss of a part of his troops, he had been saved from hazarding the lives of the remainder.

Fully aware of the danger by which he was menaced, the Marquis de Vaudreuil, with that remarkable energy which seems to have been a characteristic of the French governors in Canada, made every preparation in his power to meet it.

He called around him his faithful allies, and having strengthened Quebec and the posts below on both sides of the river, sent out trusty spies to watch for the first appearance of the British squadron. When he became aware from the intelligence which reached him that Quebec was no longer threatened, De Vaudreuil hastened at the head of three thousand men to Chambly, in order to protect Montreal against the advance of the provincial army under Nicholson. His apprehensions of an attack in the latter quarter were, however, speedily put to rest. Nicholson no sooner heard that Walker had set sail for England, and that the colonial transports had been sent home, than he disbanded his forces and departed from Albany, leaving the inhabitants of that city in great alarm lest De Vaudreuil should advance from his camp at Chambly and carry on a frontier war of retaliation.

To New York the shameful failure of this expedition was peculiarly unfortunate. An expense of ten thousand pounds had been incurred to no purpose; the frontiers still lay open to the incursions of the enemy; while the Five Nations, beginning to regard with contempt a people whose projects always ended unsuccessfully, evinced a disposition to form a treaty of alliance with the French, whose good fortune, spirit, and energy had won their admiration.

In England, the inglorious return of Walker

roused the public indignation. The regular officers defended themselves, by attributing the failure of the expedition to the detention at Boston while waiting for supplies; and charged the delay upon the New England people, whom they denounced as being selfish, ill-natured, sour, hypocritical, and canting. The latter retorted by asserting the enterprise to have been a tory device intended to fail, and gotten up for the sole purpose of fleecing and disgracing the eastern provinces. Parliament next took up the quarrel, and Harley, separated from his former colleagues, accused St. John and the Chancellor Harcourt of having contrived the project, for the purpose of putting twenty thousand pounds into their own pockets. "No government," said Harcourt, "is worth supporting that will not admit of such advantageous jobs."

While this controversy was raging, Governor Hunter was contending with a refractory assembly. The latter, abiding by their previous determination to make no appropriations for a longer term than one year, refused to pass the bills as altered by the council. Warm discussions ensued. The council contended that, as a coordinate branch of the legislature, deriving, in like manner with the assembly, their authority from "the mere grace of the crown," they had a right to make such amendments as they thought proper. The delegates replied boldly: "The inherent right the assembly have to dispose of the money of the freemen of this colony, does not proceed from any commission, letters patent, or other grant from the crown; but from the free choice and election of the people, who ought not to be divested of their property, nor justly can without their consent. Any former condescensions of other assemblies, will not prescribe to the council a privilege to make any of those amendments; and, therefore, they have it not. The assembly are sufficiently convinced of the necessity they are in, not to admit of any encroachments so much to their prejudice."

Another cause of complaint at this period was the erection of a court of chancery, and the assumption of the chancellorship by Hunter himself. The assembly disputed his authority to establish such a court without their consent, and contended that the fees exacted under such circumstances were contrary to law. They appealed to the Lords of Trade, but met with a pointed rebuke, the act of Hunter and his council being fully sustained.

At the session of 1712, Hunter again vainly endeavoured to prevail upon the assembly to grant a permanent revenue. They would allow no more than an annual appropriation, specifically applied. Nothing could be more gloomy than the aspect of affairs at this period. The assembly, governor, and council were at issue; the

Iroquois, tempted by French emissaries, were wavering in their allegiance; an invasion was anticipated by sea; and, to add to the general alarm, a negro insurrection broke out in the city of New York, by which several persons lost their lives. It was speedily suppressed, however, and nineteen of the real or supposed conspirators were executed. During this year, the Tuscarora Indians, having been defeated in an attempt to exterminate the English in North Carolina, took refuge among the Iroquois, by whom they were received into the confederacy, which became known thenceforth as the Six Nations.

At length, in 1713, the second intercolonial, or Queen Anne's war, was terminated by the peace of Utrecht. France, humbled by the successive victories of Marlborough, ceded to Great Britain the territory of Hudson's Bay, the whole of Newfoundland and Acadia, and the island of St. Kitts in the West Indies. The subjection of the Five Nations to the English crown was also acknowledged; but as neither the boundaries of the Iroquois territory, nor those of Louisiana and Acadia were defined by the treaty, they became, in after years, a fruitful source of dispute, which engendered repeated acts of hostility, and kept the frontiers of the English colonies in almost continual warfare, until the conquest of Canada was finally consummated by General Wolfe.

But though the close of the war relieved New York from the pressure of an active enemy, the province still continued agitated by the differences existing between the governor and the assembly. Finding, after several successive sessions, that neither threats nor blandishments, nor the decision of the Lords of Trade, could move the delegates to grant a revenue in the manner demanded by the crown, Hunter resorted to artifice to obtain his ends. Personally a favourite with all parties, and ably supported by Colonel Morris, his confidential adviser, a gentleman of great influence in the province, he at length succeeded, by intrigue and concession, in accomplishing the orders of his superiors.

At the session of 1715, "a well-disposed majority" granted a revenue for five years; and two years afterward, authorized a new issue of paper money to the amount of forty-eight thousand pounds, for the alleged purpose of liquidating long outstanding public debts, which had not been provided for previously.

From this period until the return of Hunter to England in 1719, every thing worked harmoniously. Victorious on the only important point at issue, the governor, always disposed to conciliate matters, could well afford to be generous. He permitted the naturalization of the Dutch inhabitants, a privilege which had previously been denied; consented that British imported goods should be taxed for the benefit of the colony, and to the imposition of tonnage duties on foreign vessels. The failure of his health demanding a change of climate, Hunter surrendered the government of the province into the hands of Colonel Schuyler, and embarking for England on the 31st of July, 1719, carried with him, from the respective assemblies of New York and New Jersey, testimonials expressive of their high appreciation of his public services, and of his private virtues.

CHAPTER XII.

Arrival of Governor Burnet—His character—Old assembly continued—Sale of Indian goods to the French prohibited—Mercantile opposition—Petition to the king—Reply of Colden and Alexander—Activity of the French—Indian policy of Burnet—Fort Oswego built—Administrative difficulties—Alienation of Schuyler, Philips, and Delancey—New assembly demanded by the people—Removal of Burnet to the government of Massachusetts—Montgomery appointed governor—Harmonizes with the assembly—Meets the Indians in convention at Albany—Fort Oswego threatened—Burnet's Indian policy repudiated—Boundary fixed between New York and Connecticut—Seizure of Crown Point by the French—Cosby succeeds Montgomery—Ingratiates himself with the assembly—A free school established—Violent and arbitrary conduct of Cosby—Political quarrels—Imprisonment of Zenger, printer of the Weekly Journal—His trial—Defended by Hamilton, of Philadelphia—Liberty of the press vindicated—Illegal career of Cosby—His sudden death—Bitter party feuds—Clarke appointed lieutenant-governor.

SCHUYLER administered the government of the province with great prudence and honesty for thirteen months. On the 17th of September, 1720, he was superseded by William Burnet, a son of the celebrated bishop. Though a gentleman of fine literary acquirements, and an industrious student, he was nevertheless of a lively and social disposition. By no means averse to mending his shattered fortunes, which had been greatly reduced by the bursting of the South Sea bubble, he exchanged with Hunter the comptrollership of the customs at London, for the government of the colonies of New York and New Jersey. Desirous of conciliating the affections of the people, Governor Burnet rendered himself accessible to all; while, in his frequent visits to the principal families, whose friendship he assiduously courted, he delicately avoided every appearance of parade or ostentation. Such conduct was well calculated to win the strong personal esteem with which he soon came to be regarded, and tended in a great degree to soften the political asperities by which his administration was subsequently distinguished. As Hunter had taken the precaution to prevent a dissolution of the "well-disposed" assembly during his absence, Governor Burnet, contrary to custom, continued it in existence after his arrival, and obtained thereby, through the influence of Colonel Morris, a renewal of the grant of a revenue for five years.

But if this retention of the old assembly was of service to Burnet in one respect, it unfortunately lost him the support of Schuyler and Philips, both of whom, as members of the council, had strenuously advocated the propriety of a new election.

In this measure, however, Burnet only conformed to his instructions; but he acted from his own just and enlarged views, when he procured from the same assembly the passage of a law prohibiting the sale of Indian goods to the French

As the principal commodities required in the Indian trade were of British manufacture, the retaining of those commodities in their own hands, was not only of vast benefit to the province in a pecuniary point of view, but it was also well calculated to effect a political change in the relations previously existing between the Canadians and the distant Indian tribes, who, subsequently, could only obtain their customary supplies at the hands of English traders.

The act, however, being productive of great opposition from interested parties, and eliciting a memorial to the crown praying for its repeal, Burnet was soon after called upon to answer the objections of the petitioners. A long and able report was accordingly drawn up by Colden and Alexander, two members of the council, which triumphantly justified the course pursued by the governor, but entailed upon its authors the lasting enmity of those merchants who had formerly carried on a lucrative traffic with the French.

Indefatigable as ever, the latter were making every effort to extend the dominion of France, from Canada westwardly, by ingratiating themselves with the Indian tribes of those regions, through the influence of their traders and missionaries. Penetrating their projects, and well acquainted with the geography of the country, Burnet sought to intercept the intercourse between the Canadians and the Indian tribes settled on the great lakes and the numerous tributaries of the Mississippi, by building, during the year 1722, a trading-house at Oswego, which he subsequently strengthened by a fort erected at his own expense; thus extending the limits of the province of New York to the south shore of Lake Ontario. The situation was judiciously chosen, and the Miamis, the Hurons, and unknown tribes from the distant west, soon became frequent and profitable visitors.

But while the wisdom of Burnet's Indian policy was regarded with approval by all those who were most nearly interested in the prosperity of the province, his domestic administration was a turbulent one. The old dispute respecting the chancellorship was revived. This was touching the governor nearly, for he prided himself greatly upon the exercise of the office of chancellor, as it afforded favourable opportunities for the display of his erudition. His integrity was unquestionable; but whether he was altogether suitable for a judge may be doubted, as his rapid decisions gave him but little time to reflect upon the merits of the cause. "I act first, and think afterward," said he; a dangerous admission, which, doubtless, had its weight in the scale of opposition. But he had other sources of annoyance. Unaccustomed to dissemble his thoughts, his free speech had alienated Schuyler, Philips, and Delancey, all three persons of influence in the province;

while the continuance of an assembly, which had already existed for eleven years, was regarded by many as unconstitutional. The assembly themselves, changed by the decease of old, and the election of new members, were also becoming insubordinate. In 1726 they refused to grant a revenue for a longer period than three years. The people were clamorous for a new election, and Burnet reluctantly yielded to the general wish.

The new assembly, which met in 1727, consisted of members wholly disaffected to the governor. His decrees in chancery, his conduct in relation to a dispute in the French church, and the prohibition of the Canada trade, being made subjects of severe animadversion, he took the earliest opportunity of summoning the delegates into his presence and dissolving them.

The commission of Governor Burnet expiring by the decease of George I., his opponents exerted their influence to procure his removal, on the plea that his longer continuance in office would be dangerous to the public tranquillity. Their efforts proving successful, Burnet was transferred to the government of Massachusetts Bay, and was succeeded on the 15th of April, 1728, by John Montgomery.

Educated to the profession of arms, Governor Montgomery had subsequently occupied the more peaceful post of gentleman of the bedchamber to

George II., prior to that monarch's accession to the throne. His abilities were very moderate, and preferring a life of ease to the turmoil of politics, he won the favour of the assembly by conceding their right to regulate salaries, and by declining to sit as chancellor until specially directed to do so by orders from England. Even then he obeyed with reluctance, and only as a matter of form, as he confessed himself unqualified for the station.

Having procured from the assembly the grant of a revenue for five years, he proceeded to Albany, where he held a council with delegates from the Six Nations, and bestowed upon them the presents with which he was charged. At this council he succeeded in renewing the ancient league, and in engaging the Indians to assist in defending the fort at Oswego, in case of its being attacked by the French.

This judicious arrangement was well-timed; for, during the spring of 1729, Governor Montgomery received intelligence from the vigilant Burnet, that an expedition was organizing in Canada for the purpose of destroying the obnoxious trading-post. The garrison was immediately reinforced by a body of men taken from the independent companies, and the Six Nations having proclaimed their determination to join in repelling the enemy, the prospect of success being thus rendered doubtful, the Governor of Canada broke up his preparations, and abandoned his design.

Unfortunately, at this period the wise policy of Burnet was repudiated by the king, who, through ignorance or intrigue, repealed the acts prohibiting the Canadian trade, and thereby restored to the French those advantages of which they had been deprived by the judicious but unpopular measures for which Burnet, trusting to time for his justification, had willingly incurred so much odium.

In the month of May, 1731, the long disputed boundary question between Connecticut and New York was finally settled. On the 1st of July following, Governor Montgomery dying, the administration devolved upon Rip Van Dam, president of the council. In the short period during which Van Dam held the office of acting governor, the French, in defiance of previous treaty stipulations, entered the territory of the Iroquois, and seizing upon Crown Point, proceeded to build a fortress there. This daring and dangerous encroachment, which secured the command of Lake Champlain, and laid open to the enemy the frontiers of New York, Massachusetts, and New Hampshire, was regarded with singular apathy by the assembly of New York. No attempt was made to counteract it until 1737, when a scheme was projected for settling a body of Scotch Highlanders on Lake George, to serve as a military colony in the defence of the province. It was partially carried out, but owing to the selfishness and ill faith of the provincial government, was finally abandoned.

In August, 1732, William Cosby arrived at New York, commissioned to succeed Montgomery in the government of the province. The character of Cosby had preceded him. Previously Governor of Minorca, he was charged with having illegally seized and confiscated the property of a Spanish merchant, evading a judicial inquiry into his conduct by secreting the papers which would have enabled the owner to prove the criminality of the act. Having, however, been active in opposing the measures brought forward in Parliament the preceding year for the encouragement of the sugar islands, the assembly evinced their gratitude by continuing the revenue for five years, by fixing his salary at two thousand pounds a year, and by presenting him with the sum of seven hundred and fifty pounds for the assistance he had rendered their agents in London. Indignant at receiving so small a remuneration for his services, he broke out into violent abuse of the assembly, and sarcastically asked Morris, one of the members, why they did not add pounds, shillings, and pence? "Do they think I came from England for money?" said he. "I'll make them know better." This display of temper gained for him an addition of two hundred and fifty pounds, but he lost from that time the confidence of the assembly.

Provision was made at the same session for the first free school established in New York. The bill for this purpose, drafted by Phillips, the speaker, and introduced by Delancey, occasioned no little merriment, from its preamble containing the singular declaration that, "the youth of this colony are found, by manifold experience, to be not inferior in their natural genius to the youth of any other country in the world."

Avaricious and arbitrary, Cosby was no sooner placed at ease in respect to a revenue, than, casting off all restraint, he exhibited himself in his true colours. He suspended Van Dam and others from their seats in council without authority. He deprived Morris, the chief justice, of his office, which he bestowed upon the younger Delancey. He quarrelled with Alexander, the secretary of state, and with Smith, one of the leading lawyers in the province. When reminded of his illegal proceedings, he answered flippantly, "I have great interest in England." He took care, however, to write to the Lords of Trade, defending his measures as necessary for the preservation of the king's prerogative; charging the assembly, and part of the council with being tainted with "Boston principles."

Finding remonstrances of no avail, the opponents of the governor at length made known their political grievances through the columns of the public press. Prior to 1733, Bradford's New York Gazette was the only newspaper published in the province. As this was in the interest of the governor, a new paper, called the Weekly Journal, was issued by John Peter Zenger, as the organ of the popular party. It soon became filled with articles in which the measures of the government were criticised with great severity. Among these, certain "low ballads" were charged by the chief justice to be libels. Not being able to obtain the concurrence of the assembly in a prosecution of the printer, Cosby and his council, on the 2d of December, took upon themselves to order four of the journals to be publicly burned by the common hangman, and imprisoned Zenger, on the charge of publishing false and malicious libels.

The grand jury refusing to indict him, Bradley, the attorney-general, filed an information. Alexander and Smith, the counsel for Zenger, having excepted to the commissions of the judges on the ground of illegality, the court ordered their names to be struck from the roll of attorneys.

At that period there were only three lawyers of distinguished legal reputation at the New York bar. Smith and Alexander were among those most prominent; the third, Murray, was a fast friend of the governor, and could not therefore be expected to risk the favour of the latter by acting as counsel for the prisoner. Under these circumstances, the friends of Zenger sent secretly to Philadelphia and engaged the services of Andrew Hamilton, a jurist of great learning and experience. When the trial came on, Hamilton, admitting the fact of publication, boldly asserted that the matters charged were true, and therefore no libels. Being under no awe of the court, he ridiculed the decision of the judges, that a libel was the more dangerous for being true, and by wit, sarcasm, and invective, and by an eloquent appeal to the jury to protect, in the cause of the poor printer Zenger, the nobler cause of liberty, he so effectually diverted their minds from the question at issue, as to obtain for his client a verdict of acquittal.

The instant the decision was made known, the hall rang with triumphant shouts. The wrath of the judges, who threatened a commitment of the ringleaders, was met by a significant rejoinder, and Hamilton was hurried from the court to partake of a splendid dinner prepared for his reception. He received from the corporation a gold box, enclosing the freedom of the city, and on his return to Philadelphia the next day, was escorted by a large concourse of people to his barge, which he entered under a salute of cannon. The other colonies also rejoiced at an issue which strengthened and encouraged the growth of liberal principles; but the contest proved in the end unfortunate to the "poor printer" Zenger. Elevated for a time into a bewildering notoriety, he launched out into an extravagant expenditure, and, neglecting his business, sank finally into poverty and neglect.

Setting at defiance all laws which interfered with his pleasure or rapacity, Cosby still pursued his arbitrary and unprincipled career. He continued the assembly against their own petitions for a dissolution, and in direct opposition to the known wishes of the people. He increased the public discontent by insisting upon a re-survey of old grants and patents, and by infamously destroying important documents placed in his hands for inspection by the corporation of Albany. On the 10th of March, 1736, greatly to the relief of the province, he died suddenly. The rejoicings which followed this event had not subsided, when a bitter contest arose between Van Dam and Clarke, each of whom claimed the right to administer the government. Their respective partisans took up the quarrel. Morris, the former chief justice, lately arrived from England, espoused the cause of Van Dam, and placed himself at the head of the popular party. The feud had already risen to such a height, that Clarke had withdrawn into the fort, and called around him the military for his protection. Upon being asked for his advice in this state of affairs, Morris replied significantly, "If you don't hang them, they will hang you." Fortunately, however, the crisis was averted by the arrival of despatches on the 12th of October, which confirmed Clarke in his authority, and which were followed shortly after by a commission advancing him to the rank of lieutenant-governor.

CHAPTER XIII.

Character of Lieutenant-governor Clarke—His policy—Conduct of the provincial party—Their reply to his opening address—Extraordinary issue of paper money—Disfranchisement of the Jews—Snare laid for the popular leaders—Its success—Permanent revenue refused—Negro plot in New York—Terror of the citizens—Evidence of Mary Burton—The conspiracy doubted—Judicial murder of Ury—Arrival of Governor Clinton—His quarrel with Chief Justice Delancey—Difficulties with the assembly—War between England and France—Activity of the French—Capture of Louisburg—Settlements around Saratoga ravaged—Invasion of Canada projected—Assembling of the provincial levies—Boston menaced by a French fleet—Subsidence of the alarm—Political feuds in New York—The village of Saratoga burned—Peace of Aix-la-Chapelle.

ENGLISH by birth, though for a long time resident of the province, the new lieutenant-governor was no sooner fairly installed in office than he evinced a politic disposition to overlook past differences, and to disarm opposition by smooth words and a specious courtesy.

Owing his first minor appointment in the province to the court influence of an uncle, he had sedulously improved his opportunities until he had reached his present elevated position. Though labouring under the deficiencies of a limited education, he was a man of talent, and had made himself thoroughly conversant with the condition and affairs of the colony. Cunning rather than sagacious, cool and cautious yet active, he preferred to win his way by address rather than by force, and while serving the crown with a reasonable degree of fidelity, seized every advantage which his station gave him to improve his own fortune. The first act of Governor Clarke was a popular one. He dissolved the old and convened a new assembly. This measure, as indicating a design to cast off his old political associates, was regarded with alarm by the old government party, while the provincials, hailing it as a triumph, easily secured a majority at the ensuing election. After a session of two days, during midsummer, they adjourned until the 23d of August, both parties anxiously watching the course of the governor, and desirous of securing his support.

But however much the provincial party might have wished to obtain the countenance of their chief magistrate, they did not, when the assembly met in autumn, show any disposition to purchase it at the expense of the principles they had espoused.

Their reply to the opening address of the governor rigorously defined the policy they intended to pursue. In answer to the usual demand for appropriations for revenue, and other purposes, they said boldly: "You are not to expect that we will either raise sums unfit to be raised, or put what we shall raise into the power of a governor to misapply, if we can prevent it; nor shall we make up any other deficiencies than what we conceive are fit and just to be paid, or continue that support or revenue we shall raise, for any longer time than one year; nor do we think it convenient to do even that, until such laws are passed as we conceive necessary for the safety of the inhabitants of the colony, who have reposed a trust in us for that only purpose, and which we are sure you will think it reasonable we should act agreeably to; and by the grace of God we will endeavour not to deceive them." The session was prolonged for nearly four months, during which a grant of revenue for one year was passed, and a bill for holding triennial assemblies; but the latter was soon after rejected in England.

But by far the most important act of the session was the passage of a bill authorizing an issue of paper money to the amount of forty-eight thousand three hundred and fifty pounds. Forty thousand of this was to be loaned to the respective counties, in small sums, for twelve years, at five per cent.; while, to secure the signature of the governor, the remainder was ordered to be applied to public uses.

One other occurrence took place during the assembly of 1737, which strongly indicated the prejudices of the period. The seat of delegate for the city being contested by Van Horne, the son of a deceased member, against Phillips, the late speaker, the house ordered that neither should sit until the conduct of the sheriff had undergone an examination. The latter was speedily acquitted of having acted improperly, upon the testimony of the petitioner; but Smith, who, with Alexander, had been invited to resume his practice at the bar, acting as counsel for Van Horne, disputed the qualification of Jews as electors, and after a brilliant speech, in which his extensive theological learning was brought to bear upon the case with great effect, the assembly decided that Jews were not entitled to vote, and a law was passed soon after to disfranchise them. Though steering a middle course between the two great parties, Clarke had failed in obtaining a grant of revenue for a term of years; but he concealed his chagrin, expressed himself satisfied with the conduct of the delegates, and assented, with great apparent cheerfulness, to the bills which required his signature.

In the mean time, however, he was secretly maturing a stratagem to render the popular leaders odious in the eyes of their constituents. Affecting to regard them with great favour, he offered them places under the government, promising to exert his influence with the council to secure their appointment, well knowing at the same time that the nominations would be rejected. The scheme, artfully laid, was completely successful. Morris, Johnson, and others, fell into the snare, and not only lost office, but were viewed with hatred and contempt by their former supporters. Confidence in the popular party being thus weakened, the elections of 1739 resulted in favour of the government.

But the new assembly, though importuned to do so, would not pass a grant of revenue for any longer term than one year, and this policy was for the future strictly adhered to. Thus, after a vehement struggle, which had lasted for thirty years, a great popular victory was consummated.

Fully restored to the confidence of his council, whose countenance was necessary to the success of his land speculations, Clarke continued to administer the government, if not without occasional excitement, yet without provoking the opposition of succeeding assemblies beyond his power to allay.

In the year 1741, the city of New York, then numbering some twelve thousand inhabitants, was fearfully agitated by the pretended discovery of a negro plot. On the 18th of March, the chapel and buildings in the fort were consumed by fire, which was at first attributed to the carelessness of a workman employed in repairing the gutters of the governor's residence. A report was spread shortly after that the fire was premeditated, and seven fires occurring in succession, amidst the general alarm suspicion soon ripened into certainty. Several slaves were accused of having a knowledge of the plot, and during their examination two other fires took place, from one of which a negro was discovered in the act of making a precipitate escape.

The evidence of Mary Burton confirmed the general impression of a conspiracy. This woman, an indented servant to one Hughson, the keeper of a low tavern to which negroes were in the habit of resorting, testified that certain slaves, in her presence and in that of Hughson, his wife, and another woman, had consulted together to burn the city and massacre the whites. Improbable as her relation was, it was eagerly believed, and although in subsequent examinations she varied materially from her previous statements, the terrified citizens still persisted in giving credence to her testimony. Twenty-one whites and one hundred and sixty slaves and free blacks were committed to prison. The whole summer was spent in prosecuting these unfortunate people. Rumours were magnified into facts, and the wildest assertions accepted for proofs. Thirteen negroes were burned at the stake; eighteen were hanged, and seventy transported. Hughson and one negro were gibbeted. The wife of Hughson, their woman-servant, and Ury, a nonjuring schoolmaster, were also executed.

Condemned upon insufficient evidence, in the midst of a tumult of passion, fear, and prejudice, it has become a grave doubt whether any of the victims were really guilty of the crime for which they suffered an ignominious death.

The execution of Ury, who died asserting his innocence, was unquestionably a judicial murder. He was accused of covertly exercising the office of a Catholic priest—itself a capital offence in the province—and of urging on the plot by offers of absolution to the conspirators. He was convicted on both indictments, though neither of the charges were legally proved, and the last was rendered totally unworthy of credence by the character of the witnesses. How many more persons might have suffered from the combined effects of terror and religious intolerance, it is difficult now to say; but when the woman Burton, the principal informer, bewildered by the frequent examinations to which she had been subjected, began to extend her accusations to persons of spotless reputation, a reaction took place in the minds of the citizens, and all further convictions were stayed.

In the autumn of 1743, Governor Clarke was superseded by George Clinton, an admiral in the British navy, and uncle to the young Earl of Lincoln. Desirous of improving his fortune, and neither sensitive nor scrupulous, but easy and good-humoured, the new governor, with the exception of being retiring and unsocial, seemed well calculated to effect a good understanding with the assembly. Having taken Chief Justice Delancey into his confidence, the vast influence possessed by that arch-intriguer tended to produce more harmonious action in the government than had been exhibited for many years. This calm was, however, but the prelude to a storm. Quarrelling with Delancey, the governor became estranged from his former confidant, and took Colden, a bitter opponent of the chief justice, into his favour instead.

The latter, placing himself at the head of opposition, and strong in having a majority of his relations and friends in the assembly, commenced a series of violent and incessant attacks upon the executive, which lasted during the whole period that Clinton remained in the province.

In the mean time war had been declared between England and France. Acting with their accustomed promptness, a French expedition was immediately organized for a descent upon Nova Scotia. Fort Cansean was easily captured; but Annapolis, formerly known as Port Royal, though twice invested by a mixed body of French and Indians, was fortunately saved by a timely reinforcement of troops from Massachusetts.

Conscious that while the French held possession of Louisburg, a strongly fortified post on the island of Cape Breton, the New England States would be subject to constant annoyances from that quarter, Shirley, the governor of Massachusetts, proposed its reduction by the colonial troops alone, and called upon the other provinces to co-operate. The assembly of New York were at first inclined to render no assistance, but at the session of 1745, they reluctantly voted three thousand pounds toward the expenses of the expedition, which they shortly after increased to five thousand. Clinton, ashamed of their lukewarmness in an affair of so much moment, forwarded to Shirley ten pieces of field ordnance, and a supply of provisions obtained by private subscription. The result justified the boldness of the enterprise. On the 17th of June, after a siege of forty-nine days, terms of capitulation were agreed upon, and the garrison, amounting to six hundred and fifty men, with thirteen hundred inhabitants of the town, capable of bearing arms, surrendered to the conquerors.

In the mean time, owing to the disputes existing between Clinton and his assembly, the frontiers of New York lay open to incursions from the enemy. Burning to revenge the loss of Louisburg, a party of French and Indians were despatched from Crown Point, and entering the territory of Massachusetts, captured the fort at Hoosick, in Berkshire county. Penetrating thence to within forty miles of Albany, they surprised, during the night of the 16th of November, the settlements around Saratoga, massacred a number of the inhabitants, and carried others into captivity.

Smarting under these disasters, and inspirited by the conquest of Cape Breton, with its almost impregnable fortress, the old project for an invasion of Canada was revived. Many of the provinces at once agreeing to furnish their respective quotas, levies were promptly made as far south as Virginia. The New England troops were collected at Louisburg, in readiness to co-operate with a British fleet and army, while those from Connecticut, New York, and the provinces farther south, assembled at Albany. The chief command of the latter was given to Clinton. The British fleet failing to arrive, the New England levies were partially disbanded; but reluctant to give up wholly an enterprise for which such vast preparations had been made, fifteen hundred of the Massachusetts troops marched for Albany to form a junction with Clinton. They were speedily recalled by the unexpected appearance of a French fleet off the coast of Nova Scotia, commanded by the Duke D'Anville, and instead of advancing on Montreal, the levies at Albany returned to assist in the defence of their respective provinces. The French squadron consisted of forty ships of war, besides numerous transports, having on board four thousand regular troops. Boston being menaced, an army of ten thousand men was collected in the vicinity, and the fortifications on Castle Island were strengthened and extended. But the danger, imminent as it was, soon passed away. The French fleet, weakened by storms, by shipwreck, and by sickness among the troops, was in no condition to undertake offensive operations. D'Anville died suddenly, and the second in command committed suicide. Another storm off Cape Sable completely dispersed the remainder of the armament, and such of the ships as escaped the tempest returned singly to France.

The fierce feud existing between Clinton and the assembly still continued to rage as hotly as ever, and charges and countercharges were constantly being made, couched in language alike discreditable to both parties. The governor accused the assembly of wilful neglect in securing the protection of the frontiers. The latter retorted by imputing the distressed condition of the province to fraud and mismanagement on the part of Clinton. In the midst of these violent agitations, which were prompted neither by patriotism nor integrity, the province suffered greatly. During the year 1747 Saratoga was a second time attacked by a party of French and Indians, the village burned to the ground, and the inhabitants barbarously massacred. The peace of Aix-la-Chapelle, which took place the following year, at length brought these alarming incursions to a close.

CHAPTER XIV.

Treaty with the Six Nations—Shirley's conspiracy—Action of Clinton—His violent disputes with the assembly—Demands a permanent revenue—Their able reply—Clinton appeals to the English government—Movements of Shirley and Belcher—Walpole's bill to strengthen the king's prerogative—Colonial protests—Its defeat in parliament—Cautious policy of New York—Dismissal of Colden—Clinton's letters to the Board of Trade—Taxation by parliament suggested—Encroachments of the French—Exploration of the Ohio valley—Attempt to restrict the limits of Acadia—Patent of the Ohio company—Trading house built at Brownsville—Indian council at Albany—Duquesne descends into the valley of the Ohio—Alarm of the western Indians—Instructions from England—Sir Danvers Osborne appointed governor of New York—His character, conduct, and death.

In July, 1748, three months previous to the final ratification of the treaty, Clinton, accompanied by his chief adviser, Colden, attended a convention of delegates from the Six Nations, at which Shirley, the governor, and Hutchinson and Oliver, commissioners of Massachusetts, were by previous concert also present. The conference terminated satisfactorily, the Iroquois and their allies agreeing neither to send deputies into Canada, nor to allow any French emissaries within their territory.

Soon after the convention was dissolved, Shirley arranged with Clinton a secret scheme for shaking off the dependence of the provincial governors upon their respective assemblies, by forcing them to grant permanent salaries and a revenue at the disposal of the crown; or, failing in that, to foment existing disputes to such a height as to compel the British parliament to interfere. The project thus secretly formed was vigorously pressed by Clinton. When the assembly met in October, 1748, he demanded a revenue for five years, and the annexation of fixed salaries to the offices in the gift of the crown, but not to the officials by name. He defended his acceptance of annual grants previously, on the ground of the existing war, and his desire to promote harmony; but that now the time was come to resist the innovations which had weakened the king's prerogative.

The assembly, in reply, refused to grant a support for any longer term than one year, or to make any change in the method of voting salaries. Their address, coarse and bold, closed with a vituperation of Colden, who was characterized as "mean and despicable," and a censure of Clinton for admitting him into his confidence. Charging them in return with a violation of decency, the governor refused to receive the address, of which a copy had been sent him for perusal. The assembly then appealed through the newspapers to the people, for which they were pointedly rebuked by Clinton, who threatened to send their address to the king.

At the session of 1749 the dispute was renewed. A permanent revenue was again insisted upon, and a positive answer required of the assembly whether they would or would not, grant it agreeably to the royal instructions. The response was, that "the faithful representatives of the people can never recede from the method of an annual support." Clinton now shifted his ground, and claimed the right to disburse the moneys voted for public purposes, on the plea that, under the English constitution, the powers to grant and to distribute were vested in different branches of the government. Admitting that such was indeed the usage in England, the assembly denied that it ought to be made applicable to the provinces. "In the one case," they said, "the disposition of the sums raised was intrusted to the king, who was supposed to have an interest in the welfare of his subjects, and whose officers in that country were amenable to justice. With provincial governors the case was different. They were generally strangers, who, holding no land in the colonies over which they were appointed to rule, seldom regarded the welfare of the people. Uncertain how long they would be permitted to retain their offices, they were eager to seize every opportunity of improving their fortunes, and would never want pretexts for misapplication if they had the disposition of the money. This they could do with impunity, as the people, thus plundered, had no mode of redress, inasmuch as their representatives could neither call the governor to account, nor suspend the council."

This able vindication of their course roused the indignation of Clinton. Charging them with being guilty of disrespect, he refused to receive the address; and until it was accepted the house declined entering upon the business of the session. Against conduct so resolute the governor had no remedy but a prorogation.

In the mean time Clinton had not been idle in keeping the English ministry well informed with regard to the dissensions which agitated the province. He charged the assembly with usurping parliamentary powers; with restricting the prerogatives of the governor, by assuming to themselves the sole authority to disburse the public money; with keeping the crown officers in a condition of dependence, by granting the salaries annually, and by naming the persons to whom the salaries were to be paid. As an effective remedy for this disordered state of affairs, he urged that parliament, whose right to control the colonies had never been disputed, should be called upon to interpose, and take from an intractable assembly the power to slight the king's instructions, or to weaken the authority of their governor. Shirley was equally active, and Belcher, the Governor of New Jersey, entered warmly with his council into the conspiracy. Chief Justice Morris, at enmity with Delancey, embarking for England on business connected with the boundaries between New York and New Jersey, undertook to support the allegations of Clinton, and Shirley set sail about the same time to quicken, by his personal influence, the action of the ministry.

But the representations of the confederated governors had already produced the desired effect in England. On the 3d of March, 1749, under cover of suppressing the evils of colonial paper money, the Board of Trade, through Horatio Walpole, reported a bill "to make all orders by the king, or under his authority, the highest law in America."

The agents of Massachusetts, Connecticut, Rhode Island, and Pennsylvania, immediately protested against the proposed measure as "repugnant to the laws and constitution of Great Britain," and their own privileges and charters. Their objections being sustained by Onslow, the Speaker of the house, the bill was finally passed, shorn of its most obnoxious clauses.

But, though unsuccessful in this insidious attempt to strengthen the royal prerogative, the Board of Trade determined to persevere. In New York, however, the introduction of so important a measure into parliament had the effect of rendering both parties more temperate and cautious. To guard against misrepresentation, and to protect the general interests of the province, the assembly, as early as April, 1748, had appointed an agent in London with instructions to correspond directly with the Speaker of the house. This agent, Mr. Charles, owed his appointment to the recommendation of Admiral Sir Peter Warren, related by marriage to the Delancey family. Active in the interests of his employers, Charles was soon enabled to inform them that the attention of the Board of Trade had been particularly directed to the disturbed condition of New York, and that they were preparing a voluminous report on the state of the province, to be laid before the royal council. The receipt of tidings so alarming induced the assembly to assume a more moderate tone.

Clinton also had his own causes for uneasiness. He dreaded a recall; and from the failure of the most important clause in Walpole's bill, was either led to doubt the success of the ministry in their endeavours to give additional force to the royal orders, or he feared to push matters to extremity before he was confident of receiving efficient support. Under these circumstances, he thought it best to conciliate opposition by dismissing Colden, and submitting himself to the cooler counsels of Alexander. But in the midst of the temporary calm which succeeded, Clinton did not fail, during the spring of 1750, to press upon the attention of the English government the absolute necessity of securing obedience to the royal authority, and relieving the crown officers from their condition of dependence upon the colonial assemblies, by a system of parliamentary taxation to be made general over all the American provinces. Adopting the same commodities advocated by Colden a year previous, he suggested that imposts on wine and West India produce would be sufficient to defray the expenses of the civil list. Preferring to attain the same ends by strengthening the king's prerogative, the Board of Trade were at first disinclined to adopt any other mode of reducing the colonies to obedience. But the inefficacy of royal orders becoming every day more apparent, they finally came to the conclusion, in the spring of 1751, to bring the question to an issue in New York by the appointment of a new governor, strictly charged to demand of the assembly a fixed revenue, and the surrender of its disposition. A revenue from the whole of the colonies, to be obtained by Acts of Parliament, was at the same time resolved upon. Dissensions, however, in the English cabinet, delayed for a time the prosecution of measures so dangerous to the liberties of America.

During this period of intrigue and dissension, the French were steadily persevering in their efforts to extend the limits of their dominion over the regions watered by the Ohio and the Mississippi. In 1749, the Count De la Gallisoniére,

Governor-General of Canada, despatched an officer, with three hundred men, with instructions to explore the region of the Ohio, to bury leaden plates, engraved with the arms of France, at the mouths of important creeks, to take possession of the country by formal verbal process, and to forbid the Indians from trading with the English.

On the north-east an attempt was also made to restrict the disputed limits of Acadia to a part of the peninsula now known as Nova Scotia, and the old French inhabitants were invited to remove from the ceded territory and open settlements upon the newly-established frontier, where forts had been established for their protection. In the west the military station at Niagara was improved and strengthened, and permission obtained from the Iroquois to build a trading-house in the vicinity of the Mohawk country.

In the mean time, to secure the valley of the Ohio to the English, a company, organized in England and Virginia, had obtained a grant of five hundred thousand acres of land between the Kanawha and Monongahela, on condition of settling thereon one hundred families within seven years from the date of their patent. In order to effect their purpose with advantage, Christopher Gist, an experienced trader, was employed by the Ohio company to examine the region west of the mountains, as far as the falls of the Ohio. His report of the country, and the amicable disposition of the western tribes, proving favourable, a trading house was erected in 1751, at Brownsville, on the Monongahela.

To traverse the designs of the French, Clinton, acting upon the advice of his council, invited the governors of all the provinces to meet deputies from the Six Nations in congress, at Albany, but only Massachusetts, Connecticut, and South Carolina responded to the call. The convention met in July. Old differences were harmonized, and a new treaty of alliance, offensive and defensive, was formed, in which the Catawbas also joined.

Notwithstanding these ominous preparations for resistance, the Marquis Duquesne, the new governor of Canada, determined to maintain the claim of France to the valley of the Ohio. In the summer of 1752, he sent a party of French and Indians to Sandusky, to punish the Miamis for trading with the English; and early the following year pushed forward a body of twelve hundred men to establish posts at Erie, Waterford, and Venango. The latter being on the main stream of the Alleghany, the western Indians, alarmed at these encroachments, entreated the Governor of Virginia to check the progress of the French by building a fort at the junction of that river with the Monongahela, promising to assist in its defence. Dinwiddie wrote to England for advice, and was ordered to repel intrusion by force.

While the steady and resolute movements of the French were rapidly tending to a renewal of hostilities, the Board of Trade were busy with schemes having in view the better "regulation" of the colonies. The long-pending difficulties in New York first claiming their attention, they determined, before appealing to the direct action of parliament, upon making a final effort to re-establish the executive authority by means of arbitrary instructions. In order to carry out this purpose with effect, Sir Danvers Osborne, brother-in-law to the Earl of Halifax, was commissioned to succeed Clinton in the government of the province, while at the same time, to conciliate the refractory assembly, Delancey was appointed lieutenant-governor.

Osborne was strictly and imperatively charged to maintain in its fullest integrity the royal prerogative, and to demand of the assembly "a permanent revenue, solid, indefinite, and without limitation," to be disbursed by the governor alone, under the advice of his council.

No person could have been selected more illy fitted to perform this arduous service than Sir Danvers Osborne. Naturally mild, amiable, and gentlemanly, the recent loss of a beloved wife had utterly overpowered the little strength of character he originally possessed, and had subjected him to a constant depression of spirits nearly allied to lunacy. He reached New York on the 7th of October, 1753, and on the 10th, after taking the oaths of office in the presence of the council, his commission was publicly read at the town hall. Returning thence to the fort with Clinton, his sensitive nature was deeply wounded by the contumelious expressions vented by the people against his predecessor. "I expect the like treatment," said he, gloomily, "before I leave the government." On his return to the council chamber, the bold address of the city corporation disturbed him still more. "We are sufficiently assured," said they, "that your excellency will be as averse from countenancing, as we from brooking, any infringements of our inestimable liberties, civil or religious."

Meeting with Delancey at dinner the next day, Osborne complained of indisposition, and said, with a smile, "I believe I shall soon leave you the government—I find myself unable to support the burden of it."

The following day he convened the council, and laying his instructions before them, desired their opinions. "The assembly will never yield obedience," said they. With great emotion Osborne next addressed Smith, who had hitherto remained silent: when, receiving a similar answer, "he sighed, turned about, reclined against a window frame, and exclaimed, 'then what am I come here for?' "

Pleading ill health, he returned to his lodgings in great mental distress, and during the course of the evening consulted a physician. After dismissing his servant about midnight, he burned a number of private papers, enclosed and directed a sum of money to the person from whom he had borrowed it, and retiring to the garden of the house just before the break of day, deliberately hanged himself.

CHAPTER XV.

Lieutenant-Governor Delancey—Royal instructions—Course of the assembly—George Washington—Movements of the French—First skirmish—Death of Jumonville—Surrender of Fort Necessity—Congress at Albany—Franklin's plan of union—Rejected by the colonies—Disaffection in New York—Establishment of a college—Liberal grants by the assembly for the defence of the frontiers—General Braddock appointed commander-in-chief—Congress of governors at Alexandria—Plan of campaign—Success in Nova Scotia—Rout of Braddock's army—His death—Crown Point expedition—Fort Edward built—Approach of Dieskau—Skirmish with the provincials—Battle of Lake George—Rout of the French—Capture of Dieskau—Honours awarded to Johnson by parliament—Neglect of Lyman—Inactivity of Johnson—Fort William Henry built—Niagara expedition—Reverses and disappointments of Shirley—Sickness of troops—Fort Oswego built.

By the unexpected death of Sir Danvers Osborne, the arbitrary measures he was commissioned to enforce failed of their intended effect. Delancey, the new lieutenant-governor, having been so long in the confidence of the assembly, was not disposed to weaken his popularity by insisting upon obedience to instructions which he well knew would never be complied with. Even the council, although a majority of them were opposed to the extreme views of the popular party, were not inclined to acquiesce in the demand for a fixed revenue. Thus supported, both by his friends and opponents, Delancey merely urged, as a matter of form, obedience to the royal mandate, and having discharged his duty to his superiors, left the assembly free to act as they thought proper. Under such circumstances their course may readily be conjectured. They respectfully declined making any change in the rule they had adopted respecting annual appropriations, but conceded to the governor and council the authority to disburse the public moneys.

This firm and steadfast opposition to the royal commands might have given rise to serious consequences, had it not been that the attention of the English government was diverted from the question of prerogative by the threatening aspect of affairs upon the frontiers.

The colonies, generally, had received orders to repel the advance of the French; but it fell to Dinwiddie, as governor of Virginia, to take the initiative. Desirous of avoiding hostilities, if possible, he commissioned George Washington, then in his twenty-first year, a native of Virginia, and a surveyor by profession, to cross the mountains with a message to the French commandant, demanding that the French should withdraw from the territory of the Ohio, and release the traders captured at Sandusky. After a dangerous and painful journey of eleven weeks, Washington returned. He had held a friendly conference with Tanacharison, the half-king, and various Indians assembled at Logstown; had carefuly examined the point of land formed by the junction of the Alleghany and Monongahela with the Ohio, with a view to the construction of a fort at that place; and had delivered his message to St. Pierre, the commandant of Fort le Bœuf at Waterford, a few miles south of Lake Erie. The answer of St. Pierre, and the unguarded conversation of his officers, rendering it certain that the French were determined not to recede from the territory of which they had taken possession, Dinwiddie convened the assembly of Virginia in January, 1754, and obtained from them a grant of ten thousand pounds towards the defence of the frontiers. Forty-one men were despatched to build a fort at the forks of the Ohio. The military force of Virginia was increased to six hundred men, and Washington, commissioned as lieutenant-colonel of the regiment, was ordered to Alexandria to enlist recruits.

The other colonies being called upon for assistance, the assembly of New York voted, during April, one thousand pounds to Virginia, and despatched two companies of regulars to support the militia of that province; but declined giving any further aid, on the ground that it was doubtful whether the French had actually encroached upon any territory belonging to the colonies. To strengthen their own frontiers, they granted four hundred and fifty pounds for an additional garrison at Oswego, and agreed to become responsible for the repairs of that fort, and to bear their proportion of the expenses which might be incurred in the erection of such new forts as should be found necessary for the common defence.

While these resolutions were under debate, Washington, at the head of one hundred and fifty men, was marching for the forks of the Ohio, to assist in building the fort already commenced at that point. On the 17th of April, three days before he reached Wills' Creek, the French, one thousand strong, descending the Alleghany from Venango, had driven off the workmen at the forks of the Ohio, and were strengthening and completing the works already began there, naming the post of which they had thus taken forcible possession Fort Duquesne.

Washington had no sooner received this alarming intelligence, than he resolved to push forward and fortify himself at the mouth of Redstone Creek, on the Monongahela, until reinforcements should arrive. Moving but slowly by reason of the ruggedness of the way, and the deep fords which had to be crossed, he was met at the crossing of the Youghioghany by a message from Tanacharison, the half-king, warning him of the approach of a French detachment, and their avowed resolution to attack the first English they met. Hastening to Great Meadows, he threw up an intrenchment, and after sending out a small mounted party on wagon horses to reconnoiter, encamped for the night. On the morning of the 27th, Gist, who had been the companion of Washington on his journey to Fort le Bœuf, and who had opened a plantation on the Youghioghany, brought fresh tidings of the vicinity of the enemy. Late in the evening, an express arriving from Tanacharison, Washington marched with his command, through the rain and darkness, to the Indian camp, and early the following day, accompanied by the half-king and his warriors, proceeded in search of the enemy. Having discovered the place of their concealment, he attacked them by surprise, routed them with the loss of ten killed and took twenty-one prisoners. Among the killed was Jumonville, the commander.

Reinforcements coming up soon after, an independent company was left at Great Meadows to build a stockade, called Fort Necessity, while the Virginians were employed in opening a road to Gist's plantation, and a path to the mouth of the Redstone. In the midst of these labours the French advanced in force, and Washington was compelled to fall back upon Fort Necessity. On the 3d of July the fort was assaulted, and after nine hours fighting a capitulation was agreed upon, by the terms of which the garrison were permitted to retire across the mountains, bearing with them their arms and baggage.

While these events were transpiring on the western frontiers, a convention of delegates from the colonies north of the Potomac, with the exception of New Jersey, assembled at Albany to meet the Six Nations in council, and to concert measures for the common defence. It was at this congress that Franklin, one of the delegates from Pennsylvania, brought forward his celebrated plan of union. He proposed to establish a grand council, to consist of forty-eight members, who were to be elected triennially by the provincial assemblies of all the colonies, not any one of which was to be represented by more than seven, nor less than two delegates. The head of this federal government was to be a president-general, commissioned by the crown, with power to nominate military officers, and a negative on the acts of the council. The federal government was to make peace or war with the Indians, regulate the Indian trade, purchase lands from them, raise soldiers, build forts, equip vessels to guard the sea coast, the lakes, and the great rivers, to enact laws, and levy such taxes as might be equal and just.

This plan of union, though adopted by the convention, was rejected by the colonial assemblies as giving too much power to the crown; while in England it was regarded by the Board of Trade as favouring the independence of the provinces.

At this period there were many causes operating to render New York disaffected to the authority of England. The original European settlers, the Dutch, and their descendants, had never been disposed to submit patiently to the jurisdiction of their conquerors, and the breach had been widened by the preferences shown to the Episcopalian form of worship. The restrictions in their commercial relations were also severely felt, and as constantly evaded whenever an opportunity offered. Nor were those who held large and dubious grants of land better disposed, for while some feared an inquiry into the validity of their titles, others dreaded the operation of a land tax.

The establishment of a college in 1754, the presidency of which was limited to such as were in communion with the Church of England, the members of which did not constitute one-tenth of the population of the province, weakened in those of other religious denominations that sentiment of loyalty which many had hitherto entertained, while it inflicted the first serious blow upon the popularity of Delancey.

Notwithstanding the growing disaffection toward the lieutenant-governor, the assembly, alarmed at the successes of the French in the Ohio territory, readily acquiesced in his wishes to provide for the defence of the province, and for undertaking such other operations against the enemy as might be thought best conducive to the common interest. In February, 1755, they voted forty-five thousand pounds in bills of credit; and in May, after the plan of the campaign had been agreed upon, they ordered eight hundred men to be enlisted, to co-operate with the forces raising in the other colonies, and appropriated ten thousand pounds toward defraying the expense of the enterprise.

The British government having received tidings of Washington's expulsion from the Monongahela, were no less active. Although there had been no formal declaration of war, they anticipated approaching hostilities by appointing General Braddock commander-in-chief in America, and by sending with him two regiments of regulars to assist the troops levied in the provinces. On the fourteenth of April, the governors of Massachusetts, New York, Pennsylvania, Maryland, and Virginia, met Braddock in congress at Alexandria, and concerted with him the plan of the campaign. Four expeditions were agreed upon. Lawrence, lieutenant-governor of Nova Scotia, was to expel the French beyond the supposed limits of that province. Johnson, the Indian agent in the Mohawk country, was to conduct a mixed force of provincials and Iroquois against the fort at Crown Point. Shirley, the second in command to Braddock, was to assault the post at Niagara, while the latter in person undertook the reduction of Fort Duquesne.

The operations in Nova Scotia resulted in the

capture of Beau Sejour, and the occupation of the settlements at Minas and Annapolis; but the inhuman abduction of the peaceful Acadiens from their happy homes, and their distribution among the English colonies, where they pined gradually away in misery and destitution, has fixed a stain upon the projectors of that barbarous act which time can never efface.

In the mean time Braddock was slowly moving toward the Ohio. Holding the provincials in utter contempt, and profoundly ignorant of the Indian mode of warfare, he refused to throw forward scouting parties in advance of the army, and imprudently suffered himself to be surprised by a small body of French and Indians lying in ambush within seven miles of Fort Duquesne. Fighting in masses, exposed to the deadly fire of a concealed enemy, the troops fell by hundreds. Braddock himself, after having had five horses disabled under him, was mortally wounded. The troops at length becoming thoroughly disorganized, broke and fled, having sustained a loss in killed and wounded of sixty officers, and near seven hundred men. The Virginians under Washington taking to the trees, and fighting with their accustomed coolness and courage, assisted in covering the retreat of the regulars until nearly the whole of them fell a sacrifice to their heroism. The retreating forces were not rallied until they reached the rear division commanded by Colonel

Dunbar. On the 13th of June, four days after the battle, Braddock expired of his wounds, and was buried at the road-side, near Fort Necessity. Finding the spirit of the regulars utterly broken, Dunbar abandoned the expedition, and recrossing the mountains, halted awhile at Cumberland, and proceeding from thence to Philadelphia, finally reached Albany, where he went into winter quarters.

At the period of these disasters on the Ohio, the New England troops, under General Lyman, of Connecticut, in conjunction with the levies from New York and New Jersey, had assembled, on their march to Crown Point, at the portage between the Hudson and Lake George, where, by the 8th of August, they had built Fort Edward. When Johnson arrived from Albany, with stores and artillery, he assumed the command. Leaving a garrison at Fort Edward, he crossed the portage with the remainder of his force, amounting, with the Indians, to some thirty-four hundred men, and encamped on the southern shore of Lake George.

Aware of the dangers by which they were threatened, the French had not been idle. Shortly after Braddock had sailed from England for the Chesapeake Bay, Baron Dieskau embarked on board the French squadron at Brest, with four thousand troops destined for America. Eluding the British fleet cruising off the Banks of Newfoundland, he landed a thousand men at Louisburg, which had been restored to France by the treaty of Aix-la-Chapelle, and sailed with the remainder to Quebec. Having been instructed to reduce Oswego, Dieskau proceeded to Montreal for that purpose, but was diverted from his object by learning that Crown Point was menaced by the provincial forces encamped on the margin of Lake George. He immediately determined to break up the latter expedition by an assault upon Fort Edward, but as his Indian allies were reluctant to attempt the reduction of a work strengthened by artillery, he was persuaded to change his design, and attack Johnson in his camp.

Unconscious that Dieskau was advancing upon himself, Johnson sent Colonel Williams with one thousand men, and two hundred Mohawk warriors, commanded by the brave Hendrick, their aged chief, to the relief of Fort Edward. At a distance of about three miles from the camp, while marching carelessly, and without any apprehension of meeting the enemy, the detachment fell into an ambuscade, and was speedily thrown into confusion. Williams and Hendrick were both slain, but the troops being rallied by Whitney, the next in comand, they fell back in good order to the camp.

Flushed with this success, Dieskau pressed immediately forward against Johnson. The camp of the latter was secured from assault on the flanks by impassable swamps, and in front by an imperfect breastwork of trees hastily felled for that purpose, and by the wagons and baggage of the troops. A few pieces of cannon brought from Fort Edward only two days before, were hastily mounted and disposed along the line. Dieskau, driving the fugitives before him, had hoped by closing upon their rear to penetrate the camp with them, and thus derive an advantage from the confusion which would necessarily ensue. In this, however, he was disappointed. Immediately the artillery opened, the Indians and Canadians forming his right and left flanks, halted, and crouching in the brushwood could not be prevailed upon to take any part in the battle. With the regulars alone Dieskau marched directly upon the centre, and attempted to force it. Johnson being wounded early in the action, the command of the provincials devolved upon General Lyman. For five hours, sheltered by their slender breastwork, the Americans maintained an incessant and well-directed fire. Dieskau being wounded in several places, and the greater portion of the regulars terribly shattered, orders were at length given to retreat. The pursuit being closely pressed by the provincials, Dieskau, finding himself unable, from the nature of his wounds, to keep up with his routed army, seated himself upon the stump of a tree, and ordering his attendants to place his military dress beside him, dismissed them. In this position he was found by one of the pursuers, who fired at and mortally wounded him.

The same evening a detachment of two hundred New Hampshire militia, under McGinnis, sallied out from Fort Edward, and intercepted a party of three hundred French, who were retreating in good order with the baggage of the army, and after a spirited conflict completely routed them. The loss sustained by the French in these engagements has been variously estimated; that of the provincials amounted, in killed and wounded, to upward of three hundred men. For this victory, subsequently known as the battle of Lake George, Johnson was created a baronet, and received a grant from parliament of five thousand pounds; while General Lyman, to whom the success of the provincials was mainly attributed, obtained no other reward for his gallantry than the honourable esteem of the people of New England.

Instead of proceeding at once to the reduction of Crown Point, Johnson, apprehensive of an attack with artillery, lingered on the borders of Lake George, where he employed his troops in building Fort William Henry. When the approach of winter precluded all further advance, he left six hundred men to garrison the newly-erected fortress, and dismissed the remainder to their homes.

The expedition of Shirley against Niagara was not even partially successful. The troops collected for this enterprise, discouraged by the tidings of Braddock's defeat, and broken down by sickness and the difficulties of the route, finally reached Oswego during the month of August, where they commenced the erection of a new fort, and constructed a sufficient number of boats to bear them across Lake Ontario. But storms, heavy rains, and a scarcity of provisions, combined to delay the progress of the enterprise until the season was too far advanced to attempt it with any reasonable degree of safety. Baffled by these untoward circumstances, Shirley left seven hundred men in garrison at Oswego, and disbanding the rest of his forces, returned to Albany.

CHAPTER XVI.

Sir Charles Hardy appointed governor of New York—His popularity—Congress of governors—Expeditions agreed upon against Crown Point, Forts Niagara and Duquesne—Surprise of Ticonderoga proposed by Shirley—Rejected by New York—Action of the assembly—Taxation for revenue resorted to—War formally declared against France—Obnoxious acts passed in England—Arrival of Abercrombie—Assembling of the troops—Arrival of Loudoun—Activity of Montcalm—Oswego attacked—Death of Mercer—Capitulation of Forts Ontario and Oswego—Loudoun abandons offensive operations—Quarrels with the citizens of New York—Campaign of 1757—Futile expedition to Louisburg—Siege of Fort William Henry—Spirited defence of Monroe—Surrender of the garrison—Indian outrages—Conduct of Webb—Of Loudoun—Campaign of 1758—Energetic course of Pitt—Louisburg captured—Abercrombie repulsed before Ticonderoga—Fort Frontenac surprised and captured by Bradstreet—Forbes marches against Fort Duquesne—Its abandonment by the French.

On the 2d of September, 1755, Sir Charles Hardy arrived at New York, and assumed the government of the province; but as the new governor, submitting to the counsel of his predecessor, did not seek to enforce the instructions with which he was charged, he soon became popular with the assembly, a majority of which still consisted of members friendly to the interest of Delancey.

Nothing could more strikingly display the necessity of union among the colonies than the want of success in the late hostile operations. With forces far superior in point of numbers to those which the French could bring into the field, the various expeditions had not only accomplished nothing of moment, but, in the case of Braddock, had sustained a terrible defeat, which encouraged the Indians friendly to the French to follow up the successes of their active ally, by ravaging and laying waste the weak and exposed frontiers.

In the midst of this deplorable state of affairs, a congress of governors and military officers met at New York, on the 12th of December, to adopt a plan of operations for the ensuing year. All of those present expressed themselves conscious that no imposing success could attend the efforts of the colonies until parliament should interfere, and, by a general system of taxation and a uniform plan of operations, give that unity and directness to the forces employed which the disorderly action of the respective colonial assemblies at present prevented.

It was, however, agreed upon by the council to raise an army of twenty-one thousand men, one-half of whom were to renew the expedition against Crown Point; six thousand to attempt the reduction of Fort Niagara; while the remaining five thousand were to be employed against Fort Duquesne and the settlements on the Chaudière. A subsequent proposition was made by

Shirley, who had been appointed commander-in-chief, to surprise, by a winter expedition, the post at Ticonderoga, and thereby facilitate the capture of Crown Point. But the assembly of New York, to whom the project was communicated by the governor, refused to assist in the prosecution of the enterprise, unless Shirley would reinforce the provincial troops by a larger number of regulars than he could spare without injury to the plan laid down for the summer campaign.

For the latter, however, the assembly voted a levy of seventeen hundred men, and issued bills of credit on the faith of the colony to the amount of forty thousand pounds. The previous appropriations having exhausted the resources of the province, the assembly, at the December session, resorted to taxation for a revenue. Duties were imposed on imports and on stamps, and such other means were adopted to meet the expenses of the war as were thought least burdensome to the people.

Great Britain at length formally declared war, and the Earl of Loudoun was appointed commander-in-chief throughout America, with a commission as governor of Virginia, and extraordinary powers. Acts had also been passed by parliament subordinating the provincial officers to those commissioned by the crown, and for quartering the troops on private houses. Both these acts gave great offence throughout the colonies, which was not lessened by the arrogance and discourtesy with which they were enforced.

On the 25th of June, General Abercrombie, the second in command to Loudoun, reached Albany, having brought over with him from England the 35th regiment and Murray's regiment of Highlanders. There also were assembled seven thousand provincials and the remains of Braddock's regiments. The forts at Oswego, by the resolute activity of Bradstreet of New York, the commissary-general, had been amply supplied with provisions and stores for five thousand men. Intelligence being brought by the latter that the French were advancing to the assault of that post, Abercrombie, who had been vainly urged previously by Shirley to reinforce the garrison, now ordered General Webb to be in readiness for that service; but his march was delayed until the arrival of the Earl of Loudoun on the 27th of July. The main army at length prepared to advance upon Ticonderoga and Crown Point, while Webb was despatched with his regiment of regulars to the relief of Oswego. It was then too late.

The Marquis of Montcalm, who had lately succeeded Dieskau as commander of the French forces in Canada, seizing rapid advantage of the isolated condition of Oswego, placed himself at the head of a mixed force of regulars, militia, and Indians, to the number of five thousand men. Ascending the St. Lawrence from Quebec, he crossed Lake Ontario with wonderful expedition, and appeared before the forts at Oswego on the evening of the 12th of August. These forts, two in number, were situated upon the right and left banks of the river from which the station was named, and at a short distance from the lake. Fort Ontario, built upon an eminence which commanded the more substantial works of Oswego, was strongly garrisoned by Pepperell's and Shirley's regiments, numbering over fifteen hundred men. Against this garrison, on the morning of the 13th, Montcalm, well supplied with artillery, opened his fire; and during the whole day the assault and defence were continued with unceasing vigour and resolution. Finding his ammunition failing, Mercer, the English commandant, spiked his cannon, and silently evacuating Fort Ontario, crossed the river under cover of the night, and occupied Fort Oswego with the greater portion of his force. Montcalm promptly took possession of the deserted work, and commenced an uninterrupted fire upon the opposite fortress. On the 14th, Mercer having been previously killed by a cannon-ball, the garrison proposed terms of capitulation. The loss in killed and wounded was not great on either side; but one hundred and thirty-four pieces of artillery, six armed vessels, two hundred boats and batteaux, and an immense quantity of stores and provisions, were captured by the French. The garrison, over one thousand in number, after enduring some outrages from the Indians, which were greatly exaggerated at the time, were sent to Montreal as prisoners of war. To propitiate the Six Nations, Montcalm razed the forts, and returned to Canada in triumph.

The alarm created by the successful achievement of this important and ably-conducted enterprise, led to the abandonment of offensive operations on the part of the British commanders. Webb, after advancing as far as the Oneida portage, fell back precipitately to Albany. Loudoun, the commander-in-chief, recalled the main army, then on its way to Ticonderoga, and after reinforcing Forts Edward and William, dismissed the provincials and ordered the regulars into winter quarters. A thousand of the latter were crowded into the barracks at New York; but the magistrates of the city declining to grant free lodgings for the officers, the imperious earl threatened, that if the demand was not complied with, he would billet the whole of his forces upon the city. This outrageous conduct produced great indignation among the inhabitants; and though the difficulty was finally arranged by private subscription, the insolent arrogance of Loudoun created toward him a general feeling of detestation.

The campaign of 1757 was equally inglorious to the British arms. The early part of the summer was wasted in preparations; and it was not until July that the indolent and imbecile Loudoun, after providing for the safety of the frontiers, was enabled to leave New York to co-operate with a fleet under Admiral Holborne in the attempted reduction of Louisburg. Sir Charles Hardy having been appointed to a naval command in this expedition, the government of New York was again left in the hands of Delancey. While Loudoun, with a well-appointed army of ten thousand men, was loitering away his time at Halifax, a French squadron of seventeen sail anchoring in the harbour of Louisburg disconcerted the proposed attack. The indignant officers, with their broken-spirited troops, were re-embarked for New York.

They had scarcely set sail on their return from what was contemptuously called "a cabbage-planting expedition," in allusion to a vegetable garden with which Loudoun had amused his inactivity at Halifax, before tidings reached them of the capture of Fort William Henry. Gathering together the whole disposable force of Canada, regulars, Canadians, and Indians, to the number of eight thousand men, Montcalm ascended Lake George, and on the 2d of August suddenly appeared before the astonished garrison. Disembarking his troops at the southern point of the lake, he sent a portion of the Canadians to cut off all communication with Webb, who lay at Fort Edward, only fourteen miles distant, with an army of five thousand men. Another strong detachment, under De Levi, was posted in the woods to the north of the fort; while the main body took up a position on the west side of the lake. On the 4th of August, Monroe, the veteran commander of Fort William Henry, was summoned to surrender; but confidently expecting to be reinforced by Webb, he determined upon a vigorous defence. Montcalm at once hastened up his artillery and commenced the attack. The conduct of General Webb in this emergency has been justly censured. During the progress of the siege, Sir William Johnson repeatedly solicited permission to march with a strong body of provincials to the relief of the beleaguered garrison; but, labouring under the apprehension that Fort Edward would be the next object of attack, Webb not only rescinded the permission which after much importunity had been extorted from him, but wrote to Monroe, stating his inability to render him any assistance, and advising him to capitulate on the best terms he could obtain.

Notwithstanding the garrison at Fort William Henry did not much exceed two thousand men, the brave Monroe protracted the defence for six days; when, his ammunition being nearly exhausted and only four of his guns remaining serviceable, he agreed to surrender, on condition that his troops should be allowed to march out with the honours of war, and furnished with an escort to Fort Edward sufficient to protect them from the vindictive ferocity of the savages. To these terms Montcalm consented; but, although both himself and his officers perilled their own lives to shield the vanquished garrison from the tomahawk and the scalping-knife, in spite of their most strenuous personal efforts many of the prisoners were massacred, and a still larger number were seized and hurried off into captivity.

Within a few days after the surrender of Monroe, Webb had received additions of volunteers and militia until the force at Fort Edward was increased to twenty thousand men. It was then, however, too late to render any effective service. Satisfied with having achieved a triumph with so little loss to himself, Montcalm, hastily reducing the fort and out-buildings to a heap of ruins, re-embarked for Canada, bearing with him the immense quantity of stores which had fallen into his hands.

In the midst of the alarm created by this successful incursion, Loudoun arrived at New York from his fruitless expedition against Louisburg, and, partaking of the general panic, proposed to encamp on Long Island for the defence of the continent. And thus, amid the sneers of coffee-house wits and the contempt of his own officers, the summer was passed. With more men capable of bearing arms in a single province than there were male inhabitants in the whole territory of Canada, and with an army of regulars amounting to twenty thousand men, the English had been shamefully expelled from the valley of the Ohio and from the borders of Lake Ontario and Lake George. The French, victorious in every engagement, not only held possession of the disputed territory, but had succeeded in coercing the Six Nations to a position of neutrality; while their own Indian allies, spreading themselves along the frontiers from Massachusetts to Virginia, scarcely met with any resistance to their ferocious and sanguinary career.

The campaign of 1758 opened under happier auspices. William Pitt, who "trampled upon impossibilities," and who had risen solely by the force of his commanding talents from the humble station of a cornet of dragoons to the head of the British cabinet, no sooner found himself in a position to act without restraint, than he sought, with all the energies of his large mind, to effect a radical change in the aspect of American affairs. Thoroughly acquainted with the condition of the colonies, he appeased the just discontent of the officers attached to the provincial levies by rescinding the odious army regulations, and allowing all, from the rank of colonel downward, an equal command with the British. By a circular addressed to the respective governors he called for all the men they could raise, to coöperate with the sea and land forces about to be sent from England; taking upon himself to provide arms, ammunition, tents, and provisions; and, while requiring of the colonists to clothe and pay their levies, he promised that even these expenses should be reimbursed by parliament.

His requisitions were promptly met by a hearty response. The governments of New England were profusely liberal. New York enlarged her quota from one thousand seven hundred men to two thousand six hundred and eighty, and voted one hundred thousand pounds to defray the charges of their service and equipment. Loudoun was recalled, and Abercrombie appointed commander-in-chief. Early in May, fifty thousand men, including twenty-two thousand regulars, were ready to take the field.

The plan of the campaign embraced three expeditions: Admiral Boscawen, with a squadron of thirty-eight ships of war and an army of fourteen thousand men under Amherst, assisted by Brigadier-General Wolfe, was to attempt the reduction of Louisburg; while Abercrombie, with fifteen thousand men, advanced against Ticonderoga; and Forbes, with six thousand regulars and provincials, marched to the conquest of Fort Duquesne and the expulsion of the French from the valley of the Ohio.

On the 8th of June Boscawen appeared before the fortress at Louisburg, and the same day the troops were disembarked and the works invested. The siege was pressed with great caution and energy until the 27th of July, when, the French ships of war in the harbour having been destroyed or taken, the garrison capitulated, and the islands of Cape Breton and St. Johns were immediately taken possession of by the conquerors.

During the progress of this siege, Abercrombie marched from Fort Edward with nine thousand provincials and six thousand regulars, and embarking in one thousand boats and batteaux, sailed down Lake George, bearing with him, on rafts prepared for that purpose, his artillery and military stores. The cloudless sun of that July morning looked down upon a magnificent array of troops in scarlet and gold, of burnished arms, and of waving banners, while the shores of the lake echoed back the inspiring sounds of martial music, by which the movements of the flotilla were accompanied. On the 6th of July, in a cove on the west side of the lake and near to its outlet, the army landed, and soon after, following the windings of the river, moved in four columns along the west bank of the stream, the regulars in the centre and the provincials on the flanks.

While advancing in some confusion over the uneven ground of the dense forest, the right centre under Lord Howe suddenly encountered near Trout Brook a detachment of three hundred men, who, having been sent by Montcalm to watch the movements of the English, had, in falling back during the previous night, lost their way in the woods. A sharp but brief skirmish ensued, which ended in the complete rout of the French. One hundred and fifty-seven men were taken prisoners, the remainder being either killed or dispersed. But this petty triumph was saddened by the loss of Lord Howe, who was shot dead at the head of his column when the firing first commenced.

After encamping in the forest for the night, Abercrombie thought of falling back to the place of landing; but by the energy of Lieutenant-Colonel Bradstreet, the bridges, which had been broken up by the enemy above and below the falls of the stream, were renewed; and a circuit of the stream being thus avoided, the army took possession of the Saw-mills, a strong military position, within one mile and a half of the works at Ticonderoga.

These works consisted of Fort Carillon, surrounded on three sides by the waters of the lake, and obstructed landward, on the north, by a morass. To defend the approach from the northwest, Montcalm had thrown up a breastwork of logs, before which an abatis had been formed of trees felled, with their branches sharpened and extending outward. The force within the lines, by the opportune arrival of a detachment under De Levi, amounted, on the evening of the 7th of July, to three thousand six hundred and fifty men.

On the morning of the 8th, Clerk, the chief engineer, who had been despatched to reconnoitre the lines, returned and reported them easily practicable. Without waiting for his artillery, Abercrombie at once determined to carry the breastworks by storm, although Mount Defiance, an eminence commanding the works, was in possession of his troops, and a few pieces of cannon judiciously placed upon it would have rendered Ticonderoga utterly untenable, with little, if any, loss to the besiegers. Having made his dispositions for the attack, the troops, with the regulars in front, were ordered to advance with fixed bayonets, rush through the fire of the enemy, and reserve their own until they had passed the breastworks. Unconscious that on the right of the French the fortifications were unfinished, the storming party bore down upon that portion of the works which was most strongly protected by cannon.

The resolute and sagacious Montcalm instantly seized advantage of the error. Stripping off his coat, he drew his sword, and forbidding, under penalty of death, a single musket to be fired until he gave the word, he waited silently until the English had become embarrassed by the limbs of the trees and by the loose logs and other entangling rubbish of which the abatis had been formed. Then, at the given signal, the fire of his artillery and musketry opened, and swept off the assailants by hundreds. Checked for the moment, but not dismayed, the troops returned to the assault, and for four hours persevered in their desperate attempt to force a passage over the breastwork; while the French, covered by their intrenchments, kept up an incessant and destructive fire with but little loss to themselves. Daring even to the extreme of rashness, the regulars, entangled at every step they took, made successive attempts upon the centre, upon the left, and upon the right; but at length becoming bewildered by the prodigious slaughter, they commenced to fire upon each other, when Abercrombie ordered the attack to be abandoned, and retreated precipitately across the lake, with a loss, in killed and wounded, of nearly two thousand men.

The army, disheartened and discontented, had no sooner reached Fort William Henry, than Bradstreet solicited permission to lead a strong force of provincials against Fort Frontenac. A detachment of three thousand men being reluctantly placed at his disposal, he proceeded at once, by forced marches, from Lake George to Albany, ascended the Mohawk River, crossed the portage to Oneida Lake, embarked at Oswego in open boats, sailed down Lake Ontario, entered the St. Lawrence, and landing within a mile of the fort, invested it on the 26th of August; and on the following day compelled the astonished garrison to surrender. By this brilliant exploit, thirty pieces of cannon, sixteen small mortars, and nine armed vessels, employed in supplying Duquesne and the other southern forts with military stores, fell into the hands of Bradstreet. Fort Frontenac, a strong stone structure, was laid in ruins; and of its garrison, one hundred men became prisoners of war, as many more having previously sought safety by flight. In twenty-four days Bradstreet was back at the Oneida portage, having lost but few men by the enemy, though some five hundred of his detachment, principally from New York, died soon after of sickness.

In the mean time, General Forbes was on his way to Fort Duquesne, marching slowly, cutting a new road as he went, greatly to the indignation of Washington, who would have pushed forward by the old route opened for Braddock's army. It was not until the 5th of November that the main body of the troops succeeded in reaching the camp at Loyal Hanna. The season being so far advanced, and a distance of fifty miles of unbroken forest yet remaining to be traversed, it was decided by a council of war to relinquish the expedition until the following year. Fortunately, at this juncture three prisoners were brought in, from whom it was ascertained that the garrison, cut off from their usual supplies by the capture of Fort Frontenac, had been deserted by their Indian allies, upon whose fidelity the hope of a successful defence had mainly depended. Inspirited by these tidings, Forbes resolved to leave behind him the heavy baggage and artillery, and press forward at once. Washington, at his own solicitation, was thrown in advance to clear the way for the main army. But the obstacles were many and the progress slow; and it was not until the 25th of November that the troops took peaceable possession of the ruins of Fort Duquesne, the French having fired and abandoned it the day previous. The structure was immediately ordered to be renewed and strengthened, and having been supplied with a garrison of four hundred and fifty men, was named Fort Pitt, in honour of the minister whose energy and decision had so greatly contributed to the general success of the campaign.

CHAPTER XVII.

Campaign of 1759—Plan of conquest—Prideaux marches against Fort Niagara—Invests it—Is killed—Attempts of the French to raise the siege—Their defeat—Capitulation of the garrison—March of Amherst—Ticonderoga and Crown Point deserted—Wolfe sails for Quebec—Takes possession of the Isle of Orleans—Quebec—Its situation and defences—Defended by Montcalm—His encampment—Attempt to fire the British fleet frustrated—Occupation of Point Levi—Wolfe encamps on the east bank of the Montmorenci—Battle of Montmorenci—The English repulsed—Murray ordered up the St. Lawrence—The heights of Abraham—Plan of attack—Daring movement of Wolfe—Its success—Incredulity of Montcalm—Preparations for battle—The English victorious—Death of Wolfe—Montcalm mortally wounded—Capitulation of Quebec—De Levi attempts to recapture it—Capture of Montreal—Final conquest of Canada.

EMBOLDENED by the advantages already gained, Pitt now resolved upon the entire conquest of Canada. His call upon the colonies for additional levies for the campaign of 1759 was met with alacrity. New York voted her previous quota of two thousand six hundred and eighty men, and appropriated one hundred thousand pounds for their levy and equipment.

The plan of conquest embraced three expeditions, separately commanded. While Prideaux marched against the fort at Niagara, Amherst, who had succeeded Abercrombie as commander-in-chief, was to advance upon Ticonderoga and Crown Point, and, after reducing those places, was to proceed, by way of Lake Champlain and the Sorel River, to the assistance of Wolfe, who, supported by a powerful fleet under Admiral Saunders, had been ordered to attempt the reduction of Quebec.

The first blow was struck by Prideaux. Leaving a portion of his troops at Oswego to reconstruct a fort at that place, he embarked on Lake Ontario with about two thousand regulars and provincials, reinforced by several hundred Iroquois warriors led by Sir William Johnson; and landing on the 6th of July, without opposition, a few miles east of the peninsula upon which the ruins of Fort Niagara are yet to be seen, invested it in form.

Anxious to preserve a station of so much importance to the safety of the interior posts, detachments from the garrisons at Detroit, Le Bœuf, Venango, and Erie, to the number of twelve hundred men, accompanied by a strong body of Indian auxiliaries, hastened to the relief of the besieged.

Receiving early intelligence of the danger by which he was menaced, Prideaux made his arrangements to meet it. Being killed on the 15th of July by the bursting of a cohorn, the chief command devolved upon Sir William Johnson, who, faithfully following out the plans of his predecessor, posted his troops between the fort and the cataract, so as to intercept the advance of the French. On the morning of the 24th of July the latter made their appearance, and the war-whoop of their Indian allies was the signal for battle. The contest was sustained with great firmness and determination for nearly an hour; but the Iroquois, gaining the flanks of the French, succeeded in throwing them into confusion, and the English charging at the same moment, a panic ensued which ended in the total rout of the relieving force, large numbers of whom, hotly pursued, were killed in the surrounding forests. The next day the garrison, six hundred and seven in number, capitulated; and communication with Erie, Le Bœuf, and Venango being thus cut off, those posts were abandoned soon after.

While the western army was investing Fort Niagara, Amherst marched for Ticonderoga. With eleven thousand regulars and provincials he descended Lake George in four columns of boats, and on the 22d of July disembarked his troops on the eastern shore of the outlet, nearly opposite to the point where Abercrombie had landed previously. The French being defeated the same evening in a skirmish at the Saw-mills, Bourlamarque, their commander, abandoned the lines from behind which Montcalm had repulsed his assailants with so much slaughter, leaving behind him four hundred men to garrison the fortress. Cautiously advancing, Amherst took possession of the deserted works; but, before his batteries were completed, the garrison blew up their magazines, and on the 26th retreated to Crown Point. On the 31st, they evacuated the latter fort also, and fell back to Isle-aux-Noix, where, thirty-five hundred in number, well furnished with artillery, and having a naval superiority on the lake, they proceeded to entrench themselves. The repair of the abandoned forts, and the construction of vessels of sufficient strength to cope with those of the enemy, occupied the attention of Amherst until the 10th of October, when, not knowing that Quebec had already fallen, he set sail for the purpose of cooperating with Wolfe; but being baffled by adverse winds, he returned to Crown Point on the 21st, and disposed of his troops in winter quarters.

As soon as the harbour of Louisburg was free from floating ice, Wolfe, having under him Brigadiers Monckton, Townsend, and Murray, all three of whom were young men of station and affluence, had embarked his army of eight thousand men under convoy of a fleet of forty-four ships of the line, frigates, and armed vessels, commanded by Admiral Saunders, and, ascending the St. Lawrence, had landed his forces on the 27th of June upon the Isle of Orleans, a few miles below Quebec.

The defence of the latter city had been undertaken by the Marquis Montcalm, whose troops, although superior in numbers to the British, consisted of less than two thousand regulars, the remainder being militia and Indians. He therefore wisely determined to avoid a battle, if possible, and to depend upon the natural strength of the country. The advantages which this gave him he had sedulously improved to the utmost.

Situated upon a point of land formed by the junction of the St. Charles with the St. Lawrence, Quebec consisted of an upper and a lower town, which, besides being protected on the north and south by those rivers, were fortified with great care and art. The lower town, washed by the river, nestling at the base of a bold and rocky precipice, forty-eight feet in height, was overlooked by the upper town and citadel, which crested the summit. This rocky and precipitous wall, extending for a considerable distance westwardly along the St. Lawrence, opposed an almost impracticable barrier to any attempt which might be made to surmount it; and for nine miles above and below the city, or from Cape Rouge to the Falls of the Montmorenci, every weak point had been strengthened and protected. To guard these extensive lines, Montcalm had encamped his troops behind intrenchments along the shore below Quebec, the centre of his position being the village of Beauport, while his wings extended to the St. Charles on the one side and the Montmorenci on the other. Such were the obstacles which it was required of Wolfe to overcome before he could hope to obtain possession of the city.

The troops had scarcely disembarked, before a furious storm arose, in the midst of which several of the smaller craft foundered. Some of the vessels of war also lost their anchors, and several of the transports sustained serious damage. Taking advantage of the confusion arising from this occurrence, the French let loose, on the night of the 28th, a fleet of fire-ships, which, floating down with the tide, created considerable alarm; but the sailors resolutely boarded them, and towing them ashore, freed the shipping in the river from the danger by which they had been menaced.

On the next night, Brigadier Murray, with four battalions, was despatched across the south channel to take possession of Point Levi, opposite to Quebec, and to commence the construction of batteries for mortar and cannon. While these works were in progress, sixteen hundred of the citizens of Quebec, foreseeing the destruction which must ensue, volunteered to cross the river and destroy them; but, being seized with a panic, they fell into confusion, fired on one another, and retreated in disorder. The artillery opened soon after with great effect; shells and red-hot balls entirely destroying the lower town, and considerably damaging the upper. The distance being found too great to make any impression upon the citadel, and the strong river-works protecting the place from assault, Wolfe, eager to bring Montcalm to battle, crossed the north channel on the night of the 9th of July, and encamped on the eastern bank of the Montmorenci, opposite to the left wing of the French encampment.

On an examination of the river, a ford was discovered about three miles from its mouth; but the opposite bank was intrenched, and so steep and woody, that the passage was pronounced impracticable. A reconnoissance was next made of the St. Lawrence, above Quebec, but the bold shore was found equally well protected by nature and art. Notwithstanding the obstacles which everywhere presented themselves, Wolfe projected an attempt to be made at St. Michael's Cove, three miles above the city; but Montcalm foiled the design by planting a mortar and artillery at that point to play upon the shipping. A landing at the cove being thus rendered too hazardous, Wolfe returned to his camp on the Montmorenci, and adopted the desperate resolution of crossing that river below the falls, where it was fordable for several hours between the latter part of the ebb and the beginning of the flood tide.

Accordingly, on the morning of the 31st of July, the brigades of Townsend and Murray were ordered to hold themselves in readiness to take advantage of the tide and pass the river on foot, while a detachment of grenadiers and a part of Monckton's brigade were descending from Point Levi to co-operate with them.

At the proper time of the tide, the signal being made, Townsend's corps was put in motion, and at the same moment the boats crossed the St. Lawrence; but the latter grounding on a ledge, were thrown into confusion, and considerable time was lost before they could be gotten off. During this interval, the march of Townsend's corps was delayed, while Wolfe, accompanied by several naval officers, pushed off in a flat-bottomed boat, and selected a better place for the troops to land. Thinking it, even then, not too late to make an attack, a disembarkation was ordered. Thirteen companies of grenadiers and two hundred of the second Royal American battalion being the first to reach the shore, were directed to form and begin the assault, so soon as Townsend's corps had crossed the ford, and the forces under Monckton had arrived within supporting distance.

But, without waiting even to form, the advance party rushed forward in impetuous disorder to storm the intrenchments. Great numbers of them being swept away by the close and well-directed fire which immediately opened upon them, the remainder were driven to seek shelter in and around a redoubt which the French had abandoned on their approach. Unable to organize under so destructive a fire, they were compelled to remain under cover until the approach of night, when Wolfe directed their recall, fearing that the returning tide would expose the troops which had crossed the Montmorenci to the danger of being cut off by the enemy. The retreat was effected in good order and without loss; but five hundred men had previously been killed and wounded; such of the latter as could not be brought off, were subsequently murdered and scalped by the savages.

Immediately after this severe repulse, Murray, with twelve hundred men, assisted by a portion of the fleet under Rear-Admiral Holmes, was sent up the river to endeavour to destroy some French ships, and open a communication with Amherst. Two different attempts made by this detachment to effect a landing on the north shore were repulsed; but on a third, Murray succeeded in surprising a weak military guard at Deschambault, and in burning a magazine containing provisions and military stores. From some prisoners captured at the latter place, Wolfe learned for the first time that Niagara had surrendered, that the forts at Ticonderoga and Crown Point had been abandoned, and that Bourlamarque, with three thousand men, was fortifying himself at Isle-au-Noix.

For a long time Wolfe waited hopefully for the approach of Amherst, until, chafing at his own ill success, and worn down by toil, watching, and anxiety, he fell ill of a fever. Even during this period of physical prostration, the ardour of his mind remained unabated, and he proposed to his principal officers several desperate plans of attack, which were respectively abandoned. At length it was resolved to proceed up the river, and attempt, by an assault on the city, to bring on a general engagement. The troops were accordingly transported from the camp at Montmorenci to Point Levi; but, after a long and careful examination, the approaches to the citadel were found to be so strongly intrenched and fortified, that although the batteries of the lower town might have been silenced with ease from the ships, the latter would have been subjected to considerable damage from the mortars planted on the heights; and so dangerous and unpromising did the undertaking appear, that Wolfe would not propose it to the admiral.

By this time the month of September had set in, and there remained only one hazardous chance of success. A close scrutiny of the north shore had revealed to the quick eyes of Wolfe, at a short distance above the city, a narrow intrenched path, very difficult of ascent, winding up the steep acclivity from the beach formed by a small cove of the river, and terminating in the Heights of Abraham. This path was protected by a battery of four guns, supported by a small force of Canadian militia, whose tents gleamed whitely on the summit of the heights. Here Wolfe resolved to disembark five thousand men secretly by night, and, climbing the bank, to form them on the plain above in the rear of the town, where the fortifications were weakest; although the rapidity of the stream, the narrowness of the landing-place, and the numerous sentinels posted watchfully along the shore, added greatly to the danger of the enterprise and the probability of an early discovery.

The troops destined for this service were accordingly transported to a considerable distance up the river, and all the necessary preparations having been made, at one o'clock on the morning of the 13th they dropped silently down the river in boats, without using oar or sail, but trusting to the force of the current only. The ships followed shortly after to cover the landing. "Who goes there?" shouted a sentinel from the shore, as the boats were gliding quietly down with the stream. "La France!" promptly responded an English captain, in the language of the challenger. "What regiment?" demanded the sentinel. "De la Reine!" replied the captain, who recollected that such was the name of a regiment which had been sent up the river under Bougainville to watch the movements of the English. "Pass on!" said the guard. They were subsequently hailed again several times, but averted detection by similar replies. One of the sentinels, however, was more suspicious. Running down to the water's edge, he exclaimed, "Why don't you speak louder?" "Hush! we shall be overheard!" said the captain, significantly, and the boats were suffered to pass without further interruption. Some struck the landing-place, and others fell a little below it. The troops from the latter, among whom was Wolfe, aided by bushes and projecting roots, clambered up the precipitous wall of rock, nearly two hundred feet in height, and dislodging the guard intrusted with the defence of the pathway, were speedily joined by their companions. By daybreak the whole of the troops had surmounted the obstacles which had impeded their progress, and stood in battle array upon the Plains of Abraham.

When the intelligence first reached Montcalm, he received it with incredulity, for he had never conceived the possibility of any large body of men succeeding in so daring and perilous an enterprise. The tidings being confirmed soon after, he sent swift messengers to Bougainville and De

Vaudreuil, the one commanding fifteen hundred and the other two thousand men, to join him with all possible despatch; but after waiting impatiently for some time without being reinforced by either, he crossed the St. Charles to dare the issue which had been thus suddenly forced upon him. By ten o'clock the two armies, each about five thousand in number, stood opposed to each other in order of battle.

The advantage of the ground was with Montcalm, but his troops, composed partly of militia and Indians, were far inferior to the English. After a cannonade of nearly an hour, from three small field-pieces on the part of the French, and two on that of the English, Montcalm, having posted fifteen hundred irregulars under cover of the corn-fields and bushes in front, advanced with the intention of outflanking the British. This movement being frustrated by Wolfe, who despatched Townsend with the regiment of Amherst to form on the left, so as to present a double front to the enemy, Montcalm, taking his station on the left of his line, opposite to where Wolfe stood at the head of his grenadiers, advanced with a dashing intrepidity to the attack.

The English troops, disregarding the skirmishers, by whom they were considerably annoyed, reserved their fire until the main body of the enemy approached within forty yards, when they opened with such a regular, incessant, and destructive discharge of musketry, that the French soon exhibited signs of faltering. Montcalm was wounded, and his second in command killed. Profiting by the terrible check which his adversary had sustained, Wolfe ordered a charge with fixed bayonets, himself leading the twenty-eighth and the grenadiers. At this prompt and well-timed movement the French gave way; but as Wolfe moved forward in advance of his soldiers, he received a musket-ball in the wrist. Wrapping his handkerchief about the wound, he continued to lead his men. He was soon after struck more dangerously by a second bullet, but intent only upon securing the victory, he concealed the knowledge of it from those about him, and still pressed on. Just as the French were becoming completely disorganized, a third bullet pierced his breast, and he was carried to the rear mortally wounded. While reclining upon the ground, supported by one of his officers, he questioned him eagerly respecting the progress of the battle. Being told that the French ranks were greatly disordered, he desired to be lifted up, that he might once more view the field, but his eyes were already growing dim. Suddenly the officer exclaimed, "They run! they run!" "Who run?" said Wolfe. "The French!" replied the officer. "What, do they run already?" he responded; and for a few moments the approach of death was suspended by the tidings he had heard. He gave rapid directions that Webb's regiment should be marched to Charles' River to intercept the fugitives, and then exclaiming, "Now, God be praised! I die happy!" he fell back in the arms of his attendants, and expired.

Monckton being dangerously wounded, the chief command fell upon Townsend. The pursuit of the fugitives was stayed soon after, and the troops recalled. This was scarcely effected before Bougainville, hastening to the assistance of Montcalm, made his appearance upon the field with a reinforcement of two thousand men; but the victory was already won. After some sharp skirmishing, he secured the safety of his detachment by withdrawing into the neighbouring woods and swamps.

The fate of Quebec was now no longer doubtful, for Montcalm, the only man whose genius might yet have saved it from capture, had also been wounded mortally while attempting to rally a party of fugitives. Expressing himself thankful that he should not live to see the surrender of the city, he wrote the same evening to Townsend, recommending the French prisoners to his humanity, and died early the following morning. In this important battle the French lost five hundred in killed and a thousand in wounded and prisoners. The loss of the English amounted only to fifty men killed, though their wounded numbered upward of five hundred.

Preparations for besieging the city were immediately commenced by Townsend, but on the seventeenth of September, before any of the batteries were constructed, the garrison capitulated. With the fall of Quebec ended the French dominion over Canada. During the following spring, a daring attempt was made by De Levi to retake the city, which, for a time, promised to be successful; but the opportune arrival of an English fleet finally frustrated the enterprise; and Montreal being taken by Amherst early the ensuing September, the conquest of Canada was completed.

CHAPTER XVIII.

Retention of Canada determined upon—Spain joins France against England—Treaty of Fontainebleau—Death of Delancey —Administration of Colden — Monckton appointed governor—Ordered to Martinique—Independence of the Judiciary struck at—Alarm of New York—Difficulties between New York and New Hampshire—Financial embarrassment of England—Action of the ministry—Stamp-tax passed—Its reception in New York—Colden burned in effigy—Stamp-tax repealed—Townsend's scheme of taxation—Action of the colonies—Pusillanimous conduct of the New York Assembly —Alexander McDougal—His imprisonment and popularity—Rapid increase of New York in population and wealth—Dunmore appointed governor—Removed to Virginia—Transfers the government to Tryon—Regulators in North Carolina—Their defeat—Disturbances respecting the New Hampshire grants—Resistance to state authority—Tea sent to America —Proceedings of the colonies—Congress at Philadelphia—Battle of Lexington.

THE expulsion of the French forces from Canada, and its occupation by the British, created a general joy throughout the provinces. The merits of Wolfe, Amherst, and their subordinate officers, were extolled in the highest terms. Congratulatory addresses poured in upon Pitt from all quarters. France, impoverished and humiliated, desired peace at almost any sacrifice. In view of this event, the American colonies were unanimous in their desire to retain Canada as an English possession. Pitt, and most of the other members of the cabinet, entertained similar sentiments; and Choiseul, the French minister, bent upon putting an end to a war so inglorious for his country, was not disposed to insist upon its restoration. Pitt, however, while lending a favourable ear to propositions for peace, steadfastly persevered in his preparations for a continuance of the war. Choiseul desired to retain a harbour in the Gulf of St. Lawrence and the freedom of the fisheries. These concessions Pitt refused, and, while negotiations were still pending, sent out a powerful fleet, which captured Belle Isle. A third party now entered into the quarrel.

Aggrieved by the establishment of English commercial posts in the Bays of Honduras and Campeachy, and conscious of being too weak to obtain redress single-handed, Spain, during the summer of 1761, entered into a secret treaty with France, under the title of the Family Compact; and, although differences in the English cabinet led at this juncture to the resignation of Pitt, war soon after broke out afresh. The British forces proving everywhere victorious, negotiations were again proposed, and on the 3d of November, 1762, peace was finally ratified by the treaty of Fontainebleau.

By the sudden death of Delancey, toward the close of July, 1760, the administration of the government of New York had devolved upon Cadwallader Colden, as president of the council.

Appointed the following year lieutenant-governor, he was superseded in the chief magistracy soon after by General Monckton; but the latter had scarcely presented his commission as governor, before he was ordered to take command of an expedition against Martinique, and Colden again assumed the reins of government.

In the mean time, the Board of Trade, in pursuance of their determination to attempt the restoration of the royal prerogative in America, had struck at the independence of the colonial judiciary by making the tenure of the judicial commissions subject to the king's pleasure, instead of during good behaviour, as formerly. The office of chief-justice of New York having become vacant, the appointment of Pratt, a Boston lawyer, was made the first test of colonial obedience. The subordinate judges, whose commissions were supposed to have expired at the death of George II., having also reluctantly consented to continue to serve, subject to the same restriction, the assembly became alarmed at the dangerous character of the innovation, and resolved to resist it, by refusing to grant the customary salaries. Equally determined to carry out the measures they had projected, the Board of Trade, in June, 1762, recommended to the king that the salaries of the provincial judges should be paid out of the royal quit-rents. The advice was adopted, and the system of a judiciary wholly dependent upon the crown, as established in New York, was directed also to be applied to the other provinces.

During this period of anxiety, serious difficulties had arisen between the governments of New York and New Hampshire, in respect to grants made by the latter of lands lying between the Connecticut River and Lake Champlain. Both provinces claimed this territory—since known as the state of Vermont—to be within the limits of their respective jurisdictions; but a royal order, promulgated on the 17th of June, 1767, decided the dispute in favour of New York. Had the government of the latter province been content to exercise the authority thus conceded without interfering with the grants previously issued by New Hampshire, and for which the settlers had already paid, the controversy would have ceased. But the greater portion of the territory in dispute being already covered by the New Hampshire grants, most of the sturdy pioneers refused to purchase their lands a second time, and organized themselves into parties for the purpose of resisting the ejectments which the executive officers endeavoured to enforce.

But a mightier quarrel was at this time beginning to engross the attention of the American people. The long-contemplated project of drawing a revenue from the colonies at length approached maturity. The remarkable series of victories which had exalted the power of England, and secured to her, by the treaty of Fontainebleau, a vast accession of territory, had, at the same time, by the enormous expenses of the war, plunged the nation into a condition of the most alarming financial embarrassment. As this distress arose in part from the heavy charges incurred in protecting the American colonies, the ministry sought to rid themselves of so great a burden for the future by attempting to draw a revenue from the provinces sufficient to defray the cost of their support and defence. By obtaining this revenue through the action of parliament, the power of the provincial assemblies would be so curbed and restricted as to be easily subordinated to the royal authority. Accordingly, in 1763, Grenville, the chancellor of the exchequer, notified parliament, in addition to minor measures devised for the same purpose, of his intention to bring forward a bill by which all bonds, deeds, notes, and various other necessary business papers used in America, should require to be drawn upon stamped paper, to be issued by the British government, and sold only by agents duly authorized.

At the ensuing session of 1764 parliament formally avowed the right to tax the colonies; and in March, 1765, the Stamp Act passed both houses with but little opposition. In addition to this, an act called the Quartering Act was passed, by which the ministry were authorized to keep up a standing army in America, the respective colonies being required to furnish quarters for the troops, together with firewood, soap, bedding, drink, and candles. No sooner did the passage of these acts become known to Virginia and Massachusetts, than, impressed with their dangerous character, they took the lead in opposition. The other provinces speedily followed their example. Committees of correspondence were formed, and a call for a colonial congress was responded to by a convention of delegates at New York during the month of October. The session continued for three weeks. A declaration of rights was agreed to; a petition to the king, and a memorial to both houses of parliament, all of them able and eloquent papers, were drawn up and signed by a large majority of the members. The principle of taxation without representation was indignantly repudiated, and everywhere combinations were formed to resist the introduction of the stamped paper.

In New York the denunciation of the stamp-tax was both fierce and vehement. Copies of the act were publicly hawked about the streets, under the title of "The folly of England and ruin of America;" and the excitement finally rose to so high a pitch, that the stamp distributor resigned his appointment, and when the stamps arrived, toward the close of October, refused to have any thing to do with them. Colden being thus in a measure compelled to assume charge of the obnoxious papers, they were by his orders conveyed into the fort for safe keeping.

On the evening of the 1st of November, the day appointed for the Stamp Act to go into operation, a party of citizens, many of whom had organized themselves under the name of "Sons of Liberty," broke open the stable of Colden, adjoining the fort walls, and seizing his carriage, marched with it in procession through the principal streets, until they reached the common. After hanging Colden in effigy, they returned with great parade to the Bowling-green, where, under the muzzles of the fort guns, they burned the carriage and effigy together. The excitement continuing for several days, Colden became alarmed, and finally agreed to surrender the stamps to the city authorities. In the midst of these disturbances Sir Henry Moore arrived, and took upon himself the functions of governor.

Up to this time, most of the wealthier inhabitants had not openly taken part in the quarrel; but emboldened by the success which had attended the efforts of their sturdier fellow-citizens, many of them now publicly joined the ranks of the disaffected. On the 6th of November they held a meeting, which resulted in the formation of a committee to correspond with the other provinces, and an agreement to import no more goods from Great Britain until their grievances were redressed.

Opposition to the Stamp Act being universal throughout America, and a change having already taken place in the British ministry, great hopes were entertained that the tax would be repealed at the ensuing session of parliament. Nor were those hopes fallacious. Pitt rose in his place, and denied the right of parliament "to levy a tax on the colonies;" and although Grenville strove to defend the bill, and charged the Americans with being in open rebellion, on the 19th of March, 1766, the Stamp Act was annulled.

But the gratification which was felt throughout America at this result was only of brief duration. Basing their repeal of the obnoxious act upon the ground of expediency rather than of justice, parliament reasserted their right to tax the colonies; and, in accordance with this assertion, Charles Townsend, the new chancellor of the exchequer, on the plea of regulating trade, brought forward a bill imposing duties on tea, paints, paper, glass, and lead. About the same time, an act was also passed to compel the assembly of New York to comply with the provisions of the Quartering Act, and forbidding them, in the mean time, to legislate for any other purpose.

The determination evinced by parliament to

raise a revenue without the concurrence of the colonial assemblies was opposed at once by the latter. Committees of correspondence again became active, and resolutions were very generally adopted not to import any goods from Great Britain but such as the wants of the people rendered absolutely necessary. The assembly of New York declining to make provision for the troops, that body was twice dissolved; but, supported in opposition by the popular voice, exhibited no inclination to submit to ministerial dictation.

Townsend's insidious scheme of taxation, though adopted under the pretence of regulating commerce, soon proved as complete a failure as the Stamp Act by which it was preceded. Opposition throughout the colonies growing more intense and vehement, the English ministry, becoming alarmed at the storm they had evoked, addressed, in 1769, a letter to the colonies, promising a repeal of all the duties imposed under Townsend's act, with the exception of that upon upon tea,—a promise which was carried into effect the following year.

At this period, distressed by the increasing differences concerning the New Hampshire grants, and rendered uneasy by the dissolution of two successive assemblies, and by the rapid growth of republican sentiments, many of the wealthier inhabitants of New York sought to retrace their steps and confirm their loyalty by the election of members to a new assembly whose political sentiments should partake of a more conservative character. In this effort they succeeded after a sharp contest; and under the influence of a triumphant majority the moderate party, as they were styled, consented to accept the conditions of the Quartering Act, and made provision for the troops.

Outraged by this pusillanimous course of conduct, Alexander McDougal, a prominent leader of the Sons of Liberty, called a public meeting of the citizens, denouncing the acts of the assembly as a betrayal of the trust reposed in them. So bold an address roused the indignation of the assembly, who declared it false and seditious, and ordered the imprisonment of McDougal. This rigorous exercise of power did but inflame the more the ardour of the patriotic party. McDougal was extolled as a martyr to the cause of liberty; while the soldiery, who undertook to become the champions of the assembly, were not unfrequently brought into collision with the populace.

Notwithstanding this untoward condition of things, the province of New York increased in population and wealth with almost unexampled rapidity. In the year 1770 it contained more than one hundred and sixty thousand inhabitants, many of whom were sturdy pioneers, who, pushing out into the forest, cleared settlements along the borders of the Mohawk, Wood Creek, and the head of Lake Champlain.

After exercising the gubernatorial authority for four years, Sir Henry Moore died, and Colden, now extremely old, again assumed the administration of the government. The following year, 1770, he was superseded by Lord Dunmore; but the latter, after exercising the office for a few months, was commissioned as governor of Virginia, transferring the chief authority in New York to William Tryon, who, as governor of North Carolina, had distinguished himself by the energy with which he had put down the Regulators—men who had banded themselves together, in the first instance, to resist the exaction of oppressive fees and the payment of taxes but too frequently appropriated to the personal use of the authorized collectors. Growing bolder with increase of numbers, these Regulators began to indulge in excesses which justly rendered them amenable to the laws of the province. Discountenanced by the assembly, and persevering in the commission of various outrages, Tryon placed himself at the head of a body of militia from the lower counties, and marched against them. The Regulators at once assembled in force, and gave battle to Tryon at Alamance, near the head waters of Cape Fear River. After a sharp contest, they were signally defeated, leaving some two hundred of their number dead upon the field.

Removed to New York, Tryon was soon called upon to exercise his abilities in a more difficult field of action. The conduct of the settlers holding lands under the disputed grants from New Hampshire had become, year by year, more firm and decided, while that of the New York officials was equally pertinacious. The lands of many who refused to take out new patents were sold over their heads, and the sheriffs received orders to place the new purchasers in possession. Armed combinations were immediately formed, headed by men of great energy and determination of character; one of the principal leaders being Ethan Allen, soon to be favourably known through his intrepid seizure of Ticonderoga.

All negotiations proving ineffectual, and the controversy threatening to break out into civil war, the assembly, at the session of 1774, passed an act declaring armed resistance to the government a capital offence. At the same time, Tryon offered a reward for the apprehension of Ethan Allen, Seth Warner, and some six other prominent offenders. But neither legislation nor proclamation availed to subdue the spirit of the mountaineers. Repudiating the title of rioters, they yet resolved, in general convention, to resist by force of arms all attempts at ejectment which might be made under the orders of the authorities; while the leaders, for whose arrest a reward had been offered, publicly proclaimed their determination to kill any person or persons who should attempt to take them prisoners.

But the long-pending controversy between Great Britain and the American colonies, by directing public attention to evils of greater magnitude, was soon to put an end to all civil dissensions. Firmly resolved to resist taxation in any shape, except such as emanated from the action of their own representatives, the people of America very generally agreed to abandon the use of tea, so long as it came to them burdened with a duty; and although that duty was merely nominal, they declined, for the most part, to purchase it, as involving in an insidious form the principle against which they had so long contended. The British government, with a view of carrying their point, having offered a drawback equal to the amount of duty, the East India Company, believing that the point at issue would now be abandoned, instantly despatched large shipments of tea to the various colonial ports. But the unyielding temper of the Americans was not so to be conciliated. In some of the ports they permitted the tea to be landed and stored. In others, the ships were compelled to return to England without being allowed to discharge their cargoes. At Boston the vessels were boarded by a party disguised as Indians, and the tea thrown overboard. At Annapolis, the people assembled in open day, and compelled the owner to set fire to the ship containing the obnoxious article. In New York, the tea-ship was ordered to anchor off Sandy Hook, and finally forced to return home. A private adventure belonging to the captain of another ship was treated less ceremoniously; the chests, fourteen in number, were seized and thrown into the river.

These daring proceedings no sooner became known to the ministry, than a bill was passed shutting up the port of Boston, and removing the seat of government to Salem. The tidings speedily reached America. Public meetings were called at various points, at which it was recommended that delegates from the several provinces should assemble at a stated time and place, and take upon themselves the duties of a Continental Congress. These recommendations met with an almost unanimous response. On the 1st of September, 1774, delegates from twelve provinces met at Philadelphia, and after many long and grave debates, drew up a declaration of colonial rights, a petition to the king, a memorial to the inhabitants of British America, and an address to the people of Canada.

In the mean time, the first serious prelude to the Revolution was rapidly approaching. On the 19th of April, 1775, and while the congress was still in session, tidings were received that General Gage, the governor of Massachusetts, having learned that a quantity of military stores were deposited at Concord, had sent out a strong force from Boston to seize and destroy them. At Lexington this detachment, consisting of eight hundred men, fell in with a small party of militia, which were fired upon and routed, with the loss of eight killed and several wounded. The regulars then marched to Concord, and destroyed such stores as were found there. The alarm speedily spreading, numbers of minute men came pouring into the village, and a smart skirmish ensued, during which several of the regulars were killed. Finding themselves hard pressed, the troops, greatly harassed by the way, retreated rapidly to Lexington. At the latter place they were reinforced by Lord Percy, who, with nine hundred men, and two pieces of cannon, had been sent by Gage to their relief. Falling back in good order, though closely pressed by the exasperated provincials, they succeeded in reaching Charlestown about sunset in the evening, having lost in killed and wounded two hundred and seventy-three men. The loss of the provincials amounted to eighty-eight. The exhausted regulars, after encamping on Bunker Hill for the night, crossed over to Boston the following day.

CHAPTER XIX.

Effect of the battle of Lexington—Doubtful position of New York—Ticonderoga and Crown Point seized—Descent of Arnold upon St. John's—War formally declared—Acts of the Provincial Congress—Opposition of the loyalists—Washington appointed commander-in-chief of the American forces—Other appointments—Battle of Bunker Hill—Congress determines upon an effectual blockade of Boston—Washington assumes the chief command—Return of Governor Tryon to New York—State of political parties—Seizure of military stores at Turtle Bay—Removal of guns from the Battery at New York—Unpopularity of Tryon—He takes refuge on board the Asia man-of-war—Invasion of Canada—Surrender of Forts Chambly and St. John—Capitulation of Montreal—Montgomery forms a junction with Arnold—Assault of Quebec—Death of Montgomery—Evacuation of Canada—Disturbances in New York—Rivington's Gazette—Lee ordered to assist in defending the city—Disaffection of the Johnsons—Joseph Brant—Declaration of Independence.

THE battle of Lexington was the unsheathing of the sword. War, though not formally proclaimed, was recognised to have commenced in earnest. Within twenty days expresses had carried tidings of the affray to every important point in all the colonies between Massachusetts and South Carolina. Volunteers soon encompassed Boston to the number of twenty thousand men. The committee of correspondence at New York, notwithstanding the Tory predilections of a considerable portion of the inhabitants, adopted a plan of association for the defence of colonial rights, and issued an address to the county committees recommending the appointment of delegates to a provincial congress. These measures were not carried without meeting with considerable opposition, and party differences at length grew to such a height, that it was thought expedient to send a body of Connecticut troops to within marching distance of the city, in order to awe the loyalists into submission.

On the 10th of May, the fortress of Ticonderoga was surprised by Ethan Allen at the head of a party of Green Mountain boys, the British commander having been summoned to surrender "in the name of Jehovah and the Continental Congress." In this expedition Benedict Arnold took part as a volunteer. A detachment led by Seth Warner took undisputed possession of Crown Point the same day. Two hundred pieces of cannon, together with a large amount of ammunition and military stores, fell into the hands of the Americans. Being joined soon after by some fifty volunteers, who had already signalized themselves by the capture of Skenesborough, and the seizure of a schooner at that place, Arnold descended Lake Champlain, surprised the post at St. John's, boarded and carried an armed sloop, and with his prizes, laden with valuable stores, returned in triumph to Crown Point.

On the 26th of May, Congress formally resolved that war had been commenced, although the idea of a declaration of independence was not at this period very generally entertained. Four days previous to this, the provincial congress which met at New York adopted resolutions for raising four regiments of militia, and for erecting fortifications. They also agreed to furnish supplies to the Connecticut regiment under Hinman, which was already in garrison at Ticonderoga. These measures were not carried without embarrassment, for the royalist party throughout the province, tenaciously averse to severing all connection with Great Britain, succeeded in carrying, in spite of warm opposition, a plan for conciliation.

On the 15th of June, the Continental Congress appointed George Washington commander-in-chief of the American forces. Ward and Putnam, already engaged in active service before Boston, with Schuyler of New York, and Charles Lee, lately a lieutenant-colonel in the British service, were commissioned as major-generals. Horatio Gates, also formerly a captain in the British service, was chosen adjutant-general, with the rank of brigadier. Sullivan of New Hampshire, and Montgomery, an Irish officer who had served under Wolfe before Louisburg and Quebec, were, with Pomeroy, Heath, Wooster, Spencer, and Green, appointed brigadiers.

While many of the preceding nominations were still pending, and two days only subsequent to the appointment of Colonel Washington as commander-in-chief, occurred the battle of Bunker Hill.

Stimulated to more vigorous action by tidings of so momentous a character, Congress immediately determined upon a complete investment of Boston, the British garrison at that place having been lately increased, by reinforcements under Clinton, Howe, and Burgoyne, to the number of ten thousand men. Washington at once departed to assume the command, and within two weeks took up his head-quarters at Cambridge.

At this juncture, Governor Tryon, who had been absent on a visit to England, returned to New York; and so nicely balanced were the two political parties by which the province was agitated, that public opinion would preponderate one day in favour of the Whigs, and the next would aid in the triumph of the Tories; for by these names the patriots and the loyalists were now beginning to be known. Even in the provincial congress, the Whig majority was small and fluctuating, though it was not long before it acquired both strength and permanence. The popularity which Tryon had previously acquired with a certain class of citizens soon began to disappear before the progressive march of events. On the very day that the city authorities welcomed the return of the governor by a complimentary address, the military stores deposited at Turtle Bay were seized and carried off by the provincials. More daring acts soon followed.

On the night of the 22d of August, Captain Sears, assisted by a body of resolute men, undertook, by desire of the provincial congress, the desperate enterprise of removing the guns from the Battery, in the face of the Asia man-of-war, then lying in the harbour. A boat which had been sent out from the latter to watch the motions of the patriots, having been inadvertently fired upon by some of the party under Sears, the Asia commenced firing with grape-shot, by which three men were killed and several wounded. Notwithstanding this serious check, Sears determined to persevere. Drawing, by an ingenious stratagem, the fire of the Asia upon a point at a distance from his working party, he finally succeeded, without any further loss, in carrying off twenty-one pieces of artillery.

During this exciting period, Tryon was exerting himself to sustain the people of Long and Staten Islands in their refusal to sign the articles of association. Other acts of a similar character rendering his further residence in the city dangerous to his personal safety, he prudently concluded to abandon his government, and toward the close of September took refuge on board the Asia.

In the mean while, Washington was engaged in blockading Boston. The Continental Congress having determined to invade Canada, two thousand men were directed to be raised for the expedition, the command of which was given to Generals Schuyler and Montgomery. On the 4th of September the latter descended Lake Champlain, and having formed a junction with Schuyler at Isle la Motte, the flotilla, containing above a thousand men, moved upon St. John's; but finding that place strongly garrisoned and fortified, it was resolved to return to Isle au Noix, and wait for artillery and reinforcements. The latter arriving soon, and Schuyler having returned to Albany, Montgomery again pressed forward to St. John's. While besieging it, Fort Chambly, lower down the Sorel River, was taken by Majors Brown and Livingston; and on the 3d of November the garrison at St. John's, consisting of seven hundred men, surrendered themselves prisoners of war. Montreal capitulating soon after, Montgomery pushed his advantage, and descended the St. Lawrence to Quebec. Forming a junction at Point au Trembles with Arnold, who had been despatched by Washington to co-operate with Montgomery, the united forces, thinned by discharges, desertions, and detachments to about one thousand men, descended the river, and on the 5th of December appeared before Quebec. Desperate as the attempt to carry the place by assault appeared, it was resolved upon. The army was divided into four corps, two of which were to make feigned attacks upon the upper town, while Montgomery and Arnold, from opposite sides, assaulted the lower.

On the morning of the 31st of December, 1775, and in the midst of a driving snow-storm, the columns advanced. Montgomery, at the head of the New York troops, marched by the bank of the river until within a short distance of the first battery on the south side of the town. As he approached, the enemy at first fled panic-stricken; but taking courage at witnessing the obstacles which the heavy masses of snow interposed to the progress of the assailants, a single artilleryman returned to his post, and fired a cannon charged with grape-shot when the Americans were within forty paces. Montgomery and his aids, Captains Cheeseman and Macpherson, were instantly killed. Discouraged by their loss, the division precipitately fell back, and made no further attempt to enter the town on that side. On the north, however, Arnold pressed forward by way of St. Roques, his advance being closely supported by a body of riflemen under Captain Daniel Morgan; but the obstructions occasioned by the great depth of the snow gave the enemy an advantage of which they were prompt to seize. Arnold fell, with his leg shattered by a musket ball; but the battery by which the barrier was defended was impetuously carried by Morgan at the head of his riflemen. The dawn of day too plainly discovered that the force by which he was sustained was wholly inefficient to maintain his conquest. A gallant attempt upon a second barrier resulted in complete discomfiture. Frozen with cold, many of their arms rendered useless by the snow, surrounded by the enemy in constantly increasing numbers, and all the avenues of retreat cut off, Morgan and his brave followers at length reluctantly consented to surrender.

Drawing around him the remainder of his troops, Arnold retired three miles up the river. Sheltering his men for the winter behind breastworks of frozen snow, he kept Quebec in a state of blockade. On the 1st of May, 1776, reinforcements, under General Thomas, increased the invading army to nine hundred men; but one-half of these being rendered ineffective by the prevalence of the small-pox, and the British garrison having, in the mean time, been strengthened by the arrival of additional troops, it was found advisable to evacuate Canada, a movement which, after a series of disasters, was finally accomplished on the 17th of June.

In the midst of these northern operations, the city of New York was thrown into a state of tumult in consequence of the obnoxious course of the editor of Rivington's Gazette, a paper supported by the influence of the Tory population, and by the patronage of Tryon, who, from on board the Asia, still kept up a constant communication with his adherents on shore. The publisher having been warned, without effect, to moderate the heat of his partisan zeal, Captain Sears, at the instigation of the Sons of Liberty, fearing to trust the local militia, mustered in Connecticut a party of light-horse, and entering New York in open day on the 25th of November, broke into Rivington's office, demolished his press, and carried off the types.

The intrigues of Governor Tryon, and the activity of the loyalists, rendering the fidelity of New York to the patriot cause a matter of considerable doubt, Washington ordered Lee to take command of a body of Connecticut volunteers to assist in the defence of the city, and to aid in restraining the factious spirit of those who still obstinately supported the pretensions of Great Britain.

These adherents were, however, too numerous, both within the city and throughout the province, to suffer more than a temporary check. Sir John Johnson, son to the conqueror of Dieskau, and Guy Johnson, the Indian agent, both living in the vicinity of the Mohawk, had contrived to keep the Highlanders, who were settled around them, for the most part favourable to the royal cause, until Schuyler, in command on the frontier, sent a detachment to disarm them, and took hostages to insure their future submission. Guy Johnson fled into Canada, whither Sir John soon followed him. The latter, accepting a commission as colonel in the British service, succeeded in raising from among his tenants and elsewhere two battalions of "Royal Greens." Joseph Brant, the half-breed, served under Guy Johnson for a brief season as his secretary, but subsequently engaged in those more active and terrible operations which have rendered his name so painfully celebrated.

Though the British troops in garrison at Boston still remained in a state of blockade, the Tory population of the provinces was far from inactive. Several skirmishes of a serious character had taken place; and as the British ministry evinced a disposition to crush all opposition by force of arms, the period for reconciliation was generally acknowledged to have passed away. On the 4th of July, 1776, the Continental Congress, assembled at Philadelphia, resolved upon a Declaration of Independence. On this occasion the delegates from New York declined to vote; but the provincial congress, which assembled at White Plains on the 9th of the same month, sanctioned the declaration, and ordered it to be engrossed and signed.

In the city of New York the proclamation of

independence was received by the patriots with the liveliest demonstrations of satisfaction. Not content with testifying their joy by shouts and acclamations, they destroyed a picture of the king which hung in the City Hall. Proceeding thence to the Bowling-green, they threw down his equestrian statue, and subsequently converted the lead of which it was composed into bullets for the use of the continental army.

CHAPTER XX.

Evacuation of Boston—Washington at New York—His embarrassments—Discovery of a plot to seize his person—Approach of General Howe—The British encamp on Staten Island—Arrival of Admiral Lord Howe with reinforcements—American defences at Brooklyn—Landing of the British on Long Island—Battle of Long Island, and defeat of Putnam—Washington encamps at Harlem—Howe takes possession of York Island—Disgraceful flight of the American militia—New York evacuated—Skirmish at Harlem—Serious conflagration in the city—Military and naval operations of the British—The Americans encamp at White Plains—Defeat of McDougal—Capture of Fort Washington—Abandonment of Fort Lee—Retreat of Washington through the Jerseys—Crosses the Delaware at Trenton—Situation of the Northern army—Crown Point evacuated—Advance of Carleton—Battle on Lake Champlain.

On the 27th of March, 1776, General Howe, with seven thousand British troops, evacuated Boston, and retired to Halifax. Confidently expecting that the next movement of the British general would be directed upon New York, Washington hastened to the latter city with the main body of his army, leaving five regiments under General Ward to garrison Boston. The earliest attention of the commander-in-chief was directed toward putting the city of New York in as good a condition of defence as his limited means would admit; but he soon found his operations greatly embarrassed by the activity of the loyalists, whom no prohibition could restrain from keeping up a correspondence with the enemy. Even the mayor of the city proved faithless to the cause of liberty. A plot was also discovered for seizing the person of Washington, and conveying him a prisoner on board one of the British ships. The principal conspirator was tried by court-martial, and ordered to be shot.

Having conceived the design of separating the northern from the southern states by the occupation of New York, General Howe, reinforced by the troops previously stationed at Halifax, set sail from that port, and on the 28th of June landed on Staten Island. In the early part of July he was joined by his brother, Admiral Lord Howe, with a fleet of one hundred and fifty sail, and twenty thousand additional troops. This overwhelming force was not without its effect, especially upon the people of Long Island, many of whom were already favourable to the royal cause. A considerable number of inhabitants immediately took the oaths of allegiance, while a portion of them organized themselves into a militia corps, the command of which was accepted by Tryon.

In anticipation of this emergency, Congress had already called upon the middle and northern states for reinforcements to the number of twenty-four thousand men. But it was the middle of August before the entire force under Washington's immediate command reached twenty thousand men, more than one-third of whom were raw levies, for the most part badly equipped and worse disciplined. To oppose these, the camp of General Howe on Staten Island contained twenty-four thousand British troops and German mercenaries, perfect in their drill and admirably appointed.

Having been commissioned to offer a free pardon to all persons who, within a specified time, would come forward and take the oath of allegiance to Great Britain, General Howe, in connection with the admiral his brother, delayed the prosecution of further hostilities until the effect of the proclamation should be ascertained. Finding the patriots firmly resolved to maintain the principles they had espoused, active operations were determined on.

To check the approach of Howe upon the city by way of Long Island, the Americans had thrown up intrenchments at Brooklyn, a point of land opposite New York, but separated from it by what is known as the East River, an arm of the sea three-fourths of a mile wide. Behind these intrenchments nine thousand men were encamped. The command of this strong detachment had been intrusted to General Greene, under whose directions the works had been con structed, and to whom the approaches were familiar; but the latter being taken seriously ill, his command was transferred to General Putnam, who, though an able and energetic officer, was but little acquainted with the topography of the surrounding country.

On the morning of the 22d of August, General Howe embarked fifteen thousand troops, in separate divisions, on board of galleys and flat-boats previously prepared for that service. Quitting his camp at Staten Island, he succeeded in landing, without opposition, on the beach near Utrecht, in King's county, Long Island, and about eight miles south of the city of New York. On the 25th his force was still further augmented by the addition of two brigades of Hessians under General De Heister. Between the American works at Brooklyn and the British position at Flatbush extended a long range of thickly-wooded hills, pierced by several passes; and upon the degree of vigilance with which these passes were guarded mainly depended the security of the American camp.

Having at length arranged his plan of operations, the British general ordered De Heister, on the night of the 26th, to take the road which led from Flatbush across the hills in front of the lines at Brooklyn; while a similar column, under Grant, marched round the western base of the hills by the river road, and approached the Americans on their right. The object of these movements was to draw the attention of Putnam from the advance of the main body of the British under Clinton, which, at the same time, was skirting the foot of the hills by an easterly route, with a view of turning the American left. Falling into the snare thus artfully laid, Putnam threw forward a strong corps under Sterling to guard the river road, while Sullivan hastened to dispute the passage of De Heister over the hills. The approach of Clinton with the main body was thus effectually masked by the movements of the other columns; and it was not until Sullivan found himself exposed to a galling fire in front and rear, that the stratagem of the British commander was detected. After several ineffectual attempts to force their way through the masses of the enemy, the troops under Sullivan broke into detached parties, and took refuge among the hills; but the greater portion of them, together with Sullivan himself, were eventually taken prisoners.

The progress of Grant by the river road met with far more vigorous opposition from Sterling.

Strengthened about daybreak by his advanced guard, which the British had driven in, Sterling posted his troops along the summit of the hills, and, as the enemy approached, commenced a severe cannonade, which was continued on both sides for several hours. Although repeatedly attacked by the brigades under Cornwallis and Grant, the Americans at this point gallantly held their ground until De Heister had routed Sullivan, and their rear was threatened by Clinton. His position becoming momentarily more dangerous, Sterling at length reluctantly ordered a retreat. Closely pressed by the enemy in front, and having in his rear a marsh intersected by a deep creek, this movement was rendered extremely perilous, from the bridge which spanned the latter having been burned in a panic by a brigade from New England. The choice of two courses alone remained. One was, to surrender to the enemy; the other, to risk an escape by attempting to cross the creek and marsh, which were eighty yards in width and of unknown depth. Sterling gallantly resolved upon the latter. Selecting four hundred men from the Maryland battalion to cover the retreat of the rest, he placed himself at the head of this small force, and in full sight from the American lines charged, with fixed bayonets, the brigade commanded by Cornwallis. Washington, who had hastened across the river from New York, was a witness to this display of heroic bravery. Wringing his hands in anguish, he bitterly deplored the fate of men who were so nobly sacrificing themselves to the safety of their companions. Four times the desperate charge was repeated. On the fifth, the British began to show signs of disorder; but at this juncture De Heister with his Hessians commenced an assault in the rear. Reduced in numbers and weakened by their exertions, a portion of the detachment, following the example of Sterling, surrendered themselves prisoners of war. The remaining three companies, having resolutely determined not to yield, cut their way through the ranks of the enemy, and endeavoured to cross the creek. A few of them were successful in making good their escape, but the greater part perished in the attempt.

The loss of the Americans in this disastrous battle has been variously estimated. Their killed and wounded could not have fallen short of four hundred. The British commander acknowledged, on his part, to a loss of three hundred; but upward of a thousand American prisoners remained in his hands.

The victorious forces, cautiously advancing, encamped in front of the American lines, and made preparations for investing them in form. In the mean time, the troops within the intrenchments had been reinforced from New York; but

Washington, after holding a council of war with his officers, determined upon withdrawing them from a situation so precarious. A retreat across the river, conducted with great silence and secrecy, was accordingly effected on the night of August the 29th, in the midst of a thick fog, and without the loss of a single man. The capture of General Woodhull, late president of the provincial congress, which occurred the day after the battle, was another severe blow to the American cause. He died soon afterward, from the gross neglect of his captors to dress the wounds they had inflicted upon him subsequent to his surrender.

The victory on Long Island exposing New York to an attack from the enemy, Washington, leaving a strong force in the city, retired with the main body to the heights of Harlem, making, at the same time, the necessary arrangements for facilitating his further retreat.

The British military and naval commanders, entertaining a hope that the recent victory would produce an effect upon Congress favourable to their wishes, again sought to open negotiations for an amicable adjustment of the dispute between the confederated states and the mother country; but Congress firmly refused to listen to any proposals of peace which did not recognise the colonies as independent states.

An assault upon New York was immediately

determined upon. Supported by the ships of the fleet, which had forced a passage up the Hudson and East rivers, Howe landed on York Island, about three miles above the city. The guard stationed there to oppose his debarkation fled without firing a gun; and two brigades of Connecticut militia sent to their support, being seized with a similar panic, disgracefully followed their example. Washington, with Putnam and Mifflin, vainly endeavoured to put a stop to this shameful flight. "Are these the men with whom I am to defend America?" exclaimed Washington. Indignantly dashing his hat upon the ground, he suffered his attendants to hurry him from the field. Orders were at once sent to the troops yet remaining in the city to evacuate it without delay. Under cover of Smallwood's Maryland regiment, almost the only one upon which any great reliance could be placed, the retreat, though rapid and disorderly, was at length effected; but not before three hundred men had been left in the hands of the enemy. Having thus easily obtained almost undisputed possession of the island, Howe directed a strong detachment to take possession of the city, and with the remainder of his forces encamped in the vicinity of the American lines.

The next day a skirmish took place, which revived to a considerable degree the drooping courage of the continental troops. A body of the enemy, three hundred strong, appearing in the plains between the two camps, Washington directed Colonel Knowlton, with a corps of New England rangers, and Major Leitch, with three companies of an untried Virginia regiment, to get into their rear, while he engaged the attention of the enemy by making preparations to assault them in front. The stratagem was successful; and although Colonel Knowlton was shot dead early in the action, and Major Leitch received a mortal wound, the companies maintained their ground. The British receiving a reinforcement of seven hundred men; two regiments of the Maryland flying camp and three independent companies from the same State were ordered to the support of the American skirmishers. Boldly attacking the enemy with the bayonet, they succeeded in putting them to flight, and were in hot pursuit, when Washington, having made the impression he desired, ordered them to be recalled. In this spirited affair the Americans lost, in killed and wounded, about fifty men; the British loss exceeded double that number.

On the night of the 20th of September, five days after the enemy had taken possession of New York amid the acclamations of their numerous partisans, a fire broke out in the city, by which Trinity Church and nearly one thousand houses were laid in ruins. The origin of the disaster was at first charged upon the "Sons of Liberty," some of whom, in the passionate frenzy of the moment, were seized and thrust into the flames. Subsequent reflection has, however, led to the belief that the fire was purely accidental.

The American lines on Harlem Heights being found too strong to be forced by assault, the two armies lay inactive for three weeks within sight of each other; but Admiral Howe having a second time succeeded in forcing the obstructions to his progress in the Hudson and East rivers, the British troops broke up their encampment, and embarking on board of flat-boats, sloops, and schooners, landed on the 12th of October at Frogs' Point, about nine miles above Harlem. These military and naval movements having the effect of cutting off the American supplies by way of the river, Washington resolved to abandon York Island, leaving behind him in garrison at Fort Washington two thousand men under Colonel Magaw. The main body of the American army fell back to Kingsbridge, where a part of the forces were left to throw up intrenchments, in order to protect the baggage and stores, and to retard the advance of the enemy. With the advanced division Washington proceeded to White Plains. Toward the end of October, the whole army was concentrated at this point, occupying a position well chosen for defence, and strongly fortified. Howe followed up closely the retreating army. On the 27th of October he attacked McDougal, who was in command of a strong detachment on the right of the American camp. The militia, making but a feeble resistance, were soon put to flight, with a loss, in killed, wounded, and prisoners, of nearly four hundred men. After this success of the enemy, Washington expected an immediate assault upon his lines; but, for reasons which have never been divulged, Howe paused in his advance until he should receive a reinforcement of six additional battalions. His delay was improved by Washington in removing to a stronger position two miles in his rear; and Howe, hesitating to risk a battle at this period, moved down the river with his forces to the neighbourhood of Kingsbridge. Here he made his dispositions for an attack on Fort Washington.

The necessary boats having been procured, the assault was made in four divisions on the morning of the 16th of November. The defence was maintained for several hours with great vigour and resolution; but the outworks being at length forced, the men were driven back into the fort. Finding themselves thus closely invested by a vastly superior force, the garrison soon after consented to terms of capitulation, by which nearly three thousand men—including the reinforcements sent over by Greene from Fort Lee—surrendered themselves prisoners of war.

The unexpectedness of this severe blow led to the hasty abandonment of Fort Lee, with all its artillery, ammunition, and stores. The next movements of the enemy indicating an intention to occupy New Jersey, and from thence push on to Philadelphia, Washington crossed the Passaic with five thousand men, leaving Lee, with discretionary powers, in command of nearly an equal number at White Plains. Another division, under General Heath, was stationed on both sides of the Hudson to defend the passes of the Highlands. Retiring slowly before his victorious enemy, Washington commenced his celebrated retreat through the Jerseys. With daily diminishing numbers, he crossed the Raritan to Brunswick, which he entered, on the 28th of November, with less than four thousand men. Marching from thence, but without loss, though closely pursued by the British advance under Cornwallis, he proceeded to Trenton, where he crossed the Delaware in the early part of December, and took up a position on the western bank of that river.

While the forces under Washington were being beaten at all points upon the southern border of New York, the northern army under Gates was scarcely in a less precarious condition. Upon the approach of Carleton from Canada, who followed rapidly the retrogression of the invading army, Crown Point was abandoned as untenable, the attention of Gates being wholly directed to strengthening the fortress at Ticonderoga. The Americans having captured or destroyed in their retreat all the vessels upon Lake Champlain, Carleton was compelled to halt his army at the foot of the lake, until the necessary water craft could be obtained. Toward the close of summer he succeeded in getting together five vessels of a larger size than any composing the fleet of Arnold, besides twenty smaller craft, and a number of armed boats. When he had manned this formidable flotilla with seven hundred seamen from the ships in the St. Lawrence, he set out in search of the American fleet. In the engagement which followed, on the 6th and 7th of October, Arnold lost eleven of his ships, and ninety men; the remainder, with great difficulty, succeeded in obtaining shelter beneath the guns of Ticonderoga. Having, by this victory, gained command of the lake, Carleton took possession of Crown Point, from whence, on being joined by his army, he threw out his advanced parties as far as Ticonderoga. Gates, however, in the meanwhile, had received large reinforcements of militia; and Carleton, fearing to risk an assault upon a fortress garrisoned by eight thousand men, withdrew his forces from the lake on the approach of winter, and returned to Canada.

CHAPTER XXI.

New York Congress—State government established—Campaign of 1777—Howe's movements—Battle of Brandywine—Of Germantown—Burgoyne's invasion—His successful advance—Takes possession of Ticonderoga—Retreat of St. Clair—Evacuation of Skenesborough—Of Fort Anne—Weakness of the northern army under Schuyler—Fort Edward abandoned—Schuyler crosses the Hudson—Advance of Burgoyne—Fort Schuyler besieged by St. Leger—Bloody skirmish with Herkimer—Death of Herkimer—Arnold advances to the relief of Fort Schuyler—Success of his stratagem—St. Leger deserted by the Indians—Breaks up the siege—Battle of Bennington—Defeat of Baum and Breyman—Schuyler superseded by Gates—Condition of Burgoyne—Crosses the Hudson—First battle of Behmus's Heights—Second battle of Behmus's Heights—Retreat of Burgoyne to Saratoga—Provisions captured on the Hudson—British council of war—Surrender of Burgoyne.

DURING the whole of the disastrous campaign of 1776, the provincial congress of New York had exerted themselves, with considerable success, to repress the spirit of the Tory population; and by judicious but energetic measures prevented them from taking up arms and openly joining the British standard.

The establishment of a state government having become necessary, a convention of delegates assembled at Kingston on the 20th of April, 1777, and adopted "the first American constitution that gave the choice of governor to the people." On the 3d of July following, Brigadier-General George Clinton was elected to fill that important office.

The early part of 1777 was wasted by Howe in dilatory movements, having for their object the capture of Philadelphia. Putting at length his forces in motion, he sailed down the Delaware, and entering the Chesapeake, landed at the head of Elk. From thence he commenced his march upon the capital of Pennsylvania. Routing the American forces posted to intercept him on the banks of the Brandywine, he followed up the retreating troops; and after surprising Wayne in a night attack near Paoli, entered the city of Philadelphia on the 25th of September. The main body of the enemy being encamped at Germantown, Washington withdrew his forces to Skippack Creek, about fourteen miles distant. Having soon after ascertained that the British army had been weakened by detachments, Washington determined to seize the opportunity of attacking the camp at Germantown. Marching by four different routes, on the night of the 3d of October, he succeeded at first in gaining an advantage over the enemy; but reinforcements arriving, and a thick fog coming on, the Americans were eventually obliged to retreat, with a loss, in killed, wounded, and prisoners, of over one thousand men.

But it was not so much upon the military

operations on the Schuylkill or the Delaware, that the hopes of the British ministry rested for success in the campaign of 1777, as upon an invasion from Canada by General Burgoyne. The plan arranged by that active officer was, to march with a strong force by way of Lake Champlain, and, after capturing the frontier fortresses in the hands of the Americans, advance to Albany. From the latter point, he expected to be able to obtain possession of the strong passes in the Highlands of the Hudson, by the co-operation of the British troops in New York; five thousand men, under the command of Sir Henry Clinton, being stationed in and around that city. By this complete possession of New York, the New England states would have been effectually cut off from all the provinces south of the Hudson River.

The march of Burgoyne was at first one series of triumphs. With an army of eight thousand British troops, and a motley array of boatmen and irregulars, he proceeded to Lake Champlain, where, after holding a council with the Six Nations, he was joined by four hundred of their warriors. As soon as he had received this accession to his force, he proceeded to Ticonderoga, before which he appeared on the 1st of July. Seizing a steep hill which overlooked the fort, he planted his artillery upon its summit, and made his preparations for an immediate attack.

St. Clair, the American commander, having under him in garrison only three thousand men, all of whom were indifferently armed and equipped, saw at once his inability to successfully contend with the force that had so unexpectedly appeared against him. No hope being left of saving the garrison but by an immediate retreat, he despatched his stores and baggage in batteaux to Skenesborough, and abandoning Ticonderoga, fell back with the troops overland, in the direction of the same post. His flight no sooner became known, than he was hotly pursued by a detachment of the enemy, eight hundred strong, commanded by General Fraser. The American rear-guard, consisting of three regiments numbering about twelve hundred men, was overtaken the next day at Hubbardton. One of the regiments taking to flight, the whole brunt of the battle fell upon the two remaining. These, animated by the exhortations of Colonels Francis and Warner, fought for some time with great bravery; but when Frazer had received a reinforcement of Germans under Reidesel, they broke and dispersed, leaving two hundred prisoners in the hands of the enemy. The post at Skenesborough having been evacuated and burned, and Fort Anne soon after sharing the same fate, St. Clair fell back upon Rutland; but succeeded at length, on the 13th of July, in joining Schuyler at Fort Edward.

Although at this period in chief command on the northern frontier, Schuyler had not been able to muster more than five thousand four hundred men, even when reinforced by the broken garrisons from Ticonderoga, Skenesborough, and Fort Anne. With this weak force he could do nothing more than endeavour to retard the advance of the enemy, by breaking up the intervening bridges and causeways, and by obstructing the navigation of Wood Creek. Upon the approach of Burgoyne, he evacuated Fort Edward, and retreated across the Hudson to Saratoga.

While the victorious army of Burgoyne was thus advancing with firm and almost unimpeded steps into the interior of the state, a detachment under Colonel St. Leger, consisting of a mixed body of regulars, militia, and rangers, joined by a number of Indian warriors commanded by Brant, entered the western portion of New York, by way of the St. Lawrence and Lake Ontario, and marching to the head of the Mohawk River, laid siege to Fort Schuyler. As soon as General Herkimer was made aware of the approach of St. Leger, he assembled the militia of Tryon county, and advanced to the relief of the garrison, which was composed of two New York regiments, commanded by General Gansevoort. Having notified Gansevoort of his intentions, Herkimer marched carelessly toward the fort, without any of those precautions which the nature of the warfare he was engaged in should have admonished him to take. Near to the road, and at a distance of about six miles from the post he was advancing to relieve, a detachment of regulars under Colonel John Johnson, and a party of Indians headed by Brant, ensconced themselves in ambush. After suffering the column to pass by, they suddenly fell upon the rear-guard, the Indians first pouring in a destructive fire, and then completing the panic by dashing upon the disordered militia with their spears and hatchets. Animated, however, by the conduct of Herkimer, the Americans succeeded in gaining a more defensible position, where they fought for some time with desperate courage. Herkimer himself, though mortally wounded, leaned for support against the stump of a tree, and continued to cheer the drooping spirits of his men. A well-timed sally from the fort, conducted by Colonel Willet, at length succeeded in changing the fortune of the day. By this diversion in their favour the militia succeeded in beating off the enemy; but not before the Americans had sustained a loss of four hundred in killed and wounded, many of whom were leading and influential men.

Gansevoort refusing to surrender the fort, St. Leger proceeded to invest it in form. As the safety of the post was of the first importance as a means of overawing the Tories of that district, Schuyler despatched Arnold to its relief. The detachment of this daring though unscrupulous officer having been joined by a reinforcement of one thousand light troops under General Larned, Arnold lost no time in ascending the Mohawk; but learning that Gansevoort was in extremity, he quitted the main body, and with nine hundred men, lightly armed, pressed forward by forced marches. As he continued to approach, he threw forward spies with exaggerated accounts of his numbers. The statements made by these men operated so effectually upon the minds of the Indians, who had already suffered severely in the affray with Herkimer, that a large part of them suddenly quitted the English camp, and fled into the woods. The remainder threatening to abandon him in like manner unless he retired from before the fort, St. Leger broke up the siege, and, hastily retreating, returned to Montreal.

In the mean while, Schuyler, being greatly weakened by the detachments sent out under Arnold, withdrew to a stronger position among the islands at the mouth of the Mohawk. By this time Burgoyne had reached Fort Edward, on the east bank of the Hudson. From thence he despatched Colonel Baum to the neighbourhood of Bennington, a small village in the present state of Vermont, for the purpose of mounting the German dragoons, and of collecting the means of transportation for the stores which had arrived at Fort George. The force ordered upon this service consisted of eight hundred men, exclusive of militia and Indians. A body of New Hampshire militia having lately arrived at Bennington under the command of Colonel Stark, the latter, as soon as he was advised of the advance of Baum, sent off for Warner's regiment, then encamped at Manchester, and for such other parties of militia as could be hastily collected.

These energetic movements alarming Baum for the safety of his command, he halted, on the 14th of August, within six miles of Bennington; and sending back to Burgoyne for reinforcements, commenced intrenching himself. Lieutenant-Colonel Breyman, with five hundred men, was immediately despatched to his assistance. The heavy condition of the roads, and the rain which fell during the ensuing day, retarded the approach both of Warner and Breyman. Some Berkshire militia, commanded by Colonel Simmons, succeeding in joining Stark on the 16th, the latter drew out his forces and advanced to the attack. As he came in sight of the enemy, he pointed them out to his troops. "There are the red-coats," said he: "they must be ours before the sun goes down, or Sally Stark sleeps a widow to-night!" This pithy expression of his own determination gave extraordinary animation to the spirits of his hardy mountaineers. The assault was made simultaneously on front and rear of the intrenchments in four columns. After two hours' hard fighting, the militia and Indians abandoned the defences, and fled for safety to the woods.

Colonel Baum received a mortal wound; but the Germans continued to offer a vigorous resistance, until nearly the whole of them were either killed or disarmed. The victory was scarcely won before the reinforcements under Breyman arrived on the ground. A new engagement ensued, which was continued until night, when Breyman, having expended his ammunition, retreated with the loss of his artillery and baggage. The victory at Bennington threw into the hands of Stark six hundred prisoners, besides a large and much needed supply of small arms, together with four pieces of artillery. Two hundred of the enemy were left dead on the field. The American loss was inconsiderable, being only fourteen killed and forty-two wounded.

The battle of Bennington formed the turning point in the fortunes of Burgoyne. Burning to revenge the cruelties committed by the Indians in the pay of the British, it needed but the unexpected success achieved by Stark to inspire the people with a determination to expel the invader. Volunteers soon began to flock into the camp of Schuyler from all quarters. Two brigades arriving about the same time from the Highlands, the army was rapidly acquiring sufficient strength for effective operations. At this juncture the patriotic Schuyler, by reason of his unpopularity with the eastern troops, was superseded in the chief command by General Gates.

The retreat of St. Leger and the defeat of Baum left Burgoyne beset with difficulties. These difficulties were not lessened by the subsequent desertion of his Indian allies and Canadian followers. Still he determined to persevere. Breaking up his camp at Fort Edward, he crossed the Hudson on the 14th of September, and took up his line of march from Saratoga. While Lincoln, with a body of militia, hovered upon the British, Gates advanced from his camp at the mouth of the Mohawk, and intrenched himself at Behmus's Heights, a strong position overlooking the Hudson, three miles above Stillwater.

On the 19th of September the light parties of the enemy approached so near to the American encampment, that Morgan was despatched with his riflemen to attack them. While driving them before him, he unexpectedly encountered the British advance, and in turn was himself driven back. Successive reinforcements coming up on both sides, the action at length became general. The battle was continued with varying success until darkness separated the combatants. The

British claimed the victory, from maintaining possession of the ground; but this equivocal honour was more than compensated by the loss they had sustained in the encounter. Nor was the dubious result of the first battle of Behmus's Heights the only source of anxiety to the British general. Two days previous to this, a detachment of Lincoln's militia, led by Colonel Brown, captured the posts at Lake George, and, after receiving an addition to their force, proceeded to Ticonderoga and invested it. Short of provisions, with his communications cut off, and opposed by an army constantly increasing in numbers, the situation of Burgoyne daily became more imminent. Could he have held out until a diversion had been created from below by Clinton, he might yet have been relieved; but the pressure of circumstances left him no alternative but to fight or retreat. In view of the former, he determined on a reconnoissance of the American lines. Placing himself, on the 7th of October, at the head of fifteen hundred men, he formed them in battle array within a mile of the American camp. This was scarcely accomplished before a furious attack was made upon his left by Poor's New Hampshire brigade. The grenadiers under Major Ackland met the assault with great gallantry and firmness. The fire of the Americans soon extended along the front, until the right wing was also implicated. The battle now deepened. Gates, as usual with him, was not present in the field; but Arnold, though deprived of his command through the jealousy of Gates, or his own insubordinate spirit, rode everywhere through the thickest of the fight, cheering on the men, and exhibiting in his own person an example of the most desperate bravery. The British right, outflanked by the riflemen under Morgan, at length gave way. A portion of the remaining troops being detached to cover the retreat of their companions, the left wing, overpowered by superior numbers, was compelled to yield the ground they had contested so long. Major Ackland was badly wounded and taken prisoner. General Frazer, while making the most active exertions to rally his men, also received a mortal wound from a rifle ball. Leaving six pieces of artillery in the hands of the victorious Americans, the whole detachment retreated to their camp. They had scarcely entered it before a body of troops, gathered by Arnold from all quarters of the field, pressed forward through a tremendous shower of grape and musketry, and commenced an assault upon the works. Arnold, supported by a few daring men, desperately forced his way within the intrenchments; but his horse being shot under him, and himself wounded, his followers fell back, bearing him with them. A much more important success attended the efforts of Lieutenant-Colonel Brooke. Leaving Arnold on his left, he led Jackson's Massachusetts regiment against a redoubt occupied by the German reserve, stormed it at the point of the bayonet, and utterly routing the enemy, maintained his conquest in spite of all the efforts of the British to compel him to relinquish its possession.

Conscious of the insecurity of his position, in the face of an army far superior in numbers and already flushed with victory, Burgoyne silently abandoned his encampment in the night, and withdrew to the higher ground in the rear. The next day was exhausted in skirmishes. On the 9th, fearful of being hemmed in, he retreated to Saratoga, with the intention of falling back upon Fort Edward; but his communications with that place were already effectually cut off. Following up their success, the Americans next assailed the boats loaded with the only supplies and provisions yet remaining to the British army, and captured a considerable number. In this strait, with an army greatly reduced in numbers, with no hope remaining of being relieved by Clinton, and with only three days' provisions remaining, Burgoyne called a council of war. A capitulation being advised, the terms were finally agreed upon; and on the 17th of October the shattered remains of the invading army, to the number of five thousand seven hundred men, surrendered themselves prisoners of war.

CHAPTER XXII.

Clinton's diversion in favour of Burgoyne—First meeting of the State legislature at Kingston—France and the United States—Effects of Burgoyne's surrender—Conciliatory propositions from Lord North—Treaty of alliance between France and the United Colonies—Howe abandons Philadelphia, and retreats to New York—Arrival of a French fleet—D'Estaing offers to co-operate in the reduction of Newport—Puts out to sea—Americans retire from before Newport—War on the frontiers—Massacre at Wyoming—American expedition against Unadilla—Indian incursion into Cherry Valley—Campaign of 1779—Predatory incursions by the enemy—Capture of Stony Point by the British—Recapture by Wayne—Sullivan's expedition against the Indians—Exploration and destruction of the Indian villages in the Genesee Valley—Campaign of 1781—South Carolina overrun by the enemy—Defeat of Gates—Arrival of Rochambeau at Rhode Island—Treason of Benedict Arnold—Execution of André—Virginia ravaged by Arnold and Phillips—Operations of Cornwallis—Battle of the Cowpens—Battle of Guilford Courthouse—Greene recrosses the Dan—Cornwallis enters Virginia—Takes post at Yorktown—Siege of Yorktown—Capitulation.

HAD it been possible for the invading army to have held out but for a short time longer, the campaign of 1777 might yet have terminated favourably for the British arms. While the Americans were pushing their advantages to the utmost, Sir Henry Clinton, with three thousand men, was rapidly ascending the Hudson to the relief of the embarrassed Burgoyne. On the 5th of October he attacked Forts Clinton and Montgomery, which, after a brief defence, were captured, with a loss to the Americans in killed and wounded of two hundred and fifty men. To General Putnam had been confided the charge of guarding the passes of the Highlands; but he was compelled to fall back before the British advance, and retreat to Fishkill, leaving Peekskill, formerly his head-quarters, together with Forts Independence and Constitution, in the hands of the enemy. The Tories under Tryon, and a strong detachment of regulars under Vaughan, ravaged and burned the shores of the Hudson almost with impunity. The surrender of Burgoyne at length put a stop to these wanton outrages. After ascending the river to within sixty miles of Albany, the British forces returned to New York, bearing with them, from the captured forts, an immense supply of artillery and ammunition.

Previous to these alarming movements on the part of Clinton, the first legislature of the state of New York assembled, on the 9th of September, at Kingston, a small village on the banks of the Hudson. After organizing the government, appointing delegates to the general congress, and making provision for the defence of the country, the assembly adjourned. On the 15th of January, 1778, the legislature met at Poughkeepsie, when an act was passed approving the articles of confederation as drawn up by the general congress, and authorizing the delegates from New York to ratify them.

It was at this period that France began to evince a disposition to assist the confederated colonies in their struggle for freedom. The American commissioners at Paris had been for many months vainly endeavouring to obtain something more than vague promises from the French ministry, when the surrender of Burgoyne impressed Louis XIV., and Vergennes his minister, with more confidence in the final issue of the struggle.

This feeling was not weakened by the conduct of Lord North, the British minister, who, on the 14th of February, introduced into parliament a plan for conciliating the colonies, by which the whole of the original ground of dispute was emphatically surrendered. Fearful that the Americans, already deeply embarrassed by debts, divided to some degree among themselves, and resting more upon the justice of their cause than the strength of their armies, would conclude to accept the olive branch so tardily tendered them by the British minister, Vergennes, actuated less by a love of liberty than by a desire to sever from Great Britain her noblest dependencies, expressed his willingness to enter upon treaties of friendship and commerce, and of defensive alliance. On the 8th of February these treaties were concluded. Impressed with the danger that now menaced him, General Howe, fearing lest the Delaware should be blockaded by the arrival of a French fleet, at once evacuated Philadelphia, and retiring across the Jerseys, closely pursued by Washington, concentrated the whole of the British army at New York. He had scarcely reached there, before Count D'Estaing, in command of a French fleet consisting of twelve ships of the line and four frigates, arrived off the Delaware. Having on board four thousand troops, D'Estaing signified his willingness to co-operate in the reduction of Newport; but being drawn out to sea in hopes of giving battle to the British squadron under Admiral Lord Howe, the two fleets, shattered by a storm, were separated, and D'Estaing was compelled to put into the harbour of Boston to refit. The Americans under Sullivan, being thus deprived of the services of their powerful ally, after waiting for some time in the hope that D'Estaing would return, abandoned the lines they had established with so much labour, and retreated from the island. The American forces under Washington were at this period encamped at White Plains; but the remainder of the campaign was not marked by any military operations of importance. A desultory warfare along the frontiers was still kept up, the settlers being constantly called upon to contend against roving bands of Tories and Indians. The beautiful valley of Wyoming was laid waste in July of this year by a party of eight hundred rangers and Indians, under the command of Colonel John Butler. Three hundred of the settlers were either killed or carried off into a captivity from which but few ever returned. The horrid barbarities practised by the Indians on this occasion excited throughout the provinces a feeling of intense indignation.

During the month of October an expedition was organized against Unadilla, a settlement of Indians and refugees near the head-waters of the Susquehannah. The enterprise was completely successful; the settlement was destroyed utterly, and its sanguinary inhabitants driven for refuge into the neighbouring forests.

While these scenes were enacting, Captain Walter Butler, a son of that Colonel Butler who led the Tories at the massacre of Wyoming, after making his escape from the jail at Albany, obtained from his father at Niagara the command of two hundred rangers, and being joined by five hundred Indians under Brant, made a descent, on the 10th of November, upon the frontier settlement of Cherry Valley. The house of Colonel Samuel Campbell, which, by increasing the strength of its doors and windows, and by surrounding it with an embankment of logs and earth, had been converted into a rude fortress, was fortunately in a sufficiently defensive condition to enable its small garrison of Continental troops to resist the attacks of the enemy; but Colonel Alden, together with many of the villagers, and such of his command as carelessly lodged beyond the walls of the fort, fell victims to the fury of the savages. The settlement around was completely devastated. Sixteen of the garrison, and thirty-two of the inhabitants, principally women and children, were killed. Between thirty and forty others were led away into a harsh and almost hopeless captivity.

The closing portion of the campaign of 1778 passed away without any military operations more memorable than the surprise and partial slaughter of Baylor's dragoons at Tappan, and of Pulaski's legion at Egg Harbour, by British detachments. At this period the numerical strength of the British and American armies was about equal; but the former were concentrated within the lines at New York and Newport, while the latter were considerably scattered. Too weak to undertake more active military operations, Washington pressed forward to a completion the important fortifications at West Point; and after arranging all his disposable forces so as to form a line of cantonments between Long Island Sound and the Delaware, resumed, for the winter, his old head-quarters at Middlebrook.

The campaign of 1779 was productive of no decisive results on either side. During the month of May, the river counties of Virginia were harassed and plundered by a strong force of the enemy under General Matthews. After remaining in that province for a month, the marauding party returned to New York with their spoils. Upon being rejoined by this detachment, Clinton ascended the Hudson in two divisions, and captured the American works at Verplanck's Point and Stony Point. Leaving a strong garrison to maintain the conquered posts, he fell back leisurely to New York.

A predatory excursion was soon after undertaken by Tryon. New Haven was plundered; Fairfield, Norwalk, and Green Farms were wantonly burned; New London escaped the same fate only by the expedition under Tryon being suddenly recalled. The Americans had surprised Stony Point.

The command of this daring enterprise had been intrusted by Washington to General Wayne. The design was well planned and admirably executed. Two columns, led by Wayne and Stewart, each preceded by a forlorn hope and vanguard, appeared before the works about midnight of August 16th, and assaulting them from opposite sides, carried them with great gallantry at the point of the bayonet. Fifty of the garrison were killed, and the remainder, one hundred and fifty in number, taken prisoners. The American loss in killed and wounded amounted to about one hundred men.

As Stony Point commanded the works at Verplanck's, preparations were immediately made for an attack upon the latter; but the British appearing in force, Washington, fearing at that juncture to risk a battle, stripped Stony Point of its artillery and stores, and after dismantling its fortifications abandoned it to the enemy.

In the mean while, an expedition had been organized to penetrate the country of the Six Nations, and avenge upon the tribes in alliance with the British the barbarities which had been committed upon the frontiers. The chief command in this important enterprise was intrusted to General Sullivan, whose army was composed of four thousand Continental troops and one thousand militia. The latter, mainly made up of the first and third New York regiments, were commanded by General James Clinton. So soon as the entire force was concentrated, Sullivan marched from Tioga on the 26th of August, throwing out flanking troops on each side, and a corps of rangers in advance. After laying waste, on the 28th, the settlements at Chemung, the army bivouacked for the night. On the morning of the 29th they encountered a large force of Indians and Tories under Brant and Butler. These being utterly dispersed after a sharp and well-contested battle, Sullivan continued on his route until he had traversed the whole of the fertile valley of the Genesee, at that time the heart of the Indian settlements. Everywhere he went, he cut down the orchards, destroyed the corn, and laid the villages in ruins.

The country of the Onondagas, Cayugas, and Senecas being thus completely laid waste, those tribes, together with the refugees they had sheltered, were driven back upon Niagara, where they became wholly dependent upon the English for supplies. Many of them never returned to their old homes; but the spirit of revenge still animated their bosoms, and though checked for a season, they resumed, after a brief interval, their former savage inroads.

The course of the war during the campaign of 1780 rolled southward. Leaving Knyphausen to protect New York, Sir Henry Clinton, who had succeeded Howe in the chief command of the British-American forces, sailed with eight thousand men against Charleston, the capital of South Carolina. The city was surrendered after a brief defence, and General Lincoln, with five thousand American troops, became prisoners of war. The remainder of the province being speedily subjugated, Clinton returned to New York, leaving Cornwallis with four thousand men to maintain his conquest.

Prompt in their endeavours to recover so important a province from the hands of the enemy, the exertions of Congress speedily resulted in the formation of a new southern army, the chief command of which was given to General Gates.

On the 16th of August he encountered Cornwallis at Camden, but his forces were routed and dispersed with great loss.

At the north, the aspect of affairs was equally gloomy. During the month of July a powerful French fleet, having on board six thousand troops commanded by Count de Rochambeau, arrived at Rhode Island; but were prevented, for some time, from co-operating with the army under Washington, owing to the rigorous blockade maintained by a superior naval force of the enemy.

It was at this gloomy period of the war that Benedict Arnold was meditating treason against his country. Desperately brave, ambitious of distinction, but vain and utterly unprincipled, Arnold, for his eminent services in the battles which preceded the surrender of Burgoyne, had been elevated to that rank in the army to which he had long aspired, and, as a further testimony to his great military merits, had been intrusted with the command at Philadelphia. Gay company and an extravagant style of living soon involved him in debts and difficulties, which were not lessened by the means he took to extricate himself. Charged by the civil authorities of Pennsylvania with resorting to improper means for the purpose of obtaining the moneys his necessities were constantly requiring, he was at length tried by court-martial, found guilty on two of the counts, and sentenced to be publicly reprimanded by the commander-in-chief. This wound to his vanity was deepened still more by the refusal of Congress to allow the entire amount of his claims against the United States, for sums alleged to have been expended by him during the expedition into Canada. Smothering his resentment, he opened a treasonable correspondence with Sir Henry Clinton through Major André, adjutant-general of the British army. About the same time he obtained from Washington command of the fortress at West Point, with the deliberate design of betraying it into the hands of the enemy. In order to make the necessary arrangements for consummating this act of treason, André was reluctantly prevailed upon to ascend the Hudson on board the sloop-of-war Vulture, and to hold an interview with Arnold within the American lines. Day beginning to dawn before the conference was terminated, Arnold induced André to go with him to the house of one Joshua H. Smith, where, after the business was concluded, the young officer remained concealed until the evening. The return to the Vulture being considered hazardous, André, disguised as a citizen, with a pass from Arnold, and having Smith for his guide, set off on horseback overland for New York.

The next morning, after parting with Smith, he was intercepted, near a small brook about a mile north of Tarrytown, by Paulding, Williams, and Van Wart, three armed scouts, to whom, deceived by their replies, André avowed himself a British officer, travelling on pressing business. He was immediately seized. Rejecting indignantly the offers with which, on discovering his mistake, André tempted his captors to release him, they instituted a search of his person, and having found papers of a suspicious character concealed in his stockings, they conducted him a close prisoner to Lieutenant-Colonel Jamison, who was in command at the nearest American outpost. Recognising the papers to be in the handwriting of Arnold, yet unwilling to believe in the guilt of his superior officer, Jamison sent a messenger to Arnold, informing him of the arrest of André, who as yet was only known by his assumed name of Anderson; while he despatched the papers found in the boots of the prisoner by an express to Washington, then in the act of returning from Hartford to West Point.

Two or three hours before Washington arrived, the letter from Jamison relating to his prisoner was put into the hands of Arnold. Instantly aroused to a sense of his danger, the guilt-stricken traitor rose hurriedly from the table, and excusing himself to his guests, hastened to the river, where he flung himself into his barge, and passing the American forts waving a white kerchief, the usual signal of a flag-boat, took refuge on board the Vulture, which still remained at anchor in the river.

The case of André excited the profoundest commiseration, even in the breasts of his judges. Young, generous, accomplished, and of high rank in the British army, he had been reluctantly induced to remain within the American lines, and to assume that disguise and false character by which, forfeiting his right to be treated as a prisoner of war, he subjected himself to the summary and ignominious punishment that military usage accords to the common spy. In spite of the earnest entreaties of Sir Henry Clinton, he was sentenced by a court-martial to be hanged; and his execution took place at Tappan on the 2d of October.

The campaign of 1781 opened at the south. While Virginia was again suffering greatly from predatory incursions led by Phillips and the traitor Arnold, Cornwallis prepared to invade North Carolina. General Greene, who had superseded Gates in command of the American army in the south, was gradually collecting a force sufficient to resume active operations. Morgan, with a strong detachment, being stationed in the western part of South Carolina, Cornwallis despatched the impetuous Tarleton to bring him to battle. At Tarleton's approach, Morgan fell back to the Cowpens, where, on the 17th of January, he made a determined and successful stand. The British, one thousand in number, were defeated with great loss. Tarleton himself was wounded, and narrowly escaped capture during his subsequent flight. Foiled in his attempt upon Morgan, Cornwallis now turned in pursuit of Greene, and, after a long series of manœuvres, a battle was fought on the 8th of March at Guilford Courthouse, in which the British were victorious. Greene retreated for safety across the Dan; but as soon as Cornwallis had retired toward Wilmington, Greene repassed the Dan, and boldly leading his forces into South Carolina, advanced upon Camden, where Lord Rawdon was in command of the British outposts. On the 25th of April the latter attacked Greene at Hobkirk's Hill, and, after a sharp contest, the Americans were compelled to give way, retiring in good order to Rugeley's Mills, where they encamped. In the mean time, Lee and Marion had succeeded in breaking the British line of communication north of the Santee by the capture of Fort Watson. They next laid siege to Fort Motte, and Rawdon, finding himself compelled to concentrate his forces, abandoned his whole line of posts, and fell back to Eutaw Springs. The battle which was fought at this place on the 8th of September determined him to retire behind the stronger defences at Charleston.

In the mean while, Cornwallis, finding it impossible to overtake Greene, left the defence of

South Carolina to Rawdon, and pushed rapidly into Virginia. Lafayette was at once despatched with a corps of twelve hundred men to oppose him; but his force was too weak to offer any effectual resistance. The army of Cornwallis, swelled by reinforcements from New York, amounted at this time to eight thousand men. Retiring from Richmond as the enemy advanced, Lafayette fell back toward the Rappahannock, where he formed a junction with Wayne, who, with one thousand troops of the Pennsylvania line, had marched to meet him.

While these movements were in progress, Clinton, becoming apprehensive that Washington and Rochambeau would attack New York in concert with a French fleet expected to arrive in August, sent instructions to Cornwallis to select a strong position upon the seaboard, and hold himself in readiness to embark at any moment. In obedience to these orders, Cornwallis retired across the James' River to Yorktown, where he fortified himself as strongly as the situation would admit.

New York was indeed the original point selected for attack by Washington; but learning subsequently that De Grasse intended sailing with his fleet for the Chesapeake Bay, he altered his plan of operations, and resolved to attempt the capture of Cornwallis. Before Sir Henry

Clinton was aware of this design, the combined French and American forces had marched with great secrecy and expedition overland to the head of Elk, and embarking in transports already collected there, formed a junction soon after with Lafayette at Williamsburg.

The retreat of Cornwallis by water having been effectually cut off by the French fleet which occupied the mouth of York River, on the 6th of October the siege of Yorktown was commenced. After defending the place with great spirit and resolution, Cornwallis proposed a cessation of hostilities; and the terms of capitulation being at length agreed upon, the garrison, to the number of seven thousand men, surrendered themselves prisoners of war.

With the capitulation at Yorktown the war of the Revolution may be said to have ended. Skirmishes between foraging parties, and occasional enterprises conducted by spirited partisan corps, still indeed took place; but England had grown heartily weary of the war. Propositions for negotiation soon followed. On the 30th of November, 1782, provisional articles of peace were agreed to by commissioners respectively appointed for that purpose. From the 19th of April, 1783, hostilities ceased entirely; and on the 30th of September the independence of the colonies was formally acknowledged and ratified.

On the 25th of November the British troops evacuated New York; and from that date not a single hostile soldier remained in arms in any portion of the disenthralled American provinces.

CHAPTER XXIII.

A national convention called—Influence of New York—Action of the state in regard to the import duties—Meeting of the national convention—Adoption of the Federal Constitution—Action of the Anti-Federalist party in New York—Popularity of Clinton—Fierce party feuds—Jay elected governor—Reception of his treaty with Great Britain—Hamilton insulted—Re-election of Jay—Foreign relations of the United States—Alien and Sedition laws—Clinton elected governor—Aaron Burr—His quarrel with Hamilton—Death of Hamilton—Proscription of Burr—His western journeys—His arrest, trial, and acquittal—Subsequent life—Increasing foreign difficulties—British orders in council—Berlin and Milan decrees—American Embargo Act—Collision between the frigate President and British sloop-of-war Little Belt—War declared—Ill success of the American forces at the north—Important naval victories—Americans defeated at the River Raisin—Capture of York, Upper Canada—Forts George and Erie abandoned by the British—Defeat of Boerstler—Victory at Sackett's Harbour—Perry's victory on Lake Erie—Naval successes and disasters—Battle of the Thames—Defeat of the Creeks by Jackson—Battles of Chippewa and Bridge water—Capture of the Capitol—Death of Ross—Battle of Plattsburg—McDonough's victory on Lake Champlain—Battle of New Orleans—Peace declared.

THE peace of 1783 found the United States staggering under a burden of debts from which there was no hope of a speedy relief. The ability to maintain the independence which had just been acquired at so much cost and bloodshed was also doubted by many reflecting minds, who, seeing the inadequacy of the old articles of confederation to perpetuate an harmonious union, were disposed to regard as impracticable the attempt to construct a more perfect scheme of confederation. Others, however, were more sanguine. Acting on the suggestion of certain commissioners from several states of the Union, who met at Annapolis in September, 1786, Congress, during the month of February, 1787, recommended that a convention of delegates should be held at Philadelphia on the second Monday of the succeeding May, for the purpose of revising the articles of the confederacy. From the selection of delegates to this important convention emanated the Republican and Federal parties.

The influence of the growing power of New York was now about to be felt. Already, as early as 1781, the state legislature had granted the import duties of New York city to the United States, giving to Congress full authority to levy and collect the same, and to appoint the necessary officers. This act was modified in 1783; the general government still received the duties as before, but the power to appoint the collectors and other officers was assumed by the state. In 1786 the act was still further altered, so as to give the state the sole power to levy and collect the duties; but still placing the revenues thus acquired at the disposal of Congress. This law Congress refused to acknowledge, and requested Governor Clinton to call an extra session of the legislature, in order that the question might be reconsidered. Disclaiming all power to convene the assembly, except under extraordinary circumstances, Clinton declined, stating his reason for so doing to the legislature of 1787. General Alexander Hamilton, a steady advocate of a strong national government, and subsequently to become so well known as the bold and able defender of the Federal Constitution, was at this period a member of the assembly. As chairman of the customary committee, he prepared an answer to the governor's opening speech, in which he rigidly refrained from any comment upon Clinton's refusal to call an extra session. This roused the friends of the latter, who offered an amendment approving the course of the governor, which, after an animated debate, was carried by a large majority. Having decided to send delegates to the general convention at Philadelphia, Hamilton, Yates, and Lansing were appointed, but with their course of action bounded by particular instructions.

The national convention met at Philadelphia at the appointed time, and on proceeding to the business before them, commenced a discussion of three separate plans, presenting marked differences from each other. The first proposed an enlargement of the powers of the confederacy; and it was this plan for which the delegates from New York were instructed to vote. Its rejection being determined upon by the agreement of a majority of the members to adopt a new form of government, Yates and Lansing withdrew from the convention; but Hamilton determined to risk the censure of his constituents by placing himself at the head of a second party, who strongly advocated the plan of a purely national government.

"The Virginia plan," which was the third, was calculated to conciliate the prejudices of both extremes, by offering a frame of government partly national and partly federal. The constitution formed upon this plan was finally adopted, though not without many ominous misgivings on the part of those delegates who reluctantly voted for it.

The Anti-Federalists in New York immediately arrayed themselves in strong opposition. They denounced the new constitution as crippling the state sovereignties, and establishing a central government with powers so extensive as to endanger the permanence of the republic. The Federalists, with Hamilton at their head, entered upon an able defence; and at the legislative session of 1788 it was resolved upon to call a convention of delegates fresh from the people, for the purpose of ratifying or rejecting the new constitution.

The election took place at the appointed time,

and on the 18th of June, 1788, the convention was organized by the appointment of Governor Clinton as president. After a protracted discussion, continued through three weeks, Mr. Jay, on the 11th of July, moved "that the constitution be ratified; and that whatever amendments might be deemed expedient should be recommended." The Anti-Federalists strongly objected to the passage of any such resolution; but, while the discussion was still warm, tidings were received that New Hampshire had ratified the constitution; and as nine states, the number necessary to its adoption, had thus already signified their assent, the action of New York was now a matter of but little moment. After entertaining, briefly, the question whether they should ratify the instrument or recede from the Union, they came to the conclusion to accept Jay's resolution, altered in such a manner as to express their "full confidence" that the amendments to the constitution, as recommended by the convention, would be adopted by the national Congress.

So warm a contest between the Federalists and their opposers naturally engendered some bitterness of feeling, which the ratification of the constitution did not wholly allay. Governor Clinton, the most popular man in the state, was decidedly averse to the surrender of so much power to the general government, and his adherents pertinaciously persisted in entertaining a similar opinion.

At the October session of the legislature in 1788, Clinton, in his opening speech, recommended the assembly to favour a call for a second national convention, for the express purpose of revising the new constitution. But the feverish excitement gradually passed away. Washington had been elected President of the United States, and so long as he remained at the head of the general government, the people were well satisfied that their liberties were secure.

By the extraordinary force of his personal popularity, Clinton was re-elected governor in 1788, over Yates, the Federal candidate; and at the election of 1792, notwithstanding the growing strength of the Federal party, he triumphed in a similar manner over Mr. Jay, a gentleman greatly beloved, and of a moral character singularly pure. The election had, however, been very closely contested; so closely, indeed, that Clinton was said to have owed his re-election to the legislative committee to whom the votes for governor were referred, the voice of a majority of the state electors being in favour of Mr. Jay. This charge, publicly made, created a feeling of intense indignation throughout the state. Fierce party quarrels ensued; and as the passion deepened, the consequences might have been of the most serious character, had not the popular leaders on both sides exerted themselves with praiseworthy activity to moderate the fury and vehemence of their respective partisans. Though at length the feud was allayed, it had not been without its effect upon the fortunes of the Anti-Federal, or, as they now called themselves, the "Republican" party. At the subsequent state elections the Federalists were in the majority; and in 1795 they succeeded in electing Jay and Van Rensselaer, as governor and lieutenant-governor, over Yates and Floyd, the Republican candidates.

Two days after his election, Jay arrived at New York from his mission to England, where he had been sent, a year previous, for the purpose of negotiating a treaty with that power. This treaty soon became a most prolific source of contention. France, plunging into the sanguinary excesses which followed her successful revolution, had inoculated quite a number of those who belonged to the Republican party in America with a portion of her intensely-levelling and ultra-democratic principles. At the same time, the Federalists were accused of striving to promote a strong conservative policy, and of a still more obnoxious leaning toward the interests of Great Britain.

Within a week after the arrival of Jay at New York, the publication of his treaty with Great Britain changed the rejoicings with which he had been welcomed into the bitterest denunciations. In Philadelphia he was burned in effigy; and throughout the confederated states, wherever the

French or Republican party was predominant, meetings were held to protest against the conditions of the treaty, and to vent fierce and unjust accusations against the now unpopular commissioners. In New York, Hamilton attempted to address the multitude in defence of his friend, but a shower of stones compelled him to desist. The meeting, carried away by passion, assented to some angry resolutions, and then burned the obnoxious treaty in front of the governor's house.

Fortunately, violent passions are usually brief in their duration. Jay quietly bent to the storm, and when it passed away gradually rose again, if not to the height of his old popularity, yet so near it as to be again elected governor in 1798, over Judge Livingston, the strongest Republican candidate. But, though defeated, the Republican party were everywhere gaining strength. Encouraged by the number of their American adherents, the rulers of the French republic had been for some time disposed to regard with a feeling allied to contempt the repeated complaints and protests of the general government. The relations between the two countries at length became critical; and, in expectation of a war, Congress passed the well known Alien and Sedition laws.

By the Alien law, no foreigner could become a citizen of the United States under a residence of fourteen years. Such as had not been in the country more than two years might be ordered to leave it, if the president believed their presence prejudicial to the peace of the commonwealth; while all resident aliens, after a declaration of war, rendered themselves subject at any moment to be seized and incarcerated.

The Sedition law, though limited in its operation to three years, was equally stringent. Each person unlawfully combining or conspiring with others to resist the measures of the general government, or to impede any law of the United States, or to control the legitimate acts of any government officer, was made liable to a fine not exceeding five thousand dollars, and to a term of imprisonment ranging from six months to five years.

Scarcely any amount of provocation would have justified the rigorous harshness of these laws. The legislatures of Kentucky and Virginia, at the instance of Jefferson, passed resolutions denouncing them with great acrimony. The assembly of New York avoided taking part in the controversy; but the elections of 1800 and 1801 were doubtless affected by it. The power of the Federalists was everywhere completely broken. Jefferson and Burr were elected President and Vice-president of the United States; while George Clinton and Jeremiah Van Rensselaer were chosen Governor and Lieutenant-governor of New York.

No marked political events occurred during the three succeeding years, although the excitement between the opposing parties was in no degree lessened. In 1804, Morgan Lewis, the Republican candidate for governor, was elected over Aaron Burr, who, being opposed by the Clintons and Livingstons, was rapidly losing his earlier political influence. It was at this period that the circumstances originated which led to the fatal duel between Hamilton and Burr.

Lying under the imputation of intriguing against Jefferson in order to secure his own election to the presidency, Burr had lost in a great measure the confidence of his party. Failing to procure the regular nomination for Governor of New York, he sought and obtained an independent one. He lost his election, notwithstanding he was supported during the canvass by a number of the Federalists, much to the chagrin of Hamilton, although he took no active part to prevent it.

Smarting under his recent defeat, which he attributed to the influence of Hamilton, Burr seized advantage of an expression in a letter written by Doctor Cooper of Albany, in which the latter assured his correspondent that Hamilton considered Burr as "a dangerous man, who ought not to be intrusted with the reins of government;" adding—"I could detail a still more *despicable* opinion which Hamilton has expressed of Burr." Fastening on the word "despicable," Burr immediately despatched a note to Hamilton, which the latter finally answered by declaring his willingness, under respectful questioning, to show that the language he had used was applied solely to Burr's political, and not at all to his private character. Burr treated the reply as "a mere evasion," and reiterated his demand for satisfaction. Reluctantly, and in defiance of his openly-avowed principles, Hamilton accepted the challenge. The parties met, and Hamilton fell.

From that moment the character of Burr was blasted for ever. Hated in New York, and indicted for murder in New Jersey, he proceeded to Philadelphia, where he took up his abode. In the spring of 1805 he started for the West, enveloping his movements in great mystery. Returning to Philadelphia, he spent the winter of 1805 and part of the summer of 1806 in that city and in Washington; but in August he again set out for the West. His treasonable designs eventually becoming apparent, he was arrested in the Tombigbee country on the 1st of March, 1807, and conveyed to Richmond for trial.

The charge preferred against Burr was that of treason against the United States, and of misdemeanour in levying troops within a friendly territory for a revolutionary expedition against Mexico. No one doubted his guilt; but as proof of an overt act, by two creditable witnesses, could not be produced, he was finally acquitted, and took passage the succeeding year for Europe. For four years he led a restless, wretched, wandering life, but in 1812 he suddenly reappeared in New York, and resumed the practice of the law. His death, at the age of eighty-one, took place on the 14th of September, 1836.

In 1807 Daniel Tompkins was elected governor, over Morgan Lewis—both the candidates belonging to the Republican party. For two years previous to this, the current of party feeling had been greatly imbittered by the critical condition of our foreign relations. During the progress of the long and bloody European war carried on by the allied sovereigns against the power of Napoleon, the Americans, as neutrals, were rapidly acquiring commercial importance by the great extension of the carrying trade. To annihilate this lucrative business, Great Britain adopted orders in council suppressing all commercial relations between America and France. Napoleon retaliated by issuing his celebrated Berlin and Milan decrees, which rendered American vessels trading to England subject to seizure and condemnation.

These high-handed measures led to protests and remonstrances, which were received with cool indifference by both the belligerent parties. Depredations upon American commerce still continuing, an embargo was laid, for ninety days, upon all vessels within the jurisdiction of the United States. The militia and volunteers were at the same time called upon to hold themselves in readiness for service. The great distress brought upon the mercantile interests of the country by the operation of the Embargo, led to its suspension until the next meeting of Congress, in July, 1808. In this year Madison succeeded Jefferson as president, and an act was passed by Congress which prohibited all intercourse with England, France, or any of their dependencies.

The Federalists opposing a declaration of war, which the growing dislike to England seemed each day to render more inevitable, the Republican party again gained the ground they had previously lost by their support of the Embargo Act, and succeeded in 1810 in re-electing Tompkins for governor. Lieutenant-Governor Broome dying soon after, De Witt Clinton was appointed his successor.

Opinions directly antagonistic, in relation to the right of impressment, had already complicated the existing difficulties between the United States and Great Britain, when, on the 16th of May, 1811, the frigate President, commanded by Commodore Rodgers, was fired into by the English sloop-of-war Little Belt. In the action which ensued, the British lost thirty-two men in killed and wounded. From this time all thought of preserving peace was abandoned; the national indignation was fully aroused, and on the 20th of June, 1812, Congress authorized a declaration of war.

The campaign opened disastrously. An attempt to invade Canada proved not only signally unsuccessful, but was followed by retaliatory movements on the part of the British. Detroit, and all the military posts in Michigan, were occupied by the enemy. Hull ignominiously surrendered the forces under his command on the 19th of August; and on the 13th of October an American detachment, one thousand strong, which had crossed the Niagara River, and attacked the British on the Heights of Queenstown, suffered a repulse; and not being supported by reinforcements from the American side, were compelled to surrender.

On the ocean, however, the navy of the United States proudly sustained the honour of the American arms. Hull, in command of the Constitution, captured, on the 10th of August, the British frigate Guerriere. Three days afterward, Porter, in the Essex, captured the Alert. On the 17th of October the British brig Frolic surrendered to the Wasp, though both were retaken the same day by a British seventy-four. On the 25th of the same month the frigate Macedonian surrendered to the United States; and on the 29th of December the Java lowered her flag to the Constitution, on this occasion commanded by Bainbridge.

On the 4th of March, 1813, Madison was re-elected president. The operations on land still continued to terminate in the defeat of the American forces. During the month of January they were signally defeated at Frenchtown, in the vicinity of the River Raisin, and many of those who had surrendered were subsequently massacred by the Indians. An invasion of Canada by General Dearborn was more successful. On the 27th of April, York, the capital of Upper Canada, was attacked by General Dearborn, supported by a small naval squadron under Commodore Chauncey. After a brief defence, the garrison capitulated. This success was speedily followed by another. On the 27th of May, Commodore Chauncey attacked Fort George; and, after setting fire to their magazines, the British retreated to Queenstown. Fort Erie was next abandoned; but a detachment of Americans, five hundred and seventy in number, commanded by Colonel Boerstler, fell into an ambuscade, and were compelled to surrender to the enemy. In the mean while, the British under Prevost had been repulsed in an attack upon Sackett's Harbour; and on the 10th of September suffered a still severer disaster in the defeat and capture of their squadron on Lake Erie, by Commodore Perry.

In the intermediate conflicts at sea, the results had not been always fortunate. On the 1st of June the Chesapeake, commanded by the heroic Lawrence, had been taken by the frigate Shannon; and during the following August the Argus had been captured by the British armed vessel the Pelican; but the following month the British brig Boxer surrendered to the Enterprise.

The tide of battle now began to turn with a steady persistence in favour of the Americans. General Harrison gained a decisive victory over Proctor at the battle of the Thames; and during the summer of 1814 General Jackson defeated the Creeks in several pitched battles. On the 3d of July General Brown crossed into Canada, and captured Fort Erie. On the next day he successfully repulsed the British at Chippewa; and on the 25th of October the Americans fought at Bridgewater the bloodiest battle of the war. The loss on both sides was equally severe, but the Americans remained masters of the field.

During the month of August, a British squadron sailed up the Potomac River, and disembarked six thousand men under Sir James Ross. Dispersing the militia assembled at Bladensburg to obstruct his progress, Ross proceeded to Washington, where he burned the Capitol. After committing various other excesses, which betrayed more of the spirit of the Goth than of the chivalric generosity of the modern soldier, he retired to his ships.

On the 12th of September the fleet reappeared in the Chesapeake, and made preparations to attack Baltimore; but General Ross being killed in a skirmish at North Point, the detachment was recalled, and the project abandoned.

On the northern frontier, one day previous to the above repulse, Sir George Prevost, with a force of fourteen thousand men, made a vigorous assault upon the American works at Plattsburg. The defence was conducted by General Macomb with so much resolution, that the British finally retired with a loss of twenty-five hundred men. Simultaneously with the attack upon Plattsburg, an engagement took place on Lake Champlain between the British and American fleets. After an action continued for more than two hours, the fire of the enemy was silenced. One frigate, one brig, and two sloops-of-war fell into the hands of the Americans, who from that time until the close of the war held undisputed command of the lake.

Hostilities between the two nations were finally terminated by the disastrous defeat of General Pakenham before New Orleans, on the 8th of January, 1815. The forces of the British commander amounted to fifteen thousand men, while those of General Jackson did not number more than six thousand. These, however, were judiciously covered by a breastwork of cotton bags, and otherwise strongly protected by the natural difficulties presented by the ground on each flank. In an attempt to storm these works, Sir Edward Pakenham fell mortally wounded. His troops, after three desperate efforts on the centre and each flank of the American line, fell back in disorder, with the loss of three thousand men.

Two weeks previous to this battle a treaty of peace had been signed at Ghent, and on the 17th of February it was ratified by the president and senate.

CHAPTER XXIV.

Political aspirations of De Witt Clinton—The Tammany Society—Its origin—Opposed to Clinton—Tompkins elected governor—Chosen vice-president—Clinton governor—Construction of the Erie Canal authorized—Decline of the old Federal party—Origin of the "Bucktails"—Clinton re-elected governor—Van Buren chosen United States Senator—Revision of the state constitution—Principal amendments adopted—Yates elected governor—Division of the Democratic party—Organization of the "People's party"—Removal of Clinton as canal commissioner—Re-elected governor—Subversion of the old political parties—Abduction of Morgan—Masons and Anti-Masons—New organizations—Formation of the Whig and Jackson parties—Death of Governor Clinton—Van Buren elected governor—Rise and decline of the "Workingman's party"—Throop elected governor—Marcy chosen—"Equal rights" party organized—How designated by the Whigs—Merged with the Democratic party—Marcy re-elected governor—Financial embarrassments—Increasing strength of the Whigs—Seward elected governor—Party fluctuations—Bouck elected governor—Election of Wright—Anti-Rent disturbances—Their origin—Progress of the disaffection—Tumults in Delaware county—Murder of the sheriff—Military called out—Arrest and imprisonment of the rioters—Breach in the Democratic party—"Hunkers" and "Barnburners"—Revision of the constitution—Young elected governor—Election of Fish—Conclusion.

BEFORE war was declared, many of Madison's friends regarded his cautious policy in relation to the dispute with Great Britain as indicating a feebleness of purpose unworthy of his high position. Prominent among these was De Witt Clinton, who himself aspired to become a candidate for the next presidency. His party, however, were not disposed to countenance his ambitious views. Various combinations were formed against him; and, among others, he was opposed by the whole strength of the Tammany Society, a powerful association which was organized soon after the peace of 1783, in opposition to the Cincinnati Society. At first it was composed of prominent members of both political parties; but it gradually took a more distinctive character, and in 1812, by a vigorous support of Madison against Clinton, materially contributed to the defeat of the latter. The members of the association were, at this period, known as "Martling's men," from holding their meetings in Martling's long room, since known as Tammany Hall.

At the gubernatorial canvass of 1813, Governor Tompkins was re-elected. De Witt Clinton, who sought the nomination for lieutenant-governor, was again defeated by the opposition of the Tammany Society. In 1816 Tompkins and Taylor were again elected governor and lieutenant-governor; but the former having been chosen Vice-president of the United States early in the following year, the choice of the Democratic party, to fill the vacancy thus occasioned, fell at length upon De Witt Clinton. A most important measure, as bearing upon the future prosperity of the state, was passed at the session of

1817. This was no other than the passage of an act authorizing the construction of the Erie and Champlain canals. To carry out this noble project a large loan was called for, the interest of which was provided for by certain specific taxes, and by appropriating to this particular use the rents of the valuable salt-springs at Onondaga.

From this period, the power of the old Federal party was broken. The Republicans also underwent a change in their organization. From an order of the Tammany Society, who wore in their hats the tail of a deer, arose the Bucktail party. The most prominent leader of this new party was Martin Van Buren, then rapidly rising into notice as a sagacious politician. The differences between the Bucktails and Clintonians arose partly from the opposition of the former to the proposed schemes of internal improvement, and partly from a personal dislike to Clinton, whom they represented as haughty and impracticable.

The elections of 1820 saw Clinton and Tompkins, both prominent Republicans, opposed to each other; but although many of the old Federalists supported the latter, Clinton, personally popular through his advocacy of internal improvements, and further strengthened by the reiteration of certain charges improperly brought against Tompkins, was re-elected. It was nevertheless evident that the Bucktail party were rapidly gaining strength. Its leader, Martin Van Buren, was the following year elected to the senate of the United States. At the legislative session of the same year, the question of revising the state constitution was ordered to be laid before the people. A majority of over seventy-four thousand voters being found in favour of a revision, the convention assembled at Albany on the 28th of August, 1821. Ex-Governor Tompkins was chosen president. The principal amendments adopted by the convention were,—the abolition of the old council of revision; turning over the veto power to the governor; the reduction of the governor's official term to two years; the extension of the franchise; the remodelling of the judiciary; the election of sheriffs and county clerks by the people; together with many other changes of less moment. In 1822 the new constitution of the state was ratified by a large majority. In November of the same year, Judge Yates was elected governor, De Witt Clinton declining to become a candidate.

The rapid numerical increase and conflicting preferences of the Bucktail, or, as it now called itself, the Democratic, party, in the winter of 1823, threatened its own destruction. For the presidential nomination of 1824, Mr. Crawford was warmly sustained by the "Albany Regency," while many others of the Democratic party formed a junction with the friends of General Jackson, or with those who supported the respective claims of Adams, Calhoun, or Clay. The custom of making presidential nominations in a congressional caucus was by this means broken down; while, to weaken the influence of Mr. Van Buren and the Albany Regency upon the legislature, by whom the presidential electors were then chosen, a new faction was organized, which, calling itself "the People's party," advocated the right of the people to choose the presidential electors by a direct vote. To this new party Clinton and his friends immediately gave in their adhesion.

At the legislative session of 1822 a bill was reported by the house, making the presidential electors elective by the people; but it was thrown out by the senate. The defeat of this popular measure, being attributed to the influence of the Albany Regency, produced a storm of indignation throughout the state; which was increased by the removal of Clinton from the office of canal commissioner, the duties of which he had faithfully performed without remuneration for a number of years. This proscription tended to elevate Clinton in the popular regard. At the election in November, 1824, he was chosen governor by a majority of sixteen thousand, over Young, the orthodox Democratic candidate. The following year Clinton had the satisfaction of witnessing the completion of the Erie Canal.

In 1826 he was again elected governor, though by a greatly diminished majority.

It was a few weeks previous to this canvass that the United States were thrown into a condition of excitement so fierce and vehement, as led soon after to the entire subversion of the old political parties. This intense fervour arose from the abduction and supposed murder of William Morgan, a member of the Masonic fraternity, by certain unknown persons, believed to belong to the same association. The evidence submitted at the subsequent trials showed that Morgan, a native of Virginia, took up his residence in the town of Batavia in the summer of 1823. Ranking high in the Masonic fraternity, his knowledge enabled him to prepare a book purporting to be an exposition of the secrets of that order. After several attempts had been unsuccessfully made to divert him from this his avowed design, a small party of Masons conspired together to remove him; and partly by force, and partly by the connivance of certain civil officers, themselves Masons, they succeeded in seizing Morgan and carrying him to old Fort Niagara, from whence, after a confinement of three days in the magazine, he disappeared suddenly. The fate of Morgan was never positively known; but although this mysterious abduction, with its dark result, was the work of a few reckless Masons only, its criminality attached itself to the whole fraternity. At the local elections of 1827 the question of "Mason or Anti-Mason" sprang up, and in a little while the Anti-Masonic party swayed the political complexion not of New York alone, but of the whole confederacy.

The old parties being thus broken up, new organizations were attempted. Portions of the Federalists, Bucktails, and Clintonians coalesced for the purpose of advocating the nomination of General Jackson for the presidency. Other fragments of the same parties supported the pretensions of Adams and Clay. New titles were respectively assumed, and from this period arose the Jackson, or National Republican, and the Whig parties.

On the 11th of January, Governor De Witt Clinton expired suddenly, while sitting in his library. The customary testimonials of public respect were paid to his memory—a weak and very inadequate expression of gratitude to one whose able and earnest advocacy led to the adoption of those grand measures of internal improvement which have since added so greatly to the wealth and importance of New York.

The election for governor in 1828 terminated in favour of Mr. Van Buren. Early the following year, being selected to occupy a seat in the national cabinet, the duties of the office thus left vacant devolved upon Lieutenant-Governor Throop.

One other political party was organized during the year 1830, which fulfilled its purpose, and then was dissolved as suddenly as it arose into notice. This was called the "Workingman's party," under whose auspices Throop was re-elected governor. In 1832 William L. Marcy, the Democratic candidate, was chosen governor, and again elected to the same office in 1834.

In the course of the ensuing summer, the "Equal Rights party" was organized. It consisted of a detachment from the Democratic party, professedly opposed "to all monopolies, to bank-notes, and to paper currency as a circulating medium." By the Whigs it was soon designated as the Locofoco party, a title which was subsequently conferred upon the whole Democratic party when, in 1837, that wing of the latter which had proclaimed Equal Rights as a rallying cry reunited with those from whom, two years before, they had seceded.

In 1836 Governor Marcy was again continued in office, by the large majority of thirty thousand votes over Mr. Bull, the Whig candidate.

During this year occurred those fearful financial embarrassments which resulted in the ruin of so many mercantile men, and in an utter stagnation of all kinds of business. This terrible crisis was charged, by the Whigs, to have grown out of the opposition of General Jackson to a recharter of the United States Bank; to his removal of the treasury deposites; and to his specie circular of 1836, by which all moneys due the government were to be paid in gold and silver.

Whatever may have been the cause of the distressed condition of the country, as it occurred during a Democratic administration, it led many persons to join the ranks of the Whigs. In New York, the latter party, after maintaining for many years an unsuccessful contest, at length succeeded in electing their candidates. The Democrats throughout the state were everywhere defeated, William H. Seward being elected governor, over Marcy, by some ten thousand majority.

Still gathering strength, the Whig party achieved a greater triumph in 1840, by the election of General Harrison to the presidential chair, and in New York by the re-election of Governor Seward.

The death of Harrison in the early part of 1841, by placing Vice-President Tyler in the executive chair, proved seriously injurious to the Whig cause. In New York, the Democratic party, at the election of 1842, reassumed its old ascendency, Bouck and Dickinson being elected governor and lieutenant-governor, over Bradish and Furman, the Whig candidates. In the election of Wright and Gardiner to the same offices in 1844, the Democratic party still evinced an undiminished strength.

Shortly after this election, the peace of the state became seriously disturbed, in several of the counties, by popular tumults of an alarming character. These tumults had their rise in the resistance offered by certain tenants of leasehold estates to the civil officers empowered to enforce the payments of rents. The cause of this serious outbreak had its origin in the early colonial times. It has been recorded in what way, during the Dutch supremacy, the manors known as Pavonia, Swanandael, and Rensselaerwyck were acquired. Similar grants were subsequently obtained from the British crown. Some of these large proprietors partitioned off their lands and sold them, either to speculators or to actual settlers. Others established manors, and claimed the customary manorial rights and privileges. As lords of the soil, they granted perpetual leases of their lands, in preference to selling them in fee, reserving certain annual rents, payable partly in produce, and partly in labour. The right to restrain was generally made a part of the contract, and the patroon or landlord retained by express stipulation the ownership of all water-powers and mines. For a long time these regulations were submitted to by the tenants. At length, however, they began to grow restive under the restrictions by which they were encumbered. Some few acts of violence occurred in the years 1812 and 1813, which resulted in the death of the sheriff of Columbia county; but the agitation partially subsided, and with the exception of occasional petitions to the legislature, asking for a change in the tenure of the lands, no absolutely violent disruption took place until 1839. In this year, an attempt to collect the arrearages of rents due to the estate of Stephen Van Rensselaer, resulted in a combination of the tenants to resist the execution of process by the sheriff. The organization becoming of a menacing character, Governor Seward called out the military, and the tenants, ceasing to resist, consented to have their complaints adjudicated by the legislature. Nothing, however, was done by the members of that body, either on behalf of the tenants or to enforce the existing laws. Thus matters remained, with but little variation, until the winter of 1844; various bands of Anti-Renters, disguised as Indians, having, during the intermediate period, successfully impeded the execution of the laws, though without resorting to actual violence. The contest now began to assume a political complexion. Certain newspapers defended the course of the Anti-Renters, and candidates were nominated for public offices because of their known sympathy for the insurgents. In December, several serious outrages being committed by the "Indians," the legislature took cognisance of them so far as to pass an act to prevent persons from appearing armed or in disguise; and authorized the governor to call out the military at any time he might think proper.

For a short time the excitement smouldered; but in the summer of 1845 nearly the whole county of Delaware was in a state of riot and insubordination. On the 7th of August the sheriff of that county, while in the execution of his duty, was murdered by a party of Anti-Renters. Governor Wright at once declared the county in a state of insurrection, and despatched thither a military force to overawe the rioters. Many of the latter being arrested, and sentenced, upon subsequent trial, to various terms of imprisonment, order was restored throughout the Anti-Rent region. A law passed by the legislature at the session of 1846, abolishing distress for rent, and taxing the incomes of the landlords, removed to a considerable degree all subsequent cause of complaint.

In the mean time, a serious breach had occurred between various influential members of the Democratic party, which, finally widening, led to separate organizations. The two factions thus created were soon after known as the "Hunkers" and "Barnburners."

A state convention to amend the constitution, having already received the assent of the people, met at Albany on the 1st of June, 1846. Under the provisions of the new constitution, nearly all the officers previously appointed by the governor were made elective by the people; feudal tenures, and all the restraints previously existing on the alienation of lands, were abolished. No lease having more than twelve years to run, in which rent or service were reserved, was declared to be valid. Important changes were made in the judiciary system, and the elective franchise was extended to all free white male citizens; the old clause with respect to the coloured population being retained.

In the gubernatorial canvass of 1846, Young, the Whig candidate for governor, was elected over Wright by about eleven thousand majority. During the two following years, the Whigs repeatedly succeeded in their judicial and other elections, owing, in a great measure, to the want of unity among the various members of the Democratic party. A similar success attended the former at the elections of 1848, when Fish, the Whig candidate, was elected governor by a large majority over Walworth, the Democratic nominee.

With the year 1848 closes, for the present, this history of the great state of New York. Possessing an admirable geographical position for commercial purposes; with a vast system of internal improvements, immensely valuable to the state, and equally conducive to the prosperity of its citizens; with a population increasing so rapidly as almost to defy calculation; and with public schools nobly provided for and judiciously fostered, a wonderful future is before her, which, if accompanied by the exercise of those virtues that always attend upon true greatness, will command the admiration of other peoples, even more profoundly than the mystery of her present progress elicits their wonder.

THE END.

STEREOTYPED BY L. JOHNSON AND CO.
PHILADELPHIA.

CPSIA information can be obtained
at www.ICGtesting.com
Printed in the USA
LVHW030124210323
742063LV00002B/501

9 783382 128968